The Winged Lion

Marion's Match

Patrick D. Carlson

First Edition

PAGE PUBLISHING, INC.
Conneaut Lake, PA

First originally published by Page Publishing 2019

ISBN 978-1-64584-283-5 (pbk)
ISBN 978-1-64584-284-2 (digital)

Printed in the United States of America

For my wife, my children, my extended family,
and those who seek a better world.

Chapter 1

Precipice

Peter sat in his cell awaiting his execution. Electrical and plasma burns blistered his arms, legs, and torso. Grime and grit were visible in his thin blonde hair, and on his pale skin. Down the corridor, Peter could hear a guard's boots striking the concrete. The boots headed his way. When the guard arrived at his cell, Peter noticed that the guard's dark-gray protective suit was mundane compared to his menacing crimson helmet. His helmet was completely enclosed, and had black eye ports that covered the identity of the man inside.

"Pick your last meal from this menu," the guard, Officer Farrows, sternly commanded Peter.

His last breakfast. Peter's execution was set by Judge Millhood for noon today, Friday, April 14, 2090.

Officer Farrows, exasperated by Peter's delayed response, bellowed through his microphone, "You're going to die hungry if you don't tell me which meal you want. You have three seconds."

Peter calmly replied, "I'm not hungry. Maybe you should consider your hunger instead?"

"Die hungry then, you dirty piece of filth!" screamed Officer Farrows. "Why should I care about you anyway? We'll soon dispose of you for what you did."

Farrows marched off to report to Commander Young that Peter refused his last meal and that the rest of the preparations could proceed.

After some time had passed from Peter's encounter with Officer Farrows, the hour was near. It was eleven forty-five in the morning, fifteen minutes prior to Peter's execution. The solitary confinement door raised upward and slammed into its overhead compartment. A squad of five guards, including Officer Farrows, stood in two-by-two formation with Commander Young front and center. Commander Young summoned Peter to walk backward toward the door with his hands behind his back. He then ordered him to kneel. Commander Young put magna cuffs on, immobilizing Peter's hands, elbows, and shoulders rigidly behind his back.

Commander Young ordered, "Offender, stand and face me."

As the commander turned around and began to march to the front of the rectangular formation, he directed, "Move forward and stay in the center of my men. One wrong move and we will shoot you. Squad, right face. Squad, forward march."

The guards used the utmost caution as they never broke formation and tightly held their rifles at their outer shoulders, away from the offender. They were stoic and intimidating. The guards couldn't afford to bring their emotions to work on death row since the Commonwealth forbid it. The rules stated that they couldn't show any degree of compassion for or sympathy with the offenders that they lead to their deaths. Besides, it was the guards's opinions that the offenders housed at their facility didn't deserve the delight of a smile or the sympathy of a tear before they expired. Peter was no different.

Peter was expressionless. No fear. No anger. He marched along with great difficulty because of exhaustion, and incessant leg and back pain. Peter struggled to pick up each foot. He struggled as if wading through a boggy marsh. No two steps were the same and there was terrible resistance to move from within the beaten parts of his small-framed body. Over the course of Peter's short incarceration at Omega 21 Detention Center, his extreme torment brought him near his breaking point.

The dark hallway they walked ended in a sleek, crimson door that opened with their arrival. Once the squad was inside, the door shut and the elevator moved down quickly to the sixth underground level. As they exited the elevator, Peter saw the Provincial Political Affairs Council sitting at a long marble table on a grand steel floor under the vast ceiling. They were surrounded by monumental pillars and ornate busts of various world leaders. Above the balcony, extending just below the ceiling and flowing down was a massive Unified People's Commonwealth flag.

Peter had seen the flag in his school, grocery markets, technology dispensaries, and his family members's home. Within the center of the flag lay the most preeminent and ubiquitous symbol on earth—the Great Seal. It lay within the white flag delineated by shades of gray, red, and yellow. The emblem had two layers, an outer hexagonal ring and an inner bottom-heavy diamond. The diamond held a vertical line stretching from top to bottom and had two lines reaching from its near middle and extending to the two bottom corners. The Great Seal within the flag ostensibly represented equality, stability, and unity on earth in a way that no other symbol in the history of humanity had yet achieved. Following the most destructive conflagration of all time, the Unified People's Commonwealth emerged as the sanctuary for humanity, but for Peter, the Great Seal of the Commonwealth represented the abhorrence for mercy and the perversion of justice on a world scale.

As Peter proceeded into the execution chamber, accompanied by the squad of guards, he saw his aunt and uncle. He knew that this would be the last time that he would lay eyes on them. If only he could hug them. If only he could feel the warmth of their embrace. The execution chamber was certainly not the sort of place to find either form of affection.

Peter's aunt and uncle, both fifty-eight years old, were the only guests present to view the execution. They sat in the front row near the execution gallery. On the wall far behind Peter's relatives were visual data collectors that would relay the execution to parts of the world as deemed necessary for teaching and propaganda purposes. Unfortunately for Peter, because of the severity of his crimes and the rapidity of his conviction and sentencing, a quick death meant that others could not make it in time for their goodbyes.

In front of Peter stood a titanium table shaped like an arrowhead, with the base of the table having two parallel holding straps. Each of the two sides had one holding strap. Finally, at the top of the table was a larger holding strap, with two thin electronic interface panels above. This will be the fixture on which Peter will take his final breath.

Commander Young veered out of formation to address Peter's aunt and uncle as well as the Provincial Political Affairs Council upon their high and majestic balcony.

"Attention all present in the Omega 21 Detention Center execution chamber. Peter Barclay stands before you guilty of infractions that have warranted his execution on this day, Friday, April 14, in the year 2090, at twelve in the afternoon, in accordance with global law and as sentenced by a judicial magistrate held in high esteem by the Unified People's Commonwealth. The offender's infractions include: primary involvement in activities that may lead to civil insurrection, defamation of the supreme authority of the Unified People's Commonwealth Premier and his High Council, as well as public display of intolerant activities and symbols, and an attempt to proselytize with forbidden ideas. Next of kin to the offender, do you have any words for the offender?"

Peter's uncle, Jim, barely able to clear his throat, stood up to his full, but short height and found the strength to utter, "I love you, Peter. I would gladly trade places with you right now—but I can't. You have been such a blessing and such a great joy to all of us." Jim paused for several gasps with tears rolling down his cheeks, knelt down to face Peter and said, "I hope that we will meet again someday and I will look forward to that day."

Melissa, Peter's aunt, stood trembling with despair and was only able to whimper, "You've made your uncle and me into so much more than we should have been. You've opened our eyes to see what our world really is. I love you so much! Goodbye, Peter. Goodbye, my wonderful nephew." Overcome by distress, Melissa needed Jim's guidance back to her chair. Jim and Melissa sat and wept, embracing one another as they attempted to prepare to watch their nephew die.

"Ready the offender," Commander Young ordered.

Peter's magna cuffs were removed, and he was escorted to the table. Peter, following the command, laid down on the table's cold and unforgiving surface, only to find himself staring up at the equally unwelcoming appearance and texture of the ceiling within the execution gallery. Each guard stationed at all four points of the table secured the holding straps until snug on Peter's emaciated and battered body. Peter winced in pain as several of the straps clamped down on the wounds and blisters on his arms and legs. The guards, still with their crimson helmets donned and in their gray uniforms, performed their duties void of any human emotions.

Another guard, Officer Hajo, said, "Suck it up, offender. You'll be dead soon, anyways."

Officer Farrows, responsible for strapping Peter's left wrist down to the table, looked over and couldn't help but notice that Peter was looking straight into his eyes. Through the black-tinted ballistic facial shielding embedded within his combat helmet, Officer Farrows felt a deep and profound presence penetrate his mind. Peter continued to beam his focus at Officer Farrows, who at this moment in time had begun to resist his own emotional sentiment. Peter conveyed a message just under his breath.

"Tanner. Tanner Farrows. I know you remember me. Please say hello to your daughter for me. Let her know that I'll be okay. You both should know that I am glad to lay down my life today."

Dumbfounded by Peter's words, Farrows looked away and carried on with his duties. Peter continued to gaze at Farrows with a friendly grin, extended the courtesy over Farrows's right and left shoulders as if seeing something unbeknownst to anyone else, and then turned his head to look up toward the ceiling.

Commander Young finished the restraining procedure by clasping the crescent-shaped, galvanized titanium immobilizer over Peter's abdomen. Peter now lay completely still, seemingly lifeless with both wrists, both ankles, forehead, and his abdomen anchored to the execution table. A motor began to hum its rumbling sound, like that of a turbine on a small hovership. The table that Peter lay on began to move. Peter's arms, which were at his sides, now began to move outward away from his body. The slow, mechanical animation kept at its steady, continuous pace until Peter's arms locked into place at ninety degree angles. Now that the segmented, icy platform became the immovable resting place for Peter, he sweat from his palms and forehead in anticipation of what was to come. Peter's unkempt blonde hair acted as a sponge, absorbing the ever-cooling perspiration along his hairline. Directly looking up from the table, Peter saw nothing but concrete and steel, and the interspersed flickers of fluorescent lights in orderly rows every ten feet or so.

Melissa and Jim sat in their chairs, uneasy and still in disbelief with all that was taking place and the terror wrought upon them by the presence of the guards. They continued to hold each other, viscerally agonized by the horror ensuing in front of them. Jim noticed the council members on the balcony peering down at Peter with their noses slightly tipped up and contempt visible in their eyes. The time was now 11:56 a.m.

Peter heard a mechanical door open a short distance behind his head but was unable to see that another guard had entered the execution chamber. This guard had no name visible on his suit. The unknown individual wore a shimmering black suit with a vibrant yellow shade lining the crevices between its numerous interlocking parts. The Great Seal was placed in the center of his chest, as well as his back. The Great Seal represented the ultimate force for jurisprudence on earth, symbolized by the striking yellow coloration outlining the guard's body. This color represented the swift punishment toward forbidden thoughts, words, and actions displayed by citizens of the world—much like lightning bolts striking down from above. The guard in black and yellow, only known in this detention center as the Venenum, was hailed as a hero for dispatching some of the world's worst criminals. What a suitable uniform for a guard whose title means "poison" in the old language of Rome.

The Venenum pulled a levitating cart with four vials of an amber solution, multiple vital sign telemetry monitors, and a syringe that appeared to have a thin tube running from its base. As the cart came closer to Peter, it became apparent to his aunt and uncle that the cart carried the instruments for their nephew's death. The time was 11:57 a.m.

The Venenum forcefully put the syringe into Peter's arm. Not a word was said by anyone. Complete silence, just as quiet often precedes an upcoming storm. Peter's countenance visibly reflected the level of pain he felt as the needle was inserted, although it was difficult to know whether the physical pain was most acute or the emotional pain of knowing that he was close to the end of his life. The needle was in place and the cart containing the lethal substance to be injected was behind the top of Peter's head as he lay more still than ever.

The executioner's deep voice monotonously declared, "The offender is ready for execution."

Within moments, the table began to move again. This time, it tilted upright so that Peter's body was moving from a horizontal position to an upright orientation. His arms were completely outstretched with palms facing outward toward the audience, which included an unknown number of people watching through the visual data collectors. His head was in place so that only his eyes could gaze into his aunt and uncle's eyes, and at the faces of the council members above. The Venenum was directly behind Peter, and at the back of Peter's legs were the controls and virtual screens projected atop the levitating cart. Commander Young's squad was in formation and at attention with their weapons on their right shoulders near Peter's right side. All the guards hidden within their suits stood facing the offender in complete uniformity. Officer Farrows stood to the left of Commander Young. Farrows slowly moved his left hand to turn his microphone off on the side of his helmet. The time was 11:59 a.m.

"Offender, do you have any last words?" asked the executioner.

Peter took several gulps, then took a deep breath in and said, "My dear Aunt Melissa and Uncle Jim, thank you for what you've done for me and taught me over the course of my time here. I'll miss you. As for the rest of you in this room, my only hope is that you will see life more clearly and love more deeply." He looked out and said, "I'm ready."

The clock turned to 12:00 p.m., and the Venenum moved each of the four digitally projected bars beneath each vial all the way to the bottom, pushing all the lethal drug into Peter's arm. Peter remained motionless, still breathing slowly and with little chest expansion. Within a few seconds, Peter's eyes looked up as he took in a large breath of air and let it all out. He expelled his last breath from his lungs, forcing out his last chance of survival on earth, and at the same time conquered the verbal and physical venom that had been so ubiquitously forced upon him in his final days. The Venenum looked at the telemetry units and saw no signs of cardiac or neurological activity. Peter was dead.

The executioner, as well as each of the members of Commander Young's squad, put their left hand over their chest with elbows hinged as they recited, "We serve and honor the premier and his high council."

All had professed their true allegiance—all except Officer Farrows. He did put his left hand in the correct position, but did not utter the binding phrase because his microphone was off. He was still vigorously crying beneath his helmet's face mask, observing Peter in his resting position with his head up, arms out, and feet together.

As the medical team arrived for immediate retrieval of Peter's body for disposal, Farrows, ashamed and repentant, repeated to himself, "I can't kill another kid. Not one more, not for this. I can't kill another kid. Not one more, not for this."

Just as the squad was about to exit the execution chamber, Commander Young received a distressing communications transmission from his superior officer, Major Hadley. "We have an unknown, previously undetected, airborne threat that has penetrated our airspace. Report to your combat stations immediately! This facility is on emergency lockdown!"

As the air raid sirens in the detention center and across the greater Chicago region sounded, Commander Young, surprised and anxious, shouted to his men. "Squad, report to your combat stations now! Mr. and Mrs. Wilby, I will personally escort you to a secure location."

Looking up toward the balcony, Commander Young noticed that the Provincial Political Affairs Council was already being hurriedly escorted by their Unified People's Commonwealth appointed Varangian Guard unit to a safe location.

Numerous explosions rocked the city's foundation, nearly knocking the guards to the floor and teetering them out of their double-quick marching formation.

"Move, move, move! We're under attack!" Commander Young shouted.

Jim and Melissa looked at each other. Still with tears in her eyes, Melissa uttered under her breath, "Peter was right. He said this might happen."

Jim replied, "You're right, my dear—he was right. He had an understanding of the world that was well beyond us. We have to be strong now because we have a job to do."

Chapter 2

FIELD TRIP

"Peter! We're late! I told you to set your alarm last night!"

"What?" Peter asked with his eyes still closed. "Ryland. Relax. It's Saturday, so we have the day off."

"Are you kidding me? Peter, Ms. Danvers is going to kill us. It's Saturday, April 8, remember we have a field trip?"

"Oh man, you're right!" Peter sat up in bed with a surprised look on his face. "Field trip. I forgot! What time is it anyway?"

"It's seven forty-five. Yep. That means we have fifteen minutes to get to the hoverbus. At least our dorm is next to the departure bay. You've got to love how things work out sometimes."

"Ryland, we've been in a situation like this before and it turned out just fine. This time won't be any different, except we're going to Central Stadium. I just wish that we didn't have to see all that blood there. I mean, the World War V Museum would be much more educational. It's bloody, but at least it's not real blood in the museum."

Peter didn't like the idea that his seventh grade class was going to a stadium used for the sole purpose of executing some of the world's worst criminals in front of an eager audience.

Ryland replied, "Maybe if you would have grown up here in Chicago you'd be used to this sort of entertainment. I know that my parents watch most of the matches for every Tri Annum at home on their registered entertainment screen. I haven't been able to see any with them, but I have at school." Peter wasn't able to get a word in, which was not uncommon when conversing with Ryland. "Didn't you watch the matches at your old school, Peter? You know all schools in the Unified People's Commonwealth have the same curriculum."

Peter, with his head hanging down as he was twirling lint particles from his blanket, replied, "No. My old school definitely didn't have us watch any matches. My parents never mentioned them either."

"I forget. Which school did you go to before you transferred here?"

"I went to a Novenican Academy up north. It's been awhile since I was up there last. No, we had nothing like the Tri Annum matches there."

"I've never heard of that school before. I guess they do things differently up north, but usually all the schools are named after famous people from recent unified history. I mean, our school is called Secretary General Darius Karlem Primary School for a reason. He was a member of the council that created the Commonwealth in the early months after World War V."

Peter replied, "I remember learning about him in history and civics classes the past couple years. My old school wasn't named after any person, so I guess it was different."

"Well, never mind. We have to get ready," Ryland impatiently interrupted.

Ryland was first to get out of his bed to hurry into the common bathroom to wash up and get dressed. Then came Peter. Peter donned his school uniform. This seemed to be a misnomer since it was to be worn by all students outside of school as well, until he or she turned twenty-one years old and moved on to occupational preparatory universities or other government-sponsored programs.

"All right, Peter—let's go. We have five minutes to get there and it's a two minute walk."

"Okay, I'm coming. I just wish they gave us boots that were a little easier to put on," Peter complained while bent over tying his laces as he sat on the edge of his bed.

"Yeah, tell me about it. The boots and suits. I swear they were designed for robots, not us. Only robots could put 'em on fast enough to make it to class on time or as the current situation may require, to make it to a hoverbus for a field trip," Ryland remarked while he was putting on his coat in anticipation of the blustery and chilly April day in Chicago.

"All set, Ryland."

"Great. Let's go."

The two friends briskly walked down the dormitory hall past the security checkpoint, when Ryland remembered that he nearly forgot one more item.

"Hey, Peter, did you bring a bag with you? You know, in case you, uh…get sick? I mean, the matches get pretty gory. Of course, the gore only comes from the offenders since the harvesters don't bleed."

"Unfortunately, I didn't, but we'll see. I hope it won't be an issue for me," Peter unconfidently replied.

"I hope you're right, man. I'll ask around once we're in the hoverbus."

"Thanks, Ryland."

"No problem. See, we're making good time. Almost there," Ryland answered as he was looking around at the other government buildings in the area surrounding their dormitory on Riverton Road.

"Come on guys the bus is about to leave," shouted Zameera, a classmate of Ryland and Peter's.

"We're coming, Zameera! Can you tell Ms. Danvers that we'll be aboard in about ten seconds?" Peter yelled as he was running alongside Ryland. Peter struggled to keep up with Ryland because of Ryland's five inch height advantage.

Zameera turned back into the hoverbus and approached Ms. Danvers. She said, "Ms. Danvers, Ryland and Peter are almost here. They're right down the street and are running here as we speak."

"Thank you for informing me, Zameera."

Ms. Danvers looked at Zameera with her full blue eyes, shoulder length brown hair, and Commonwealth issued educator's suit. She was nearly absent of facial expression as Zameera cheerfully reported that her two classmates weren't going to miss the field trip.

"Of course, ma'am."

Ryland and Peter hurried in the hoverbus. Winded and puffing for air, they slowed to a calm and discrete cadence as they walked toward the back of the vehicle.

"Boys, a little late this morning?" Ms. Danvers inquired from her seat on the right side of the aisle.

Ryland replied, "Yes, ma'am, we're sorry. We woke up late and tried to get here as fast as we could," while still trying to catch his breath after the quick succession of sentences.

"You two are lucky that the bus was willing to wait a few extra moments. It must have noticed you running toward it and figured you were part of the class," Ms. Danvers explained. "It sure is amazing to see how convenient autonomous public transportation has become. Anyway, boys you are lucky that you made it, otherwise you would have missed all the excitement and justice in action today."

Peter, visibly embarrassed, responded, "Yes, Ms. Danvers. Ryland and I are grateful that we made it just in time. I hope we didn't upset you too much."

"No, Peter, I'm not upset. Just be mindful of your time. Punctuality is valued very highly at this school. If either of you are late to another class function this year, you'll have to undergo corporal punishment in class or be sent to the school chancellor for administrative punishment." Ms. Danvers continued into one of her infamous monologues. "This time, however, I'd like you two to each write an essay about the ethics and philosophy behind the Tri Annum that we are going to witness today. I'd like you to explain to the class why the Commonwealth holds these matches every four months so that denizens from each of the twenty-four provinces of earth can watch them in the local stadium within the heart of their capitals. Denizens from the colonial territories in the solar system come to see the matches, too, albeit less frequently, but they still make it when they can. The founders of the Commonwealth established this method of punishment and entertainment ten years ago, which was in 2080. Wait. Is that right? Let's see, today is Saturday, April 8, 2090. So hmmm. Yes, that is about right. Tell your class about the reasons why we should continue this great tradition and carry on its glorious methodology. It will be due tomorrow at the beginning of our Politics through Speech class. Plan on delivering a five-minute speech. Practice, practice, practice. Oh, and, boys. You'll have to write your speech by hand and turn in your final draft to me before you present. Dismissed."

Ryland and Peter walked to their seat toward the back of the oblong hoverbus. Ryland, with a clear expression of disbelief on his countenance said to Peter, "I can't believe that we actually have to write by hand. Our oculokinetic screens write for us without even needing to push a button or touch a screen. I'm not even sure if I remember how to write with a pen or some other handheld artifact like that."

"Well, Ryland, she could have had us go see the chancellor to determine our punishment. She didn't, so I'm thankful for that."

"Of course you'd say that, Peter. You always find a way to see good in any terrible situation."

Finally seated with their safety straps harnessed, the two friends looked out the window and saw a variety of people walking about, carrying on with their Commonwealth-assigned duties. People had very little choice when it came to determining their future in society—the Commonwealth maintained that responsibility.

Now that all passengers were ready for departure, the low frequency of the four engines ramping up barely broke the silence of the disciplined class. Within a few seconds, lift turbines carried the hoverbus a few feet up off the roadway. Since the middle of the twenty-first century, there hadn't been a need for revolving tires that perilously tread on pavement.

"Hey, Zameera?" Peter asked from across the center aisle.

"Yeah, Peter?" Zameera's sparkling eyes widened in anticipation of a question.

"Can you ask Londyn who she plans to sit with at the Tri Annum today? I would ask her, but she's obviously busy listening to something because of the way she's moving her head."

As Zameera turned toward Londyn, Londyn turned toward Zameera and removed a small transmitter from her right ear.

"What is it?"

"Peter wanted me to ask you who you'll be sitting with at the matches today."

With one eyebrow raised, Londyn, seemingly confused by the question, responded, "Peter? You said Peter wanted to know who I plan to sit with today at the stadium?"

"Yeah, that's what he asked," Zameera replied.

By this time, Londyn had looked around Zameera's head to find Peter and as she looked back at Zameera, she mentioned, "He's so weird. Why would he want to sit by me? More importantly, why would I want to sit by him?"

"I don't know why, Londyn. He may be a little different, but he is really sweet. What's the harm if he wants to sit by you? Maybe he likes you."

"Are you serious, Zameera?" Londyn moved a little closer so she could whisper into Zameera's ear and avoid Peter hearing what she had to say about him. "In World History class he always asks questions that make no sense. He confuses Mr. Henji almost every day. He explains things he knows or at least thinks he knows about world history. They're things no one else knows."

Turning toward Londyn, Zameera defended Peter.

"Maybe he says things and knows things that don't make sense to anyone else because nobody has bothered to learn more about him and his point of view. He's only been in our pod for like four months. Everyone except for Ryland has turned him away as their friend. How would you feel being at school away from your family every day of the year except for a rare twenty-four-hour period and only having one friend? He must just be dying to see his aunt and uncle. I honestly feel bad for the kid."

Londyn didn't say anything at first. She examined Peter, then looked back at Zameera and said, "We'll see."

"Just think of how I felt when I transferred here last year. It was scary and lonely. Peter probably feels the exact same."

She acquiesced after considering Zameera's point of view. "Peter, to answer your question, I don't know who I'm sitting with at the matches today. It isn't that big of a deal, so I haven't planned it all out. I'll probably be by Zameera, Briley, and Malaya." Londyn haughtily snickered, "You can sit by me if you want, but just try to be kinda normal."

"Thanks, Londyn. I'll try."

As Peter leaned back in his seat and turned his head forward to sit back and enjoy the commute, he noticed a slight prick to the back of his neck. It was small and didn't last long, so he just ignored it. Within a minute, he noticed it again. This time with more pressure and some pain.

Peter looked back to see what it was and only saw two hands come forward to cover his eyes while holding his head to the headrest, and he felt another pair of arms reaching around both sides of his chair to restrain his body against the seat.

"What's going on? Who is this?" Peter asked.

"Don't you know who this is by now, Peter?"

"Slade?"

"Good guess. You know how much fun it is to mess with you. I just can't resist, but it's not just me."

"Guess who this is?" asked Maksim while Kamren held Peter's body tight to the chair.

"I can take a guess."

"Too late!"

"Ow!"

"It's Maksim, freak."

"Why'd you hit me?"

"I told you already—because you're a freak—that's why."

"You say so, but ask me if I'm a freak in a few months after you get to know me a little while longer."

"See, I told you guys, he is such a freak. He just can't resist sounding like a weirdo."

Maksim hit Peter again, this time right in the stomach. Peter had the wind knocked out of him and gasped to get his breath back.

The torturous trio have been particularly troublesome this trimester. They find a way to pick on Peter in the dorm, at school, and just about anywhere he goes. Some instances are more overt than others. Nonetheless, each time they victimize him, he thinks of himself more and more as an outcast. He certainly is someone very different than others in his class. All he did to deserve this bullying was disagree with Slade in World History class about the apparent progression of human societies from the twentieth to twenty-first centuries and its ostensible benefit to humanity.

"Does the word ignoramus mean anything to you guys?" Peter, with a completely straight face, asked Slade.

"No. What the heck does that mean?"

"Kam, Maks, any idea?" Slade desperately asked.

"I guess not, moron. Another one of your made-up words."

"I expected that sort of irony from you," Peter uttered under his breath with a subtle smirk.

"What'd you say, freak?" Slade snarked.

"It just seems to make sense. That's all. Nothing more than that," Peter carefully responded.

"Whatever," Slade said as he walked back to his seat next to Kamren and Maksim.

The brief transit craft ride ended at the docking crescent in order to allow the class to disembark and then walk along the People's Promenade toward Central Stadium. Hundreds of other hovercraft hauled spectators from every corner of the city and the surrounding areas for the Tri Annum. Some hauled other students from Secretary General Darius Karlem Primary School as well, but they belonged to different pods. Other craft transported students from different schools, including some from primary schools with children as young as five. People of all ages and all backgrounds united under Commonwealth rule gathered by the thousands in waves as a steady flow of additional hovercraft docked.

Ms. Danvers led her class in two lines along the People's Promenade. Beautiful gardens abundant with myriad varieties of flowers and other plants were arranged on both sides of the corridor. Aesthetically speaking, the gardens conveyed a serenity that was an inconspicuous, yet profound contrast to the brutal realities of the stadium nearby.

"Peter, my dad says the gardens here are so beautiful and well-kept because the remains of the offenders harvested at Central Stadium are used as fertilizer."

"Are you serious, Ryland?"

"This time I am. My dad wouldn't make that up, and I wouldn't tell you if I thought he was making it up. I've even heard Mr. Henji mention it. He said it's used to symbolize beauty emerging from darkness, or something like that. I guess it's supposed to mean our government now versus the older governments and world wars before. It's complicated."

"That's sad," Peter said with a monotonous affect.

"What is?"

"All of it."

"I guess. I just try not to think about it. Hmm. Don't tell anyone else that I told you that, though. You know. About all this."

"I won't. You're my friend, Ryland. The only real friend that I have here. You know that my cousin Jayk is away for Robotics Corps training with the Commonwealth Land Forces, so I won't see him for a while. Although I suppose you never can tell when it comes to military life. I miss him, but since I've been at school here with you, it's like having family away from home. I appreciate it and value it. Of course you can count on me to keep a secret if you want me to."

As the class continued to walk along the shimmering granite pathway, they were amazed as they looked beyond the gardens and at the approaching Vestibule of Veneration. The promenade came to several choke points that only permitted guests to walk through one by one, making it easier for security to check identification and screen them for weapons and other contraband. The class merged to form a single line to enter through the government employees and sponsors line. The insignia on the upper left chest of each student's and Ms. Danvers's uniform indicated that they were all part of the Commonwealth Educational Authority. Specific markings present on the insignia identify years of service, cumulative grade point average, rank in his or her pod, and other distinguishing characteristics.

"I have thirty-five students with me, sir," Ms. Danvers reported to the Commonwealth Security Officer. The officer, Officer M. Ripton and five-hundred others are responsible for safety and security at all events held at Central Stadium. They and several million others worldwide are charged with the enforcement of global laws at public properties and locations in each of the twenty-four provinces.

"Stand still. Raise your right hand and allow me to scan your PI2 [personal identification implant]."

Ms. Danvers turned her forearm over to expose the small metallic particle buried near her wrist.

"Scanning in progress. Look at the instrument and push your left thumb on the bioreader." After a moment, the scans completed. "PI2, retinal, and thumb scanners all match your educator's license. Move forward and wait until all your students are identified and screened."

Each student underwent the same process and moved through without incident. Ms. Danvers closely watched and then returned to Officer Ripton for her final scan.

"All students match those entrusted to you, Ms. Danvers. Enjoy the event. Please proceed."

"Class, let's go to admire the statues of the most revered harvesters and their operators here in the Vestibule of Veneration." Ms. Danvers walked a few feet toward Peter. "Peter, since you are new to the Tri Annums and to this process, I'll walk with you to explain everything."

Slade, Kamren, and Maksim walked over to the statue commemorating a harvester from the second Tri Annum of 2085.

"April 1, 2085, the day that harvester Scyther was vanquished. It served valiantly at the hands of operator Forlay Menjamin during the second Tri Annum."

"Well, Slade, who'd it kill before it lost?" Maksim asked.

"It managed to kill a former military officer with a dagger after its sword had been destroyed. Not too bad for a basic harvester with minimal weaponry."

"Kamren, maybe you should read what happened instead of us reading it to you," Maksim answered.

"Well, I thought there was such a thing as teaching others. Maybe you guys forgot to learn that lesson in class," Kamren managed to confront Slade and Maksim.

Maksim pointed up to a tall, polished brass statue, "Look at this one!"

"What's the story with it?" Slade asked.

"Pardos here, managed to kill ten offenders over its service life and finally succumbed to a strike to the neck with a makeshift spear," Kamren described.

"Well, geez. Why couldn't it finish off the last one? All offenders deserve to die. That's why they're there—to die," Slade cheerfully replied.

Kamren continued, "Zebis was able to kill eight offenders during eight Tri Annums, but the ninth offender was able to sever its motor core, which disabled its ability to manage its balance and coordination. Might as well have had a drunken sailor fighting a Spartan hoplite on uneven ground at that point in the match."

"Well, Kamren, what's the end of the story with Zebis. I assume that since there's a steel statue here it was decommissioned during the match."

"Slade, Zebis was one of the most formidable harvesters to be torn apart. Valluck, the offender from Omega 10 Detention Center in the Seventeenth Province was able to pierce its cranium with a chained electro mace. My parents watched the match in person and were amazed at the skills that Valluck Morgan had," Kamren giddily recited Valluck's astounding accomplishment.

Ms. Danvers pointed out a seven foot figure and then directed Peter and Ryland's attention to its placard.

"Peter, this statue is of Kursk, the greatest harvester serving the Commonwealth in the year 2087. The nineteenth Tri Annum was the one where it eventually met its match. I was here with another class at the time and was so excited that my students could witness such a fulfilling fight."

"Ms. Danvers, how did the offender end up overcoming Kursk in the match?" Ryland asked as he stood beside Peter.

"Kursk, operated by Pickney Zeal, was scanning the offender, Melis, for weaknesses, when it noticed that Melis was throwing a handful of gravel at its visual receptors. In defense of its visual receptors, Kursk shielded its visual field with its arm and Melis bridged the distance between them. Melis managed to grab the back of Kursk's neck and tear out its peripheral control channel with one heavy tug. Melis was then able to take his broadsword and pierce the harvester's head through on ocular receptor port. That marked the end of the match. Melis was therefore able to delay his death sentence by an additional four months. I read that he did die in the next match four months later, at the hands of an obviously superior harvester."

Peter inquired, "So if the offender is able to defeat the harvester, then he or she is able to extend his or her sentence?"

"Yes, that's correct, Peter."

"What happens if the offender manages to beat a harvester at each Tri Annum?"

"Well, that hasn't occurred beyond two years, or six Tri Annums, so I'm not sure what would happen."

"Interesting. Maybe we will witness that history making today?"

"Perhaps, Peter. We will have to see. That would certainly make Commonwealth history, and it just happens that one of the offenders at today's Tri Annum beat the harvester commemorated to the right of Kursk. Its name was Garamus, a third generation industrial assembly robot turned hand-to-hand combat specialist. Garamus's weapon of choice during that match was a tightly wound metal line that would violently unwind in the direction of its target. Once fully unwound, the tattered steel and titanium tip would break the sound barrier, easily stripping flesh with each blow."

"Who was the one that finally beat Garamus, Ms. Danvers?"

"It was offender Nathaniel Marion. Nathaniel had served the government of the old United States of America, before the Commonwealth existed. We don't teach or talk about that country, but you may have heard of it. He was imprisoned for distributing illicit property and engaging in treasonous acts that were deemed to be an existential threat to the Commonwealth. Any crime associated with undermining the integrity of the Commonwealth is punishable by death. In extreme cases, offenders are sentenced to fight in the matches held here or at a stadium in another province—so Nathaniel must have committed crimes that were unforgivable and irreconcilable. He will be one of the five offenders here today to fight a harvester, so we'll see if another extension of life is granted. That would certainly be a historical occurrence. No one has ever survived seven matches before."

Peter, turning from the statue of Garamus, gazed at the monolithic metallic marvel known as Central Stadium.

"Yes, Peter. Today, that is where your adventure begins and where the lives of five others end."

Chapter 3

CENTRAL STADIUM

Ms. Danvers walked with Peter to where most of the class was congregated. "Everyone, back into your two lines. We're going to head into the stadium now."

"But, Ms. Danvers—" Kamren whined.

"Kamren, we have to be in our seats in thirty minutes. Do you want to miss the matches because you couldn't get to your seat in time?"

"No, ma'am."

"Okay then. Let's go."

The thirty-five students in their two single file lines followed Ms. Danvers toward entrance three, which was one of the ten enormous entry points that allowed the one-hundred thousand guests to enter. The Vestibule of Veneration accessed an inner ring of fortified gates and palisades that were are completely enclosed within the outer walls extending out from the People's Promenade. The class and thousands of other guests walked through the causeway and around the inner ring to locate their designated gate of entry into the stadium.

"Class, we have another security checkpoint at the gate. Be patient and do what the security officers ask of you, just as you pleasantly did before."

"What'd ya think, Peter?" Ryland asked.

"About what?"

"You're killing me. Look around. I want to know what you think about the megastructure in front of us that happens to be surrounded by the enormous wall that is, yet again, surrounded by an even larger wall, within a sprawling metropolis with massive skyscrapers." Ryland spun in a circle with his arms extended to express the magnitude and obvious vicinity of their surroundings.

"Well, when you put it that way...it's pretty cool," Peter nonchalantly replied.

"Geez man. What does it take to impress you?"

Peter winced an eye and said, "That is a great question. I guess you'll have to wait and see. We've only known each other four months. I'm sure that at some point you'll know what impresses me."

"Girls. Girls! Zameera. Briley. Malaya. Londyn. This is not a beauty contest. Quit messing around with each other's makeup and wait in line to get through security," Ms. Danvers sternly scolded.

"Sorry, Ms. Danvers." Zameera tried to make peace for the group.

"Just try to act like adults here. This is a sacred place and is not meant to be for your vanity."

"Yes, ma'am," Zameera, Briley, and Malaya replied. Londyn just looked on with disdain.

The same security procedures happened again. Ms. Danvers came first, then the students, and then one last student verification with Ms. Danvers. There were no incidents or issues. The Commonwealth Security Officers at the gates were constantly looking for disturbances with their weapons at the ready.

"Well, class, we're in. Now that we've passed through both security checkpoints, we can go through gate D to go inside and find our seats. Remember to reference your seat numbers on your tickets if you need to. Everyone needs to be in a seat reserved for our class, but you don't necessarily need to be in your exact seat. Just be sure that you're within the lower level, section IV, rows four through six." Ms. Danvers knew that she should preemptively warn the troublesome trio.

"Slade, Kamren, and Maksim, no monkey business this time. I don't want to use punitive teaching tools again. I'm sure that you'd rather avoid bruises."

"Yes, ma'am. We'll be good," Kamren spoke for the group.

"Okay, I'm trusting you."

The class approached the colossal stadium on one of the many walkways surrounded by plush green grass and decorated with a plenitude of trees. Marble benches and statues were placed at seemingly random locations throughout the area, reminding the masses of the many public gifts that the Commonwealth would bestow if they were in her good graces. Despite the abundant beauty within the peaceful pastures, there also stood interspersed guard towers for the purposes of surveillance and intelligence gathering. The guard towers also had the capability of using lethal force.

"Ryland, stay with the group! Peter, go get Ryland for me to make sure that he goes in with us through gate D," Ms. Danvers ordered, then rolled her eyes and mumbled to herself. "He always seems to be distracted by the concessions offered here. They do have great vendors, but he needs to keep focused and stay on track with the rest of the class."

"Yes, Ms. Danvers. I'll get him," Peter dutifully responded as he moved in his friend's direction.

"Ryland! Come over here! We need to go this way!" Peter shouted across lines of guests waiting to order their pre-event food and drinks.

"Okay, Peter!" Ryland yelled back and began to make his way over to the class as they carried on toward gate D. Peter reached Ryland among the crowd's people.

"I just can't resist looking at the Chicago style dogs that Dino's offers. I know that my order will be voided when the pre-purchase PI2 scan shows that the calorie count and sodium level are too high to maintain my ideal body mass. Did you know that the vendors can lose their licenses and get prison time by selling food and drinks to people if it results in conflicting PI2 nutritional data? I just wish the Commonwealth didn't limit what you can eat and drink, but I guess it did end up stopping the obesity epidemic and it saved a ton of money on medical costs to the government."

"I hear ya there, buddy. It's a tough thing to give up so many choices and have to be told what to eat," Peter sympathized.

Entering gate D, Ms. Danvers let her class move in ahead of her so that they could experience the awe before she did. Central Stadium had the latest upgrades for large scale, live entertainment and always seemed to impress anyone visiting.

"Peter, since this will be your first time seeing the stadium, please feel free to go to the front to see it for yourself before the rest of us."

"Thank you for the opportunity, Ms. Danvers. I think I will."

As Peter began walking from the back of the line where he and Ryland were, he drew attention from some of his classmates.

"Make sure you get a good look in there, Peter," Zameera advised.

Naturally, Slade added, "Don't trip on your way in, weirdo."

As expected, Maksim replied in quick succession after his apparent superior, "If you fall and get hurt, then we'll throw you onto the field to fight a harvester. Good luck with that."

Nearing the front of the line, Peter lay witness to the vast panorama before his eyes. Looking through the gate's tunnel toward the inside of the stadium, the view only broadened and became more stunning as he walked closer to the tunnel's end.

Ms. Danvers, with tangible joy in her eyes, put her arms on Peter's shoulders and bent her knees slightly to view what Peter was viewing at his eye level.

"Just look at what lies before you, Peter. This is what Chicago is all about. Globally, this is what the Commonwealth is about. People coming together to stand for true justice. People coming together in support of the moral progress of our great society. I'm so glad that you transferred here and have the privilege of seeing your first Tri Annum matches here in Chicago."

Peter didn't have anything to say. It was an ambivalent situation. On one hand, Peter was impressed by the enormous scale of grandeur within the stadium, but he also recognized the enormity of what was being celebrated today.

Moving down to their reserved rows, Ms. Danvers directs her class to their lower level, section IV seats in front of the many tens of thousands of people already seated, waiting for the matches to begin.

"Have a seat, class." Ms. Danvers had to raise her voice to allow the message to be heard because of the volume of noise already coming from the crowd. "The opening ceremony is about to begin."

Zameera, Malaya, Briley, and Londyn were all next to each other. Peter noticed that Londyn was seated at the periphery of the group and had an open seat next to her.

"Londyn, can I sit here?" Peter asked.

"Sure, I guess." She wasn't entirely enthused, but tried to show some level of kindness by granting Peter's request.

"Thanks, Londyn."

Ryland sat next to Peter on his other side. The goon squad, comprising of Slade and his two toadies, Maksim and Kamren, sat in the row behind Peter and Ryland.

"You sittin' next to your girlfriend, Peter?" Kamren jeered.

"No. Are you?"

"Tooshay, weirdo."

Each clique from the class continued their conversations. Some talked about past Tri Annums they'd attended, others rambled on about the highly anticipated match with Nathaniel Marion. Peter and Ryland just sat and watched the nearly innumerable staff scurrying about on the vast field below and the crowd filling in every single empty seat by the minute. Everyone was ready for the show—even Peter—but for a different reason than the rest of the class.

Chapter 4

The Tri Annum Opening Ceremony

The opening ceremony began with a loud and booming voice over the audio speakers. The numerous visual monitors honed in on the center of the field where the source of the sound originated.

"Ladies and gentlemen, boys and girls, VIPs and commoners alike, welcome to Central Stadium for the second Tri Annum matches of 2090, on this splendid day, Saturday, April 8. This is Sirus Slater, the vox populi of the Tri Annum matches here in Chicago, the capital of the Eighteenth Province. It is my great pleasure to be with you once again for this exciting and glorious event. Today, you will witness the matches involving five offenders sentenced to death and transferred here to fight our very own harvesters controlled by you, the operators. In Central Stadium, as is true in any other stadium the world over, we must remember: First, there will be violence, then there will be silence. Do not fear. Do not bend. The Commonwealth way wins in the end."

Sirus, dressed in an ostentatiously decorated orange suit from one of the Commonwealth-owned stores on Lake Street, was truly a lackey for the high council and a proverbial mouthpiece for the will of the Commonwealth. Much like the other vox populi of the matches in the other twenty-three provinces, Sirus was as firm in his beliefs as the silicone supports in his shoes. The only thing firmly worth holding was his extraordinarily large paycheck for such loyal support and over-the-top grammatical grandeur on behalf of the Commonwealth.

"As you may know, the most exciting part that involves you, the indispensable audience, is to determine which of you will serve as operators and control the harvesters during the five matches today. Now, everyone please find your ticket and locate the twelve digit number in the upper right hand corner. I know this is exciting for all of you, but please remain silent so you can all hear the ticket numbers that I am about to read. Please remember to remain in your seats until I have announced all five winning numbers, and I will direct you from there. Finally, you should all be aware that the five winning ticket numbers are drawn completely at random by an impenetrable software program. There is no possibility of misrepresenting the results. It is one of our most sacred events, and thus, its integrity is of the utmost importance."

A few long seconds elapsed. Sirus looked around and found the thousands of eyes gazing upon him in such a way as to verify his vainglory. Regardless of the perceived morality associated with the stadium, the matches, and his personal role in the matches, Sirus valued the superficial. He cared most about his appearance and the appearance of the matches with their inevitable bloodshed. The disregard for human life was quintessentially encapsulated in Sirus Slater. Many in the Commonwealth thought the same way, but few had the platform like he had.

"Now, it's time to announce what we have all been waiting for."

Trumpets and drums played in an invigorating, yet suspenseful tone from the lower decks of the stadium. Dancers with beautifully ornate banners acrobatically performed on the field below. Different groups of students, cadets, and military service members lined the field in various formations and looked on to witness the results of the lottery.

A cue from Sirus led the music to stop and the entertainers to finalize their choreography.

"I have the winning numbers here in my hand."

Showing the excited audience only drew more emotion out of them. After a brief pause, the voice of Chicago began again.

"The first winning number is 430-952-025-857. Congratulations. Please remain in your seat.

"The second winning number is 501-852-103-239. Congratulations to you. Please remain in your seat.

"The third winning number is 775-102-372-502. Congratulations and good luck to you. Please remain in your seat.

"The fourth winning number is 004-462-204-401. Congratulations. Please remain in your seat.

"Now—the fifth winning number of the second Tri Annum of the year 2090. The winning number of the fifth and final match today is—763-291-777-019. Congratulations and good luck to you!

"As you all scramble to see which of you will soon be heading down to the combative field, please remember that today's final offender has survived six previous Tri Annums and is therefore on the verge of history. An operator today who holds a winning number in his or her hand will have the chance to fight offender Nathaniel Marion, the feared and unworthy victor of six prior matches.

"Please reference the screens in the stadium to more carefully review the winning numbers. Everyone, please remain in your seats and be sure that you review your ticket number and compare it with the winning numbers provided."

All the guests in the stadium eagerly scanned their tickets to see if she or he would participate in one of the five matches today. Ms. Danvers was reviewing her ticket and wondering if any of her students would have a winning number.

"Zameera, did you win?" Malaya asked.

"No. Did you?"

"Did anybody here win?" Zameera asked as she looked to her right and left.

Ryland answered, "Nope."

"Peter, how about you?"

"It looks like my number is the same as the fifth number called," Peter said with a disbelieving look on his face.

"Give it here, Peter."

Ryland compared Peter's ticket number with the fifth winning number on the screen across the stadium. Looking back and forth to verify each three digit sequence, he carefully scanned.

"Let's see. 763. 763. 291. 291. 777. 777. 019. 019. It's a match. Peter, you're in! You may get to fight Nathaniel Marion! Do you know how many people I know that would kill to get a chance to kill him? I can't believe it! This is the probably the coolest thing that's ever happened to someone I know! You'll be great!"

Zameera couldn't believe that Peter would be responsible for killing another person today by controlling a machine designed or modified to kill. She didn't say anything in response because of this terrible realization.

Peter sat and looked around. As expected, he had no excitement on his kindly countenance, but surprisingly, he didn't have a look of dread either. It didn't seem consistent with Peter's morality to have no visible apprehension with the understanding that he would likely be responsible for killing someone today.

Sirus directed, "Please listen carefully so that we can make this process as orderly as possible. Will all five of the lottery winners stand up and be recognized by the crowd?"

The five arose and were met with thunderous applause and orchestral celebration. Sirus, still standing in the center of the combative field looked around to see that all five were standing. As Sirus was looking around to view his newest picks in the sea of people, Commonwealth Security Officers were converging on the winners to escort them down to the field.

Peter looked behind him and saw that four officers with weapons in hand were coming down the stairs toward him.

The officer in charge of the group spoke, "Operator, please exit your row and stay close to us. This is for your safety. We will protect you throughout the day until the matches have concluded. Right now we're going to bring you down for the opening ceremony."

Peter, already standing, walked past Ryland and several other classmates toward the officers. Peter's class was mostly silent out of disbelief, but Slade was kind enough to shout, "Kill 'em for me, creep!"

Peter didn't acknowledge Slade as he proceeded to walk up the stairs within the protective square of guards on his way into the catacombs of Central Stadium.

Now within the bowels of the stadium, Peter and his escorting guards walked down until they found a restricted elevator which they entered. The doors shut and they began to move downward with little perceived movement. The elevator door opened, this time on ground level, and the entourage exited through a tunnel toward the combative field. As Peter walked through the tunnel and reached the combative field, he could see that there were four other tunnels that each contained a quartet of guards and a selected operator within their center. Sirus and his security team waited in the middle of the field's artificial grass. The dancers, musicians, and cohorts of troops from various organizations were along the periphery of the field, as well as dozens of additional security officers.

The five formations converged toward the center of the completely circular field, trodding through the outer sand ring, and then into the emerald colored artificial turf in the middle.

Sirus, still on camera and relishing his limelight, stood with a massive smile to greet each of the operators as they approached him.

"Operators, please keep walking toward me and then stand behind the markers located on the field in front of you so we can carry on with the opening ceremony. I am so excited for the opportunities that await each of you. You will never forget this experience as long as you shall live."

Immediately after Sirus's soliloquy, the guards stopped and retreated to the periphery of the field along with the assembly of other security officials.

"All gathered today, please stand and face our glorious Premier, Dormin S. Kerioth. He is here to enjoy the matches with us all the way from our World Capital at Trier, which is the focal point of the world's First Province. Our Excellency is also accompanied by our own Provincial Political Affairs Council. Most Honorable Premier, I know that I speak for all in attendance today when I say that we are incredibly honored that you have come to join us and that we are proud to represent the United People's Commonwealth on your behalf."

The premier replied with his vocal magnifier, "Thank you, Sirus, and to all in attendance for your sincere invitation and wonderful introduction to the matches. I am glad to make your acquaintance here in the Eighteenth Province as we celebrate the second Tri Annum of this year. The Tri Annum matches are so important to our cause for global justice that each of the twenty-four provinces are conducting their matches in the very same manner that you are. At noon, today in Chicago, after the conclusion of the opening ceremony, we will begin the first of five matches. Every other province also begins the first of five matches at noon in their own time zone, which means that over the course of twenty-four hours, there will be one hundred and twenty consecutive matches revolving around the world. This important act of solidarity has played an integral role in keeping our world unified for justice, peace, and fairness. Thank you all for your dedication to our United People's Commonwealth—and for the operators on the field, thank you in advance for your active participation in serving the Commonwealth's judicial system."

The crowd cheered for several minutes while the premier bathed in his glory. Sirus looked on with a giddy smile as he clapped and looked up toward the prized and venerable leader of the world.

After the clapping waned, Sirus announced, "Let us all remain standing and recite our International Anthem as one people of this world."

The entire stadium simultaneously projected their voices and sang along with the band and orchestral components of the stadium's ensemble. The melody went on for a couple minutes. Some cried. Some sung with boisterous conviction. Others privately diminished their apparent fervor during several quintessential sentences as the allegiance of the world's population was clearly defined and absolute. The final two sentences of the anthem eerily reinforced the implication of why people exist and for what purpose while living on earth in the year 2090.

Sirus, now wiping his ostensible tears from his cheeks, put his microphone back up to his mouth as the crowd was still standing.

"Ladies and gentlemen, now I gladly introduce to you the men and women that will be meeting their fate today. Offenders. The terrible. The intolerant. The ignorant. So many other names could describe these individuals. Hopefully, they will all be equally described as being deceased after they face our harvesters controlled by our newly chosen operators."

Sirus turned to point to one of the tunnels, "Ladies and gentlemen, please look to tunnel number one, where we will meet our first offender of the day. This man, Raith Faris, was found distributing illicit material to minors that were on sabbatical from their school. What was it that Raith was giving to our most cherished denizens? He had the gall to circulate handheld copies of a constitution from a previous era. What a silly thing to get sentenced to death over. We all know that that item is forbidden in our progressive society. He'll get what he deserves today—I can assure you of that."

As Raith walked out with his hands and feet shackled and wearing an orange prisoner's uniform, the crowd booed and jeered at him. Most of Ms. Danvers's class was ecstatically cheering, but some were silent. Some were not quite comfortable with publicly encouraging others to die.

The prison guards, wearing their dark gray suits and their distinctive crimson helmets, led him out to the first flaming cauldron, which he stood behind to await the beginning of his end.

"Now coming out of tunnel number two is offender number two, Elizabeth Gellen. She was transferred here to undergo execution for a heinous crime that she committed while providing prenatal testing for a patient of hers. Dr. Gellen, whose medical license has obviously been revoked, allowed her patient to keep the fetus through its full-term knowing full well that the fetus had Down syndrome. We all know that this malpractice is completely illegal and unconscionable, and will obviously lead to her end today. Thank goodness for the anonymous illicit activities reporting number available in all medical facilities. Otherwise, she may still be practicing medicine."

Elizabeth's guards led her to the second flaming cauldron where she stood anxiously, as anyone in her position would likely be. Witnessing so much hostility by so many strangers was what stabbed her heart at the moment. She helped to save lives during her many years in practice, and now all that was forgotten. The blight on her record, at least according to Commonwealth authorities, was all that mattered now.

"Our third offender, walking through tunnel number three is known for his inability to reconcile his impulses with our recognized code of conduct. Laiden Gillmore, once a trusted member of the International Educators Association and tenth grade teacher, was found guilty of exposing his students to treasonous ideas and ideology in his World History class. As a highly esteemed government employee, we wouldn't have expected this man to violate his students's minds to the point where he would be sentenced to death. At least he is here with us now to die so we can save his former students from his ideas of betrayal. Let us welcome Laiden to Central Stadium for his match!"

The crowd went wild again. All pity and remorse were spared. The death sentence of one-hundred thousand sets of eyes rained down upon him. He could only look up with heartbreak and fear as he stood behind the third flaming cauldron.

"Coming out of tunnel number four is an offender convicted of child endangerment and several counts of negligence of her two young daughters. Maurie Turner egotistically abused her children's intellectual capacity by keeping them at home for her to teach, instead of complying with the mandated policy of sending her kids to the nearest public school at the age of three. Maurie thought that somehow, she would know how to better teach her children than our Commonwealth licensed and trained educators—what a laughable thought. She committed this foolish mistake twice and is therefore condemned to die here for your entertainment. Once again, offender Maurie Turner!"

Central Stadium erupted again with exuberant enthusiasm echoed by the previously introduced offenders. Maurie's guards were dragging her through the tunnel as she screamed and dragged her feet on the ground. Her feeble attempts were sure to be her last unsuccessful efforts to spare her life and her public humiliation. The guards were finally able to drag her by her shackles and held her in place behind the fourth flaming cauldron.

"Ladies and gentlemen, boys and girls, now, as we turn to tunnel number five, we have the distinct opportunity to witness our persistent offender back at Central Stadium for his record breaking seventh Tri Annum. Nathaniel Marion is his name. Nathaniel once served a nation that has since been replaced. Somehow his ideas of that nation could not be erased and he decided to distribute propaganda deriding our current society with the hope that he could single-handedly help to restore the previous world order. What a silly thing to do; now he has come to finally pay the high price for his crimes against our great and reputable state. Ladies and gentlemen. Boys and girls. Once again, I present to you—offender Nathaniel Marion."

All five offenders stood in place behind his and her assigned flaming cauldron, forming a large circle around the operators. The operators were standing in an inner, smaller circle with Sirus standing in the center with seven gold-plated swords in a sheathed bundle.

"Ladies and gentlemen of the Eighteenth Province, it is now time to determine which offender each of our operators will battle today. Each operator will pull a sword from the bundle that you see in front of me. Then he or she will carry it back to his or her spot in the circle and thrust it into the center of the ceremonial marker. Once in place, the sword will beam a light up into the sky and will match the color of the colored flame in front of the offender. The location of the flame will indicate the offender that the operator will fight and the color of the flame will identify which harvester the operator will use during the fight.

"Please reserve your applause until all matches have been determined. Thank you very much for your cooperation during this exciting time as we move forward to the conclusion of the opening ceremony of this second Tri Annum of 2090."

Peter looked around at the other operators to interpret their facial expressions. It seemed to be a mixed bag of emotions among the four. A couple looked apprehensive, while the other two seemed to be more composed and eagerly anticipating the thrill of what was to come.

"Sara Westwood is our first operator today. Sara, please step forward and pick your sword."

Sara gracefully moved forward toward Sirus. Her long blonde hair wafted in the gentle breeze. Her green colored eyes were focused on the bundle of swords. When she arrived to the bundle, she picked the closest one to her, and pulled it out with minimal effort.

"Sara, please return to your place in the circle and thrust your sword down into the ceremonial marker, then we will all see which harvester you will control to fight your chosen offender."

She walked back to her spot with both hands firmly on the grip with the blade pointing up, so as not to injure herself. She circled behind the ceremonial marker, scanned the crowd in front of her, then looked to Sirus who nodded with a gleeful smile. With reception of the cue from Sirus, Sara raised her arms high over her head and turned the sword's point down toward the ground. Gathering momentum, she thrust the sword downward and pierced the soft surface of the marker until the magnetic stabilizers slowed the sword's progression to a halt.

A bright-orange beam of light shot out of the sword's pommel just above where her hands were located. The light shot as high into the sky as the eye could see. Simultaneously, a narrow column of swirling orange flames slowly spiraled up from the cauldron in front of Elizabeth. The column continued to rise until it reached the clouds.

Elizabeth now knew who was going to kill her but she did not know what was to do the killing.

"Ladies and gentlemen, our very own operator, Sara, has selected offender Elizabeth for her match. The orange color indicates that Xeethis, the harvester, will be at operator Sara's control for the battle. Congratulations to Sara!" A minute of pause ensued as the next operator's selection was prepared by the technicians while the crowd continued their roar.

"Domitian Byers is our next operator. Domitian, please step forward and choose your sword."

Walking toward the group of swords, Domitian's black shoulder-length hair was riding the wind coming off of Lake Michigan. His hazel eyes were fixed on the swords. He picked one up, brought it back to his ceremonial marker and pierced the ground.

Up went a dazzling dark-blue beam of light from the sword's pommel, just as had occurred with Sara. An identically colored blue flame swirled up from the cauldron in front of offender Raith.

"Absolutely wonderful! Domitian has chosen to fight Raith Farris with harvester Morzim, which is represented by the dark blue light and matching flame.

"Moving on to operator Centius Grey. Centius, please go and select your sword."

Centius Grey followed the same steps as the others. This time, however, a purple beam blasted into the sky along with its fiery columnar counterpart.

"Can you believe it, ladies and gentlemen, Centius has chosen harvester Radalt to battle offender Maurie Turner! My, my, my, how great these matches are turning out to be.

"Operator Quinn Papreys, please step forward and choose your sword."

Quinn looked to Sirus with a wide-eyed smile as he walked over to the bundle of glistening, golden swords. Sirus returned the smile, but looking into his eyes and seeing the angle of his expression made it seem much less sincere.

The proud Papreys held his chosen sword with pompous affect as he marched back to his ceremonial marker for sword emplacement. A zing into the terranean scabbard was followed by a bright-green beam of brilliance from the sword's pommel, into the ever expanding azure of the spring sky. Synchronously, the tall tourbillion of green flame rose out of its cauldron in front of offender Laiden Gillmore.

"As you can now see, my fabulous spectators of Central Stadium, operator Quinn Papreys will face offender Laiden Gillmore in a trial of combat while operating the harvester, Cybrus.

"I can feel the excitement growing as we come to our final match configuration. As you already know, operator Peter Barclay will face the highly lethal and battle hardened Nathaniel Marion. The only remaining question that we have now is which harvester will Peter choose to slay his victim? We have several swords from which Peter will choose. Then, and only then, will we all know which harvester Peter will choose to finally end Nathaniel's record hiatus from death.

"Peter, we are simply dying for you to pick your sword. Now which one will it be?"

Peter did not want to make this decision. He had three swords left to choose from. Each of them would allow for Peter to participate in Nathaniel's death in its own, unique way. Each harvester had its own offensive and defensive attributes. There was no apparent way of knowing any particular strategy in selecting a sword—it was random, completely random. As was his selection to be an operator for the matches today. Or were these coincidences random?

Peter cautiously walked over to the remaining swords and looked down at them one by one. After several seconds, he picked one and raised it up. Now, walking to the ceremonial marker with all eyes in the stadium gazing down upon him, Peter could only wonder which harvester he selected. Or could he? He hoped that it was one that could be beaten since he knew he couldn't murder a human being.

"Now, the moment we have all been waiting for—Peter, which harvester have you selected to operate?"

Peter raised the sword up and looked high into the sky. He looked as far as his eyes could see and hoped to see beyond. He only hoped that beyond the sky would be the answers to his anxiety for the day. After a pause, he quickly thrusted the sword into the ground.

"Yes, ladies and gentlemen! Look at the wonderful red beam of light and its dazzling, red-flamed counterpart. Red is the color of—Kreetis—one of the most advanced, and, may I say, lethal harvesters ever created. We had an anonymous donor with a fine imagination and equally remarkable engineering skills donate it to us for the very purpose that we shall see during the fifth match today. Congratulations, Peter!"

Peter did not gratefully accept Sirus's congratulatory remarks.

"I think that a round of applause is in store for all our operators and harvesters today."

The crowd went wild again. The thundering applause was nearly deafening to the operators down below, but it didn't seem to bother them as they bathed in their glory. Peter saw nothing honorable, much less glorious, in any of this.

"Just take it all in, folks. The five columns of twirling flames and their five matching beams of light. What a day. What a beautiful day in Chicago."

Ms. Danvers's class was mesmerized. They had all gone before, but each Tri Annum has different color schemes and choreography, so the spectators never know the combination of beauty that will accompany the opening ceremony. The tyrannical trifecta were bickering over their envy of Peter being the only one in the entire stadium selected to fight such an infamous opponent. Zameera and her cadre oohed and aahed at the visual spectacles since they were not so much interested in the matches.

"Thank you, all, for your spectacular applause as our opening ceremony comes to a close and we begin the transition to the matches of this year's second Tri Annum. Operators, I am speaking directly to each one of you."

Sirus beamed his artificial and angulated smile to the operators, panning his head to look at each of them directly.

"Operators, you will now be escorted back to your seats where you will choose two people to accompany you in your operator's suite throughout the matches. Your selectants will be there to encourage you as you prepare for and engage in your match, as well as to celebrate your victory with you, should you prevail. They will be able to see you directly in the operator's chamber within your suite. It is a great honor for your two selectants, so please use your best judgement to determine who deserves this distinct opportunity."

The guards converged upon their assigned operators on the field and prompted each of them to vacate through the same tunnel that they entered. Just as the guards moved while escorting each operator onto the field, the exit from the field was equally precise and flawless.

"Class, Peter is on his way back to us, so I hope you all prepare yourselves for potentially being selected." Ms. Danvers could hardly contain herself.

"I will also get ready for the moment, should it come. I have never had a chance like this in my lifetime. Oh, would it be a dream come true to be so close to an operator and so close to the matches."

Ms. Danvers began talking under her breath to herself, but naturally some students near her heard what she was saying.

"Shi-shi-shi, hooh. Shi-shi-shi, hooh. I am going to faint, I'm so excited and nervous at the same time. Shi-shi-shi, hooh."

"The dweeb is a teacher's pet, so he'll probably pick Ms. Danvers," Slade cynically deduced to his equally cynical companions.

"Zameera, you should get ready. You know that Peter likes you," Londyn informed her unsuspecting friend.

"I don't think so. No way."

Peter made his way to his class's block of seats with his assigned guards, and made eye contact with his best friend, Ryland.

Ryland instantly knew he would be selected. It was a given to him. Who else would Peter possibly pick? Slade? Not a chance. Ryland definitely knew it was going to be him.

Saying to himself, Ryland uttered, "I know he's gonna pick me. I just know he is."

"Welcome, Peter. I mean operator Peter. I mean operator Peter, future slayer of Nathaniel Marion. There. That sounds much better," Ms. Danvers said with a shrill voice.

Without acknowledging his teacher, Peter spoke.

"Ryland, I choose you to be my first selectant."

The class began to clap and cheer for Ryland. Ms. Danvers eagerly looked around to see who else could possibly be chosen instead of her for the second selection.

"For my second and final choice, I choose—Londyn."

"Me?" Londyn pointed to herself as she looked at Peter, then to her friends.

"Yes, Londyn, you."

Ryland began making his way over to Peter and his cohort of guards. Londyn slowly began to stand since she was obviously more hesitant to accept Peter's decision to choose her instead of the so many other seemingly more qualified people in the class.

Peter looked on with a bright smile as he watched his two selectants respond to his call. This was the first time that Ryland had seen his friend smile with a palpable degree of delight. Ryland took it as a compliment to his dedication and support of their friendship. Londyn wasn't too sure what to think.

The five groups consisting of the operator, selectants, and accompanying guards all made their way to the inner workings of the stadium from their respective locations within the vast crowd. As they departed, the stadium erupted with excitement for the pre-match acrobatics show on the combative field.

Chapter 5

A Suite Experience

Peter, Ryland, and Londyn were escorted to the ground level of Central Stadium through a series of secured, labyrinthine passageways. Only authorized persons could gain access to the guarded doorways and halls through which they traveled. After going through the last door and through scanners and identification measures, the three finally arrived at their destination.

Standing beyond the ornate marble columns on each side of the entrance, the teenagers gazed in amazement at the level of opulence in front of them. Central stadium and the surrounding grounds were certainly sophisticated, but not to the level of the operator's suite. Automated water fountains were available for each of the three VIPs, each capable of dispensing various drinks—flat and effervescent alike. A full accompaniment of wait staff eagerly waited in the kitchen located in the right hand corner of the suite. In front of the custom cookware were three chairs that looked more like thrones at a first glance. The slight elevation and grandeur of the middle seat compared to the other seats indicated where Peter should sit.

"Oh my gosh. Are you seeing this, Peter?"

"Yep. I see it, Ryland."

"They have deep dish pizza, lemon meringue pie, and geez, they have Triple T's—Templeton Tornado Tostaditos."

Ryland was quickly overcome by the ambrosial ambiance of the suite and its culinary amenities.

"You're always thinking with your stomach," Londyn chimed.

"Of course I am. Look at this buffet. I'm thinking about all of this food and sitting my butt down in one of those chairs to enjoy myself. Why aren't you?"

"Don't you think there is more to us being here than eating and sitting in a fancy chair? I mean, people die right before our eyes here, Ryland. We're going to sit here and eat our fancy food while offenders are being torn to pieces in front of us," Londyn remarked with great disappointment.

"It's a game, Londyn. You've got to remember that these people deserve to be here, so them dying is just part of it. I plan on enjoying my time here. Especially since Peter chose you and me to be here with him as he fights in the final match."

"It is a game, but it's a terrible, awful game," Londyn rebuked with disgust. Her face teemed with anger and disbelief that her classmate would speak so nonchalantly about the brutality of the matches. Although, Ryland's sentiment was considered not only to be normal, but state sanctioned.

Peter completely understood the content of the exchange between Londyn and Ryland. Their contesting angles. Their differing viewpoints. He knew who stood for true righteousness.

"Peter, my name is Felder, and I am the maître d' of this operator's suite. These are my serving staff members, Vyler and Doters. Would you like a refreshment or any delectable food?"

"No, thank you," Peter answered the charming autonomous robot and his two other manufactured compadres. "I think I'll get settled in first. Maybe a little later I can eat some of your pizza for lunch. It does look good."

"Very well, sir. Peter, would your selectants like to dine at this time?"

"Guys, are you hungry or thirsty?"

"I'm starving, Peter. Yeah, Felder. Can I get a few of your tostaditos that I see over there and a glass of whatever cola you have? Do you need to scan my PI2 before I can eat?"

"Excellent choice, sir. Doters, please serve the male selectant as he wishes. To answer your question, no. In operator's suites, the personal identification implants have no influence, as these places are so highly esteemed by Commonwealth authorities that there are many more liberties granted. You are free to enjoy yourself as you wish."

"Awesome!" Ryland exclaimed with a big smile.

"Miss, would you like anything?"

"I would like an ice water with cucumber and lemon if you have it."

"Yes, miss. We have a very large inventory at your disposal. Vyler, please tend to the female selectant."

"I do have a name. My name's Londyn," the bold brunette scolded the humanoid attendant that stood a foot taller than her. "He has a name too. His name is Ryland."

"My apologies, Londyn and Ryland. My staff and I will address you as such from this point on. Operator Peter, do you have any preferred name or title?"

Peter looked with a puzzled facial expression, not expecting this level of subservient gratuity.

"Peter is just fine. Thanks."

"Very well, sir."

Ryland looked on with a surprised stare at the entire tense interchange. He just chewed his treasured tostaditos and remained silent.

The three students, two with food and drinks, moved away from the kitchen and sitting area to the left side of the operator's suite. Ryland was still busy devouring his food, so he could only point with his free hand at the vast operator's chamber's niceties. Londyn finished her sip of water and spoke with amazement.

"Look at that, guys. Peter, I guess that's where you control your harvester."

"It sure looks like it, Londyn."

Finally, Ryland was ready to let his voice out after his food had gone down.

"Oh my gosh! I've heard about it before but I never knew how cool it actually was. Londyn, they even have seats right up next to the plexiglass for us to watch Peter in there."

"It looks like you'll have an up close view of the action," Peter replied.

"Sweet!" Ryland ecstatically shouted.

Londyn wasn't completely sure that she wanted to be that close to see the fight. At least in the chamber the fighting was virtual and not the actual thing like could be seen from the other chairs in the suite.

"It looks like the techs are getting ready for the matches to start." Ryland noticed as several Commonwealth technicians were testing the heads-up displays in the operator's chamber and the sensors in the operator's combatant suit.

The chief guard in the suite let the operator and the selectants know that the matches would start in five minutes, so they needed to be in their seats by then. Since Peter's match was last, he did not need to report to the operator's chamber until the end of the fourth match.

Felder subsequently announced, "Since the first match of the afternoon will commence in less than five minutes, we, the culinary staff here, will gladly bring your additionally requested compliments from the kitchen to your seats."

Doters also advised, "Please be seated for the first match. You never can tell how long a match will be. Some are ten seconds. Others can be thirty minutes. You may feel free to use the lavatory in the back of the suite prior to and throughout the matches."

The three teenagers walked over to their seats. Peter sat in his center throne. Londyn sat to his right and Ryland to his left.

"Wow, these are even more comfortable than they look," Ryland uttered.

"Yeah, you're right. Very comfortable," Londyn said as she sat down and reclined back into her chair.

"I can get used to this. I'm not sure what it's made of, but it sure feels nice to sit in such a comfortable chair after all the walking today," Peter said.

"Yeah, Peter, totally agree," Ryland chimed in his trance-like state from the overwhelming satisfaction induced by the combination of his comfortable chair and his happy stomach.

Londyn just nodded her head in agreement, which was something she was still getting used to. She had felt acrimoniously toward Peter and Ryland at school and even during this field trip. It was hard for her to let go of her past negative feelings about them, but she was willing to try.

Chapter 6

THE FIRST MATCH

"Ladies and gentlemen, boys and girls. Again, this is your vox populi, Sirus Slater, and I'm back to join you at Central Stadium here in the beautiful city of Chicago, the capital of the world's Eighteenth Province. I am excited to announce that our first match will be starting shortly; however, before it begins, I must remind you, our irreplaceable audience here today, of some basic formalities that require your adherence during the matches.

"First of all, please respect others around you by refraining from standing and leaving your seat while a match is in progress. You may feel free to stand, stretch your legs, go purchase food and drinks, and use the restroom during our twenty minute intermissions between each match. Thank you.

"Second, please keep conversation to an absolute minimum during the matches. Conversation is completely suitable for intermission times. Cheering, yelling, and screaming are all completely acceptable and encouraged during the matches. The operators certainly appreciate your support. Thanks.

"Third, for those of you sitting in the lower level, particularly from rows ten and up, remember to put on your safety goggles. You and I know that the protective glass around the inner walls of the stadium cannot possibly stop all bodily fluids and parts that may become—how shall I say—displaced during the matches today. The goggles will help you remain safe by protecting you from biological contamination. Thank you for your understanding and commitment to safety during our matches.

"The last rule is to have a great time! Just think of the extraordinary level of unity all across the world. Every person in his or her seat at each of the twenty-four stadiums across all twenty-four provinces will be celebrating the same civic experience. That means that over two and a quarter million other people will be enjoying themselves just the way that you are today. It is certainly a wonderful feeling to know that so many other citizens are having in many instances—a time of a lifetime. Meanwhile, our one hundred and twenty operators worldwide are united in their dedication to justice while carrying out their civic duties for the Commonwealth.

"Be safe! Have fun! Enjoy! And always remember: First, there will be violence, then there will be silence. Do not fear. Do not bend. The Commonwealth way wins in the end."

An ensemble of brass sounded with a roar so loud that the entire city could hear, probably even people living beyond the city limits well into the inner suburban districts. After a few seconds, the woodwinds began. Finally, the strings combined to emanate into a unified, powerful mouthpiece to portray the magnitude of the upcoming matches and synchronize the pulse of the crowd.

Next came the visual spectacles to compliment the music. The fire and lasers dazzled the eyes and mesmerized the minds of the people gazing at them. The warmth of the fountains of fire and bursts of cylindrical flames touched each person in a different way.

"Look at all the different colors," Zameera commented to Briley.

"It's crazy cool," Briley responded without even turning her head away from the brilliant opus of optical excellence.

The reflection of the streaming beams of light bounced off Malaya's glasses and were easily seen by Zameera as she looked over to her friends.

"Malaya, isn't this beautiful?"

"It's even better than the last one."

"I thought the same thing."

"Zameera, what'd you think the next one will be like?"

"That's a good question. Maybe they won't have one?"

"Why do you say that?"

"Just a thought. I think it's difficult to find new ways to outdo the prior Tri Annum every single time. I just mean to enjoy the moment. Never mind. Like I said, it's just a thought. I'm probably wrong anyway."

"Hmm," Malaya pondered with a curious expression.

The three best friends returned to quietly observe the pre-match show and could only wonder about Londyn, their other besty. The rest of the class continued to gaze with awe.

Ms. Danvers had a satisfied look on her face as she stood at attention. The percussion from the loud booms and blares of the brass instruments and drums rippled the water in her hydration container. The showering sparks from the explosive pyrotechnics rained down to meet their flickering ends, including one ember that landed in the palm of her left hand. The radiant light of the lone ember was extinguished the instant that it met the cool, inhospitable surface of her hand.

"What an absolutely spectacular performance! Come everybody—let's all give our outstanding performers a round of applause," Sirus Slater said as he resumed his vox populi narration from the comfort of his own VIP suite on the ground level.

"Ladies and gentleman. Boys and girls. VIPs and commoners alike. Now is the time. What we've all been anticipating is finally here. The first of five matches at today's Tri Annum will begin—right now!"

The crowd erupted with a powerful outburst of hollering, clapping, and yelling.

As the applause volume lowered, the kids in Ms. Danvers's class as well as the others in attendance noticed that the ground in the center of the stadium started to move. Of course there was nothing natural about the ground to begin with. It was an engineering and technological marvel that allowed its surface to change color and texture with the press of a button by its teams of engineers and technicians. Multiple elevators were capable of carouseling offenders to and from the combatant grounds. The catacombs beneath the stadium were an upgraded version much like the old Roman Colosseum. These subterranean recesses were teaming with life, movement, and equipment meant to captivate the spectators who only expect carnage.

The surface of grass and soil that was featured on the combatant ground moved away from its center. Much like a conveyor belt, the ground slid from a center focal point into crevices at the base of the interior walls. The natural greens and browns of the earth gave way to increasingly revealed artificial materials. A gray man-made material gradually covered the entire area.

"What an engineering feat, class," Ms. Danvers exclaimed to her students.

Maksim whispered to Slade, "I just don't know why she is so in love with this place?"

"No kidding, Maks. It's pretty gross."

"All I care about are the shows and the fights."

"Isn't that what most of us care about when we come here?" Slade asked rhetorically.

Ms. Danvers looked at the faces of her class to see if they were as jubilant as her. The children seemed to have mixed expressions. She hoped that as they aged that they would revere the matches as she does.

The ashen colored combatant surface now fully in place, began to separate in two equidistant locations. As the gaps grew wider, the novices in the crowd grew more curious as to what would happen next. Ever wider, ever wider, the fissures grew. A grinding sound accompanied the halt of further mechanical movement. Rising up from what seemed to be two rectangular pits twenty feet apart were two figures. Raith, the offender, and Morzim, the harvester rose to ground level and looked around to see the stadium going wild.

Raith made eye contact with the premier up in his balcony suite. The premier, standing with a rigid posture and serious countenance, was timidly clapping along with the rest of the audience. Now crossing his arms and making a snickering half smile, the premier gave his brief attention to the offender below.

"You're gonna pay for this," Raith slowly enunciated so his nemesis on high could clearly make out the words on his face.

The premier broke eye contact and carried on with his feigned enthusiasm. His Varangian Guard enveloped him as if to cast a titanium and steel wall between himself and everyone else. Wearing modern adaptations of late Corinthian hoplite helmets, the Varangian Guard served both as the premier's personal protectors and his own small army. They took no order from anyone but the premier, nor did they spare any life in the way of fulfilling a command.

Domitian's operator chamber came to life. His selectants sat and waited for the momentous event that was about to unfold. With all sensors in place, Domitian moved his arm, so Morzim moved its arm. Domitian turned his head. Morzim turned its head. Domitian scanned the crowd and saw the gathered masses in great detail with what seemed to be his own eyes, but he was seeing it all through Morzim's eyes. Now, taking several steps in place, he moved in the safety of the operator's chamber. At the same time, the machine moved its feet up and down on the combatant ground. The operator's combatant suit facilitated a nearly perfect symbiosis between the operator and the harvester.

Selectant Aareez, one of Domitian's good friends, saw the images from the inside of the stadium and Domitian's motions right in front of him. The precise synchrony of movements between Domitian and his harvester, Morzim, was stunning—making it difficult for his mind to conceptualize.

"This is awesome! Absolutely incredible!" Domitian exclaimed to his selectants, Aareez and Wendy, who were on the other side of the clear, ballistic walls containing the operator's chamber. Domitian forgot that the harvesters had voice synthesizers that relayed all audible input from their operators, so his passion was known to those in the stadium that were able to discern his voice.

Raith, now relatively attuned to the task before him, started to bang his sword and shield together. The high intensity energy on the blade and outer shield surface collided and released small bursts of blue and white repelling lights, along with a quick crackle of electromagnetic repulsion. Raith practiced some while in the bowels of the stadium before he came up for the match, but the exact capabilities of the hardware were still mostly foreign to him.

Similarly, Domitian had a brief introduction to the basic operations of his harvester and its capabilities. The technicians gave a tutorial to Domitian before his match. Training wasn't as necessary for the operator since he or she was safely using a machine to fight the offender. The operator felt some of the physical aspects of the fighting, but not nearly as much as the offender did. The offender had his or her own flesh and blood on the line in a fight to the death.

"The stadium has transformed. The first harvester is here. The first operator is here. All that is left is to begin the match!" Sirus's own twisted fervor began to show through his masquerading smile.

"All spectators, please sit and dutifully observe the first match in accordance with our previously mentioned rules."

A stark juxtaposition in sound began to play. Earlier, during pre-match fanfare and exposition, jubilance was easily the most palpable expression associated with the music. Now, a darker morbidity was a growing theme encapsulating the stadium and all its guests.

"The first match to the death is very significant to all of us. It signifies the beginning of the Commonwealth. A time when superior human values systematically overcame those that stood in the way of true justice, guaranteed protection, and the rectification of all inequity.

"Always, always remember. First, there will be violence, then there will be silence. Do not fear. Do not bend. The Commonwealth way wins in the end. Enjoy and may the operator win on our behalf!"

It starts. Public execution-turned-entertainment before crowds by the thousands all over the world. At Central Stadium, Raith and Domitian square off. One has blood, the other has hydraulic fluid.

The explosions of fired munitions into the air sounded the beginning of the match.

"Come get it you piece of scrap," Raith taunted.

"All right, if you say so," Domitian said with his facial expression distinctly realistic on Morzim's mechanical face.

Raith's orange uniform was not by any means meant to protect him, only his shield and sword could do that. On the contrary, Morzim's blue toned titanium and galvanized alloys protected its vital components quite well, except for several locations that were designated weak spots to give the offender a slim chance to defeat it.

Raith stood with a defensive posture. His shield in his left hand and sword in his right. Sweat dripped down his brow. Some of the beads of sweat managed to hit the ground, and almost instantly evaporated on the hot and lifeless combatant grounds.

All offenders had managed to evaporate into oblivion for as long as the matches had gone on. The only exception was Nathaniel Marion. He managed to avoid the evaporation and managed to avoid the evisceration. He managed to avoid the mutilation as well as the public humiliation of a terrible death. He will try once again to survive today's match at the end of the Tri Annum.

Morzim ran at Raith with its rotating Scythian blades overhead to come down for a death blow.

Raith lifted his shield and sword to absorb the charging machine's immense downward force.

"Ahhhh!" Raith yelled as he opposed the razor-sharp blades spinning just inches away from his head.

"Just let me do it!" Domitian snarled from within his operator's chamber and transmitted through Morzim's vocal processor. "The less you struggle, the quicker your death will be. It's up to you. You can choose a slow and painful death, or a quick and relatively painless one."

"Go to hell you cowardly bastard! Come out here and fight me for yourself!"

"That's where you'll be soon enough, scum. What you did was offensive to all of us. What I'm doing is justice."

Raith managed to create enough space between the merciless robot and himself, so he could retreat for several steps.

Raising its Scythian pike, Morzim slashed down onto Raith.

The offender quickly countered the blow with his shield and managed to strike Morzim's elbow with his sword.

Raith regrettably saw that no damage had been done. This match was going to take everything he had. Despite giving every ounce of energy he could possibly muster, it still seemed quite likely this match will take his life.

"Nice try," Domitian sardonically let out.

Morzim lashed sideways. One of the half dozen blades cut a deep gash into Raith's outer thigh on his shield side. A splash of blood spurted out onto the anemic, gray grounds of the combatant field.

"Arrrrgh!" Raith let out as he moved nearly all his weight to his other side as blood was running down and covering his entire left lower leg.

"I smell blood. You know what that means, Raith—don't you?" Domitian snarked with a truly sinister tone.

"Your whole family will know what it means to smell blood after you kill me today, Domitian. I promise you that. They'll see you as the monster that you truly are."

After several long minutes, blow after blow from Morzim to the wounded offender took their toll. Raith lost a hand and had blood gushing out of a few other considerable wounds. Raith was getting woozy. Hypovolemic shock was setting in. The match was nearly over.

Raith collapsed to the ground without a word. Still barely holding on to life, his eyes looked up to the sun, which was shimmering brightly.

"Get him, Dom."

"Yeah, finish him off," Domitian's selectants, Aareez and Wendy, insisted.

Morzim cocked its weapon back, pointing the speared tip toward Raith and thrust it down through his chest. The match was over. Raith's lifeless body laid out and exsanguinated on the combatant grounds as the entire crowd stood up and cheered.

"What a wonderful beginning to our Tri Annum today!" Sirus interrupted the crowd's voluminous applause.

"An offender harvested. An operator victorious. This is what we all want to see. This is why we are all here.

"Our first intermission has now begun. Please be back to your seats in no more than twenty minutes."

"See, Peter, that's all you have to do. Piece of cake," Ryland reminded his friend.

"Yep. That's all, Ryland. I just have to use a robot to kill a man. That's it," Peter sarcastically derided.

"I just don't know what other choice you have, Peter," Londyn worriedly said. It wasn't that she wanted Peter to kill Nathaniel. She just didn't see him having any other alternative.

"We all have choices to make. You have choices. I have choices. To say that I don't have a choice isn't true, Londyn. I do have a choice. The real question is whether I am willing to accept the consequences of my choice. I know what I have to do to make this right."

"You know, you're right, Peter. You do have a couple of choices. One choice is to kill Nathaniel and live the rest of your life as a hero. The other choice is to let him live and then you will probably spend the rest of your time in prison or possibly end up getting executed."

"There's another choice."

"What?"

"There is almost always one more variable to consider, Ryland. There is almost always one more decision at play."

"Okay, Peter. Whatever you say."

Ryland almost pretended that he didn't hear that particular answer from Peter. He just shrugged it off and continued watching what was happening out in the stadium as he snacked.

Back at Ms. Danvers's class section she asked her students with a half-hearted smile, "Does anyone here need to use the restroom? Or get any food or drink?"

"No, ma'am," Zameera answered for her cohort.

"We're good, Ms. Danvers," Slade shouted out.

Ms. Danvers looked at the others for any contrarian opinion.

"All right then. Let us all stay for the second match. I hope this next match brings us as much excitement and satisfaction as the first." She couldn't help but mention one piece of vital information before letting her class resume their conversations.

"Class, you should know it is perfectly normal to need to use the restroom after seeing the expected human destruction we saw here in the first match. As we see more today, just know that it is normal for you to—"

"Oh my gosh, Ms. Danvers. We know. We know. I think I'm getting more sick by the way you're trying to tell us this than by the terrible things we just saw happen to Raith," Malaya blurted out.

"Okay. Okay, Malaya. If you need to talk, I'm right over here. You'll be fine." Ms. Danvers didn't seem to understand Malaya's point or have any degree of introspection.

Malaya looked on as she subtly shook her head in disregard for what her highly esteemed teacher offered as helpful advice. Zameera and Briley just stared at each other after hearing the strange interchange.

Chapter 7

THE SECOND MATCH AND THE SPARK

"Ladies and gentlemen, boys and girls, the first intermission has concluded. We will commence with the second match of the day in a moment. Please make your way to your seat if you have not already done so."

People hurried to their seats with their food and beverages. Sirus waited a few minutes and then resumed his announcements.

"Let me remind you of one basic philosophy that we share. Our harvesters are designed to kill, and we all know why it's so easy for our operators, picked from among you, to use them without difficulty or hesitation. We have all been educated to recognize those in our world that do not adopt our values and moral superiority. Those that do not conform must pay a price."

Some in the audience didn't relate to Sirus's words, but they had to keep their views to themselves.

"It's time. Our operator, Sara Westwood, and her harvester, Xeethis, are ready. Their randomly chosen adversary, offender Elizabeth Gellen, is as ready as she can be. Let the match begin!"

The crowd erupted again. The enthusiasm was deafening and shook the floor of the stadium.

Mirroring what happened in the previous match, the harvester and offender slowly rose up from the already opened doors in the ground. Sara's voice could be heard coming from Xeethis's vocal amplifier. Similar to Domitian's response, but with a different experiential quality.

"I can't believe this. Look at all the people—so many. Wow! So cool!"

Elizabeth was sitting on the ground as her elevator platform rose to a halting stop at the combatant ground level. She was crying vigorously. Her shield and battle ax laid beside her as her hands covered her face. Drops of tears ran down her forearms, dripped off her elbows and sizzled as they evaporated upon impact on the gray combatant surface.

Peter remained sitting between Londyn and Ryland in his operator's suite. Ryland was quite excited for the next match. He had a second helping of his favorite foods available and a large glass filled with a sugary, carbonated beverage that was outlawed outside of the very room in which he was enjoying it. Londyn was not looking forward to another lopsided duel. She could barely stand it.

"Peter, I can't watch this," she uttered under her breath into Peter's ear.

"I know it's difficult to see, Londyn. Believe me, I know what you're thinking. I completely agree with you, but you need to watch the rest of the matches today."

"What? Why?"

"There's something that is not easily understood, but I will show you why it's important to watch the matches."

"What do you mean?"

Peter turned to Ryland and asked him for a favor.

"Our servers went to go get more food since you ate much of what we had. Can you go and get me some pizza, and possibly wait for the servers to return so I can have one of the pieces of pecan pie that they spoke so highly of?"

"Sure thing. Anything for you on your big day, buddy."

"Thanks, Ryland."

"I'll just use the restroom first, then I'll get your order, sir operator."

Ryland stood up with great difficulty from all the various delicacies that he had so gladly devoured, and sauntered on his mission.

"Londyn," Peter whispered in her ear.

She turned to him with an uncertain and curious look.

"I need you to see something—it's important."

"Peter, you're kinda creeping me out."

"It's not what you think. I can promise you that."

"Okay. Still weird."

Londyn's mind curiously wandered to strange places. She could only wonder if he had a thing for her. She needed to know what he needed to show her, but at the same time it was somewhat troubling to her to think about what it could possibly be. Of course, Ryland conveniently left the area, so she was alone having this awkward conversation with Peter.

"Londyn, take my hand here, and I will put my other hand over your eyes."

"Do you have any idea how weird that sounds?"

"I do. I completely understand. Londyn, this isn't what you think it is—I promise you."

Londyn moved her head back and away from Peter. She wore a markedly skeptical expression in sharp contrast with the still, innocent countenance that Peter had.

"Okay, Peter. Whatever it is, just do it before Ryland gets back. I don't want him to see anything and tell anyone else. I had better not regret this."

"You won't look at me the same after this. I think you'll think of me in a different way."

"What'd you mean?"

"Londyn, I know what you and some of your friends say about me. I know it's difficult for you to talk to me and even be around me."

Londyn began her rebuttal, but Peter kept talking.

"I know what you're trying to say. I realize that I'm not like the others in class. I am different—I know. I also know you have been fairly tolerant of me during the time that we've been in the same pod, and I appreciate that."

"Peter, you don't have to say that. I could have been more open to talking to you when you transferred to our school. I'm sorry."

"You don't have to be sorry. Thank you anyway, though."

"Okay, let's do this, Peter."

Peter took Londyn's left hand and reached his left hand up to cover her eyes.

"Londyn, please close your eyes for me. This should only take a few seconds."

"All right."

As she tightly closed her eyes she could only imagine what Peter was up to.

Peter closed his eyes and slowed his breathing. He was in a deep and contemplative state. Finally, he saw a bright flash underneath his eyelids. It was this dazzling white spark that prompted him to open his eyes.

"Okay, Londyn. Open your eyes."

Peter slowly took his hands away from her hand and face. He looked intently into her eyes, looking for any reaction or response.

"Peter! What is that behind you?"

"Don't be afraid. You don't need to be afraid. It's all right. This is my guardian angel. His name is Adrio."

Londyn was completely terrified to see such a bright, luminous presence standing behind Peter's left shoulder. She'd never seen such a thing. She'd never heard of anything like it.

"He's a what?"

"He's my guardian angel. He looks after me. He's been with me my whole life. You have one too."

"It has a name?" she incredulously asked while staring.

"Yeah, he let me pick out a name so I wouldn't be so scared of him. That was when I was very little and had just begun seeing him."

"You said he's an angel? What's an angel?"

"Well, there are many kinds of angels. Each person has at least one that looks after them. They're not humans. They're spiritual beings that are charged with protecting humans and aiding them in their journey to heaven. They communicate with and carry out orders from God. I'm sorry, Londyn. I know all this is completely new to you. I'll teach you more in time—I promise."

"Peter, you said I have my own guardian angel."

"Yes, that's right."

"I do?" Londyn, already scared at her wits end, slowly turned and let out another shriek.

"Oh my gosh, oh my gosh."

"Londyn, you're okay. Your angel is no stranger to you—he's always been with you. You may not be accustomed to him being near you, but I can assure you that he has been quite accustomed to being near you at all times."

Peter looked at Londyn's supernatural companion and asked what he'd like to be called. "See, Londyn, his name is Chasin."

"How do you know that's his name?"

"He just told me. He thought you might like that name," Peter said with a great big smile.

"He's been assigned to you for your whole life."

"My entire life?"

In complete shock, Londyn could barely formulate a sentence.

"And why haven't I see him before? I mean, I think I'd remember seeing something this bright with me all the time. I mean, how could I even sleep with something this bright being in my dorm room at night?"

"You haven't been capable of seeing him. That's what I helped you do a few moments ago."

"I don't understand. How can that be?"

"There are many things that you have to learn before you can begin to understand. First of all, just know that I helped to restore your sight. There are many things and people in this world that encourage the blindness. The Commonwealth tries to keep the entire world blind to the truth."

"Okay?"

Londyn was so awestruck that she couldn't believe what had just happened. She could hardly speak. She could hardly think.

Peter couldn't tell if he had shown Londyn too much and overwhelmed her.

"It'll make more sense as time goes on. I can promise you that, Londyn."

Londyn grabbed Peter's hand and gave him a smile so big that he could hardly recognize her.

"Peter, who is the other angel with you? He looks different than Adrio. I thought you said each person only had one?"

"I said each person had *at least one*. I should have been a little more specific. I am trying to keep it fairly simple so it's easier for you to take in. Each person has a guardian angel, but sometimes others angels look after a person, too, if needed."

Peter turned to his right and looked behind him to see the other angel as he answered Londyn.

"Londyn, this is Michael."

Chapter 8

DEATH AND LIFE

"Get up, Elizabeth. I would hate to summon the security officers to make you stand," Sirus publicly warned as Elizabeth continued to weep with her face in her hands while sitting on the combatant grounds.

She took her hands away, revealing her face as she looked out to where Sirus stood in his booth in full view. Tears ran down her face as she begged for mercy.

"I'm a doctor. I was trying to save my patient's baby. A baby that she was looking forward to have and to hold, to love and to raise. It didn't matter to her or me if the baby wasn't as perfect as you apparently are. I helped both of them." Her rationalization fell on hardened hearts.

"It's too late for plea bargains now, Elizabeth. You are guilty as charged. In the eyes of the Commonwealth, you are as worthy of death as the man before you and the other offenders after you. Your sentence is final. This is your end. You can choose to be killed sitting or standing. I know Sara will not care what your choice is—she will kill with the assistance of her harvester, regardless."

Sirus received an urgent message from the premier's top aide. Sirus was ordered to expedite the match, preventing the offender from sharing her views with the audience present and those watching on the global Commonwealth-run viewing networks.

"Okay, Sara. You may commence."

The crowd cheered in anticipation of the quick death that was about to greet Elizabeth.

"What do you see, Londyn?" Peter asked.

"I can see that offender Elizabeth has several angels with her. One looks so sad and the other two look a little more stern. Why does she have so many?"

"My guess is that her guardian angel is sad that Elizabeth is facing so much persecution and a certain death. The other two angels appear to be from the choir of Thrones by the look of them. They offer courage and spiritual protection during times of intense persecution."

"Choirs? Do they sing or something?"

"No. By *choirs*, I mean the different types of angels. There are a total of nine choirs of angels. Each choir has many angels of the same kind that perform duties, which are different from those performed by angels in other choirs."

"Duties? Like they have jobs?"

"Yeah, they have jobs. Each one of them has a specific job. Some have more than one responsibility. Some deal with the laws of the cosmos. Some deal with the forces of nature. Some are responsible for humans and the nations of the earth. Each type of angel is placed in a hierarchical order."

"What about our guardian angels?"

"They're in the lowest order of angels since they are the closest to the material world and humans."

Xeethis began to slowly walk toward Elizabeth. Each step that it took made small particles of dirt bounce up from the ground. Xeethis had two swords, each with three blades. It had no shield. Its vicious offense was its primary defense.

Elizabeth continued to sit on the ground in protest. She refused to pick up her ax and shield even as the death machine came toward her.

"You don't want to do this. Sara, I know you can hear me. I'm a woman just like you. You know I don't deserve this."

Sara, in the safety of her operator's chamber replied through Xeethis.

"Of course I have to do this. You're an offender. What other option is there? You've been condemned to die and I have the duty to ensure that your sentence is carried out."

"Have mercy!"

"No mercy for an offender like you!"

Xeethis extended both arms back with all six devastating blades facing Elizabeth.

"No! Please!" Elizabeth screamed.

Sara screamed, "Ahhhhhhh!"

Xeethis's swords slashed in toward each other and then crossed. One sword went high, the other swung low. They sliced effortlessly through Elizabeth. Only a dozen scattered pieces of flesh and bone remained.

The crowd went wild, and Sirus continued announcing as if nothing had happened.

"I'm sorry that we did not have any adversarial fighting during that match. Sometimes the offenders just don't have it in them to fight for their own survival. We should still be grateful that we were able to see one more of our vile offenders dispatched in a manner suitable for her crime. Enjoy your second intermission."

At the moment of Elizabeth's death, Londyn noticed an odd occurrence. There was movement taking place. It seemed to be a third angel that appeared.

"Peter, what's happening?"

"I'll have to be brief. Ryland is almost ready to come back with our pizza and pie. He can't hear about any of this."

"Okay, that's fine," she hurriedly said.

"Londyn, do you see the brightly shining figure in the middle of Elizabeth's two angels?"

"Yes, I see it."

"Well, that's Elizabeth's soul. It's her spirit that transcends bodily death and leaves the physical world in which we live."

"So, that's Elizabeth, but it's not the Elizabeth who was just cut to pieces?"

"They were one in the same at that time, now her body is left behind and her soul is being escorted to the afterlife as we speak. Do you see the angels guiding her soul up toward the sky? They are taking her into the afterlife."

"So, they just float away? To where?"

"We'll have to continue this discussion later—he's coming."

Ryland walked up to Peter and slammed his hand down on Peter's left shoulder.

"My all-star, famous friend. I got your pizza slices and the pecan pie."

"Thanks, Ryland. I'm sorry you had to miss the match while you were waiting to get my food."

"Awe geez, it wasn't so bad. I ate plenty while I was waiting. Plus, that loser second offender didn't even put up a fight, so it wasn't much to miss."

"Hey, buddy, do you think you could help me out? Since my match is the last one today, there are only two more to go until I'm up. Can you go back and ask Ms. Danvers where we're supposed to meet after the Tri Annum's done? I guess after being picked and then selecting Londyn and you, I lost sight of what happens afterward."

"Yeah, sure thing, Peter. I guess I don't know what we're supposed to do either. How about after the next match?"

"Sure. That sounds good."

While putting a slice of pizza to his mouth, Peter turned to Londyn and gave her a wink.

The two matches went on just as the previous two had. There was some variance in the length of time spent fighting. Different weapons. Different wounds. Always death in the end for the offender, which was quickly followed by the ostensibly omniscient voice of the stadium with his ingratiation of the crowd and denigration of the deceased.

Londyn's worldview was slowly and methodically being expanded as her blindness was lifting. Peter's calm and compelling descriptions of the truth about life on earth were radically challenging Londyn's previous fourteen years of schooling and teaching.

Chapter 9

THE FINAL MATCH

"Ladies and gentlemen, this is our last intermission of the day, which can only mean one thing—our final match is nearly here. The highly anticipated duel of the day between operator Peter Barclay and offender Nathaniel Marion. Peter's harvester is Kreetis, a highly advanced and especially lethal robot specifically designed for this fight by a defense firm that wishes to remain anonymous. What a great match this shall be! See you all in twenty minutes."

After he donned his combatant suit, Peter started getting orientated to his harvester controls in the operator's chamber. It had all the state-of-the-art integration technology for full control over his harvester, Kreetis. Commonwealth techs were readying other equipment for the match in Peter's operator chamber. Each of them was ensuring that all the sensors, communications systems, telemetry units, and other critical elements of the operator's chamber functioned properly. They could ill afford any mishaps during the match, especially with the fate of such a highly-valued offender on the line. Nathaniel Marion was a highly skilled veteran with warfighting experience, and since Peter was a novice in hand-to-hand combat, he needed to have as many technological advantages as possible.

Ryland and Londyn moved to their alternative seats to view inside the operator's chamber.

"This has to be the coolest thing I've ever been able to do in my whole life," Ryland said to the unusually quiet Londyn.

"Londyn, did you hear me? What's the matter with you?"

"I heard you. I'm just thinking, that's all. I can't wait for this last match to be over. I just don't want to see any more death today, especially if Peter has to kill Nathaniel."

"Well, how else do you think this is going to end? Get a grip. This'll be fun and will be something that our class will talk about for months, maybe years. You and I are Peter's selectants. He picked us out of the whole class. You should be proud of that."

"I am very proud that he picked me," Londyn said with a smirk, knowing how strange it sounded. "Prouder than you'd think."

The crowd settled in for the big match. Ms. Danvers's class was exceptionally well-behaved, eagerly awaiting their classmate to fulfill an honor that many of them could only dream of doing themselves.

"It's time. This is the pinnacle of today's Tri Annum—the fifth match between a young operator and a six-time winning offender. What a match this shall be. What a time it is to be here to witness this. I am sure we are all feeling the same level of excitement, a level of excitement that can only be contained for so long. Ladies and gentlemen. Boys and girls. I must say this one more time. No, no, no. How about you say it with me?"

The crowd jumped in with Sirus, "First, there will be violence, then there will be silence. Do not fear. Do not bend. The Commonwealth way wins in the end."

"Excellent! Extraordinary! Absolutely wonderful! Thank you all so much for your participation! Now let us all cheer on Peter for his role in our finale today! It's time for the final match—to begin!"

The elevators began to rise. This time they rose as fireworks and shells fired into the air. The showering sparks and fading embers carved out trails within the sky as they steadily disappeared into the day's crisp air.

Nathaniel rose from one side, Kreetis from the other. One was biological, the other was mechanical. One was born to survive, the other was built to kill.

"All right, you bucket of bolts. Ready to get scrapped? I hope you didn't cost too much to make. It'd be a real pity," Nathaniel taunted.

Peter, fully aware that he could verbalize through his harvester, chose to remain silent. The task at hand was difficult enough for him to endure without his emotions getting the best of him by speaking.

"What I'm gonna do is take this here halberd and disassemble you piece by piece."

Peter remembered the brief description of Nathaniel that Ms. Danvers had given when they were moving about in the Vestibule of Veneration prior to entering the stadium. He was the most successful offender of any match in Commonwealth history. There was a great deal of pressure riding on Peter's shoulders to do the right thing. Peter debated whether he should act upon his own idea of what was right or do what was right in the eyes of the Commonwealth. It was his choice to make.

"I just can't imagine Peter killing someone. It just seems so contrary to what he stands for," Londyn said to Ryland while they sat outside the operator's chamber viewing Peter readying himself for battle.

"Believe me, I know him better than you. He is definitely a little different than most of us, but he knows what's good for him. He's pretty new in town. If he does this right, he'll be a hero for the rest of his life. It's not like he can just give that up, that's not how it works," Ryland countered.

"I know he's your friend, Ryland, but there's more to him than you'd think."

"What's that supposed to mean? Suddenly you know him better than I do?"

"No, I didn't say that."

"Well, I've been his friend since he moved here four months ago. How many times did you talk to him before today? Maybe twice?"

"I know, Ryland. I know. Being in this position brings people together. That's all I'm saying."

"Fair enough. I can only imagine how close I'll be to my Commonwealth rock star after today. He'll be a celebrity and I'll be his trusted sidekick. It'll be great. Heck, maybe he'll be able to pull some strings and get me to be an operator at a different Tri Annum?"

"I just hope he makes whatever decision is best for him and doesn't think about what anyone else wants him to do," Londyn said with a sigh.

The crowd grew restless. People were ready for the excitement to start. The sun's beaming rays came through the clouds, seemingly driving apart the white nebulae and exposing the light blue sky again.

"Guests of the glorious Central Stadium, I invite you to stand and honor our final operator of the day—Peter Barclay!"

Peter's image from within his operator's chamber instantly came to each monitor in the stadium, from the smallest to the large center holographic monitor above the combatant ground.

"Are you ready, Peter?" Sirus anxiously asked.

Peter, looking directly into Sirus's eyes from the screen most visible to him said, "I've never been more ready to fulfill my duty."

"That a boy! That's what I like to hear! How about the rest of you in the crowd? Isn't that what you like to hear?"

The crowd boomed with applause and shouting.

"It's time. Let the fighting begin!" Sirus bellowed as he pointed to the two combatants standing ready to tear into each other.

Nathaniel and Peter's harvester, Kreetis, began to slowly step in a clockwise direction. They didn't have enough speed to catch one another, but instead studied the other to determine what action to take. Nathaniel had both of his hands on his halberd, which didn't leave any room to carry a shield for additional protection. Kreetis had two maces that had rotating tips. The cyclonic weapons spun expeditiously. The spikes along their edges didn't have to be sharp to inflict devastating damage because they spun at such a high rate of revolutions per second.

Kreetis's shimmering, red-tinted, chrome-lined armor was impeccable. Not a smudge or scratch could be detected by the spectators seated in any direction around the stadium.

Nathaniel bounced to the right, and did a seven-hundred and twenty degree twirl with his halberd extended. The rotational speed at the tip of the electro-augmented halberd was so immense that when it made contact with Kreetis's left flank it knocked it to the ground with a hard thud.

The crowd went wild. Not to support the offender, but in awe of the masterful attack that he so meticulously executed.

Peter, now laying on his back in the racquetball court size operator's chamber stared up at the ceiling, unsure of what had just happened.

"Wow," Peter said with a muffled voice as he tried to get his breath back. He didn't expect to bear this much of the physical trauma absorbed by his harvester.

"Oh, so the mighty operator has decided to speak," Nathaniel gloated.

Peter rose to his feet and stared Nathaniel down, with Kreetis moving in the exact sequence that its operator did. Peter took a broad jump with both cyclonic maces overhead and then crashed them down on top of Nathaniel.

Nathaniel was barely able to stop the onslaught of its nearly insuperable power. The integrity of the halberd felt like it was starting to give way, so he rolled out to avoid certain demise.

"Nice try, Barclay. You almost had me there," Nathaniel remarked.

Peter didn't respond. He did, however, perform several somersaults to counter the offender's acrobatic tendencies. Then, to surprise Nathaniel, Peter took two long bounds and slashed across his body. Nathaniel managed to deflect the blow and quickly veered the other mace coming from the opposite direction.

Nathaniel went on the offensive, thrusting the halberd into Kreetis's thorax right in an infinitesimally small seam between its armor plating. Peter bent down with a dull pain in his chest. Nathaniel quickly withdrew his weapon to turn a one-eighty and strike Kreetis across the head with the electro-bladed halberd, which sent it spinning to the ground.

Peter wasn't sure how many more hits he could take. Even with the harvester taking the blows, the operator still felt much from the mechanical strikes to its outer armor. He slowly put one knee forward, then rose up onto both legs again, not knowing what his agile opponent had in store for his next move.

"I don't know how much more of this he can take," Londyn anxiously said to Ryland.

"I'm beginning to think so too. Just imagine how much force that harvester is absorbing. It's gotta be like ten times what Peter feels. No wonder Nathaniel won six matches before this one."

Nathaniel was pacing a few steps in front of Kreetis, trying to calculate his next and hopefully final move to end the match and launch him further into Tri Annum infamy.

Peter looked at Nathaniel intently, trying to predict what he might do next.

"Here we go," Nathaniel uttered to himself as he slashed low, across both of Kreetis's legs. Then, without halting momentum he sprung into an oblique three-hundred and sixty degree spin and landed right behind Kreetis.

Peter didn't have time to react. The instant he knew Nathaniel was behind him, he felt pressure followed by a sharp pain at the base of his head. Nathaniel had seamlessly pulled out a small, sharp device from the end of his halberd and jammed it into the base of Kreetis's metal cranium.

Nathaniel cranked to the right and then removed the dagger-like object. Peter felt something click as the crank stopped and felt immense pressure relief when the object was retracted. Something didn't seem right, though. Peter lost all control over Kreetis.

Peter didn't say anything, but he noticed that his visual, tactile, and kinesthetic symbiosis with his harvester was completely gone. He looked at a monitor in his operator's chamber and saw what was taking place.

Kreetis fell face-first to the ground. Nathaniel opened a small compartment on its lower right calf and punched in some sort of code and then Kreetis began to move—this time without Peter controlling it.

The reanimated harvester's arms and legs bent to ninety degree angles as Nathaniel stepped onto its back and sat on a small seat that punched up out from underneath the dorsal armor. Happening within a timeframe of less than a few seconds, a small, single passenger fuselage conformed around Nathaniel, including a lightweight protective suit with a flight helmet. Then, it lifted up off of the ground. The newly configured craft with its wily pilot hovered a few feet above the ground atop its three engines that were pulsing a steady flow of deep blue flames.

Commonwealth Security Officers rushed from all directions toward the reconfigured harvester with their weapons raised.

"Nathaniel, we have you completely surrounded. We will shoot if you do not disengage the machine and surrender. This is your only warning," the senior officer sternly warned.

"Sorry, officer, this is your only warning. You had your chance. I must be going now," Nathaniel calmly advised with a brief smile.

The now fully formed and operational aircraft quickly accelerated straight up into the sky. Once the craft reached a high enough altitude outside of the stadium, its main thrust powered on and it screamed higher yet. Anti-aircraft missiles and hyperkinetic munitions were on its tail, but were destroyed by Nathaniel's escape craft's countermeasures or missed their target from evasive maneuvering.

All eyes in the entire crowd looked up and saw the rapidly evolving aerial pursuit. Each one of them saw a larger and even faster aircraft moving toward a location that looked to intersect with the trajectory of Nathaniel's aircraft.

Peter watched on the monitor as Nathaniel and his escape craft, formerly known as Kreetis, were swallowed up in a docking bay within the larger aircraft. Once the convergence took place, the larger host craft disappeared out of the atmosphere without a trace. Nathaniel Marion was gone. Sirus and the rest in the stadium were completely speechless. The premier, still quickly being hurried to a secure location deep within the stadium by his formidable Varangian Guard, knew that losing his most prized offender would only come back to haunt him.

Sirens in the greater Chicago area blared. Combat patrols over the skyline monitored for further conspiratorial activities and threats. Soldiers and security forces patrolled the streets around critical infrastructure and landmark locations citywide.

Sirus received an immediate directive from military command assets in the region, who were secured in fortified positions underground.

"Ladies and gentlemen, boys and girls. I have just received an urgent message to relay to you from the Eighteenth Province Military Commander. It reads as follows: Citizens of the Commonwealth. Due to the unforeseen and unusual occurrences you have just witnessed, this entire incident is being classified as above top secret. The global security ramifications of this phenomenon are unknown for the time being, but there are many concerns within our political and military command structure. All of you citizens of our United People's Commonwealth are hereby sworn to silence regarding anything to do with this day's events. This Tri Annum never took place. You were never here. Any violation of this dictum will be met with swift and harsh punitive measures. Thank you for your compliance. You are dismissed from the stadium."

After Sirus's closing message, Peter turned around and looked at his two selectants.

"Well, Londyn, do you believe what you saw today?"

"Of course I do."

"Good."

Naturally, Ryland wanted to give his opinion on the matter.

"Peter! Dude! You just made history! Your harvester turned into a spaceship and was taken over by the offender! This has to be the most incredible thing I've ever seen."

"I'm glad to have been a part of history. But remember, Ryland, none of this officially happened. That means we don't have any handwritten paper due for class tomorrow."

"Oh my gosh, you're right. If we're sworn to silence, how can we legally write a paper about it? Sweet!"

Peter smiled back at Ryland and then switched his focus back to Londyn. His smile turned to a smirk that could only mean one thing—satisfaction.

Chapter 10

BACK TO SCHOOL

Back in Ms. Danvers's class, everyone was completely silent. Typically, the follow-up class period after returning from a Tri Annum was meant to summarize the students's thoughts about the day's events. The judicial system was almost always praised. The glory of the operators slaying the offenders in Central Stadium cascaded like a deluge from the school administrators and teachers. Today was different. The edict forbid any discussion of the Tri Annum since the official record expunged the existence of this Tri Annum.

"I know today has been a long and exhausting day for you all. Thank you so much for your cooperation during your exit interviews with security officials. Hopefully, they'll uncover whoever is responsible for the plot. I can only hope Nathaniel Marion is captured so justice can be served the way it ought to be," Ms. Danvers monotonously addressed her class.

"Ms. Danvers, I'm not sure what you're talking about. Today never happened. We never went anywhere. The sun failed to rise this morning. The clocks stopped in their tracks," Maksim sarcastically interjected.

"I do not appreciate that tone, Maks. One more outburst like that and I will sign you up for cleaning duty again."

"Sorry, ma'am."

"Thank you."

Zameera, Briley, Malaya, and Londyn, sitting in their customary quartet configuration, looked around with their eyes occasionally crossing paths. Londyn never looked at her friends the same way. She didn't look at anyone the same way, not since her time with Peter at Central Stadium.

"On another note, I'm sure you all know we have parental visitation tomorrow. It is that time of the trimester again, so you can spend twenty-four hours with your family members and then return to your living quarters here on campus. Be sure not to say one word about today. Remember that as a Commonwealth educator, I am a mandated reporter. If there is any indication of potential for Commonwealth subversion, I will report you as I have reported others in the past. Reporting subversion has been a rarity, but I take this responsibility very seriously and will not hesitate.

"Thank you for fulfilling your civic duties today, class. You are all dismissed for your evening routines. See you tomorrow for your parental visitation and transport at 0800, sharp."

The class stood, learning beacons in hand, and walked down the long hallway outside the classroom in a single file line. Other classes let out at precisely the same time. All together, all wearing the exact same uniform, and all heading down to eat the same Commonwealth sanctioned meals with some variation for individual nutrient and caloric needs.

"How can it be humane for them to feed us this garbage?" Ryland questioned while juxtaposing his school dinner with the gourmet food that he enjoyed in the operator's suite. "I know it's meant to keep us healthy, but geez. You'd think they would have the courtesy to at least consider giving it a little flavor. It's not healthy to want to throw up after choking down every apparently nutritious meal."

"Yeah, it's not too pleasant, is it?" Peter responded.

"That's a bit of an understatement," Ryland fired back.

Zameera sat with her friends several tables away from Peter and Ryland. She looked back at the two boys and then back to Londyn. She was trying to see if Londyn would get the hint to initiate conversation about the Tri Annum.

"So what'd you think about being a selectant?" Zameera came out forthright.

"Remember what Ms. Danvers just said? We have to be quiet about what happened. I don't wanna get into trouble."

"I know. I know. Malaya, Briley? A little help?" Zameera requested.

"Londyn, if we happened to be at Central Stadium earlier today and if you happened to be chosen by Peter Barclay as a selectant—what would you imagine your time with him to be like?" Briley asked.

"Come on, guys. Really?"

Malaya asked with a big smile, "Please?"

"All right, all right. If you have to know, it was fine. It was completely different than I expected. There is much more to him than you'd think at face value. He was very nice to me. I thought he liked me or something, but I don't think so. I mean, he likes me like someone he can talk to—not like a girlfriend or anything though."

"Well, that's interesting. Isn't it, girls?" Zameera playfully invited the others's opinions.

"Very interesting," Briley chimed.

"More please," Malaya insisted.

Londyn had reservations about revealing what had really transpired. The wonderful gift she was given by Peter had to remain a secret. Peter wanted it that way. If he trusted her enough to give her sight into the spiritual realm, then she surely had to keep her end of the bargain.

"He helped me to understand more about the world—that's all I can say. He knows things that we've never been taught. He knows things that we're being shielded from. I'm not sure why, but I know that it's happening."

"What do you mean, Londyn?" Zameera whispered.

"I don't know the full picture. I just know something is going on—something beyond us."

Peter looked on with an inscrutable expression, as he often did. He certainly noticed what Londyn and her friends were saying.

Ryland and Peter continued on to their dorm room after finishing their unimpressive supper. They were pretty tired from the ordeal today, especially Peter. Not to mention Peter being sore from all the physical trauma from the match. He had so many bruises he could hardly count them all. So they got ready for bed after packing their things for the parental visitation the next day. Neither of them had the desire to play games or explore the dorm for entertainment. They just wanted to go relax.

"Peter, I'm looking forward to meeting your aunt and uncle tomorrow," Ryland said as he lay with his eyes closed on his bottom bunk in their dorm room.

"Yeah, I'm looking forward to introducing you to them. It'll be good for me to finally meet your parents too. Is it usually a pretty hectic time when families finally get to see their kids after such a long time away at school?"

"It's hectic, but it's manageable. You know how the Commonwealth is. It's pretty organized, so it works out well."

"It'll be nice to sleep in my old bed again. I'm certainly looking forward to that," Peter said with an etched smile.

"That is a nicety of going home, even though we spend far more time away at school than we ever do with our parents in their home."

The two friends and roommates carried on, and then it dawned on Peter that this would be a perfect time to bring up a subject he had not yet raised with Ryland.

"Ryland, when I was growing up, my parents used to tell me a story they wrote called 'The Winged Lion.' They started out reading it to me, but as I grew older and outgrew the original story, they would change the wording to reflect my age. The ideas were still the same, but obviously they had to tailor it to my vocabulary. It was my favorite story growing up. Would you like to hear it?"

"Sure. I'm almost asleep as it is, so that may do the trick."

"We'll see. I like it anyway. Here it goes." Peter sighed deeply as he closed his eyes, inundating himself with the story and trying to find the exact words that he needed to begin. After a brief pause, he found them. "It always takes a second to remember how it starts."

* * *

"A long time ago, there lived a pride of lions in the great expanses of the Serengeti. It was ruled by a powerful and mighty ruler. He was an unjust and domineering king who was wrought with the spoils of his splendor. The others in the pride suffered greatly but none had the courage to improve their lives—except one. He knew that the only way to help the others was to challenge the king. His name was Josh.

"Josh was a very profound lion. From the time he was a small cub he was always precocious. As he grew older and continued to mature in his early adulthood, his mother insisted that others in the pride listen to him and follow his ways. Some listened, but they did not yet trust him enough to follow his ways."

Ryland interjected, "What kind of things was Josh doing?"

"I was just about to tell you," Peter explained.

"Oh, okay. Please continue. Sorry." Ryland acquiesced.

Peter continued, "As with each meal, King Tiber ate first, then the alpha female, and so on. Each lion lined up and waited for his or her turn. That was how nearly all aspects of the lions' lives played out. The king always came first, then the rest. Josh had a different idea. An idea that no other lion dared to attempt out of fear of what the king might do.

"Josh spoke. 'Please feel free to take my place up here, miss, and your daughter too,' he offered. The lioness was awestruck with gratitude since she knew that Josh was offering her young daughter and her a chance at having access to a more nutritious and fulfilling meal. Lions just didn't do that sort of thing for each other, they looked out for themselves. Josh had been looking out for different lions for years in many different ways. This particular situation was distinct though since it defied one of the king's rules."

Ryland's once certain appointment to count sheep was placed on forbearance as his interest grew in Peter's story.

"What'd King Tiber do when Josh gave up his spot in line?" Ryland eagerly asked while sitting attentively at the edge of his bed. Peter wasn't sure why Ryland suddenly became interested in his story. Nonetheless, he was pleasantly surprised. Maybe it had something to with the greater society? As with all other children in the Commonwealth, Ryland was raised by Commonwealth educators.

There was no lesson plan that provided bedtime story reading. Peter was not raised in this manner at all. He was quite accustomed to his parents reading to him as a child.

"Well, Peter. What'd he do?"

"I'm sorry, Ryland. To answer your question, King Tiber watched this time. He watched the young lioness and her cub move up to Josh's spot, which was third from the front. Josh then headed to the back of the line.

"As he walked past the other fifteen lions, he received many different looks of disappointment and disapproval. Some asked what happened among themselves. Others jumped to the conclusion that he must have done something wrong and was sent to the back of the line as his punishment from the king. Josh held his head up high all the way until he turned to stand at the end of the formation of hungry lions. King Tiber, obviously the first to eat, stared at Josh as he gorged himself on the newly delivered meal. The king knew full well that since he selected which lion was to eat in what order, Josh was altering the pride's hierarchy without his permission."

"So you're tellin' me that the big bad king didn't do a thing?" Ryland couldn't seem to understand the king's lack of action. The king rules over the pride, so he should know what was best, right? Under the Commonwealth's rule, he never questioned the guidance of the ruling class. It wasn't his fault. That's how the world had been most of his life. Every adult in his life reinforced the idea, so there was no alternative viewpoint.

Peter thought it was best to pause the story to answer Ryland's question. "You'll have to wait and see, but first can you explain what you mean? Why do you think the king should act?"

"It seems pretty straightforward, Peter. The king's in charge, and Josh undermined his authority by trading places in line with the lioness and her cub."

"Do you think what Josh did was wrong? Giving up his spot in line in order to, at least for one time, allow the lioness and her cub to have a better meal than they were used to having."

"Of course it's wrong. It's not his choice to change things like that."

"Even if what Josh did was kind and charitable?" Peter tried to expose the crux of Ryland's thought process.

"Even then. It doesn't matter. I'm sure the king had his reasons for choosing the order that he did. Josh didn't have the right to change the rules like that."

"Are you listening to yourself, Ryland? You're telling me that Josh needs permission to do something nice for a female lion and her cub."

Ryland started to get a little agitated, "Of course he does! The king is the king! He has the power, so he must be right!" He let out a contemptuous sigh of disapproval after his outburst.

"Just because someone has power does not make him or her an authority on morality. Sometimes they might be, and other times they might be far from it. What a ruler thinks is right might be the exact opposite of what's right. Therein lies the problem with your thinking, Ryland."

Ryland needed a moment to take in what Peter said. He'd never heard that idea before. He was always taught that those holding the most political power in society—namely the premier and others in high ranking government positions—were the preeminent arbiters of what was moral and immoral.

"Hmm—interesting," was all he could manage. "Anyway, let's continue the story."

"Sure, let's do that," Peter replied. "Now, where were we?" Only a second or two elapsed. "Okay, now I remember."

"The pride finished their day's meal and broke up into their typical small groups to rest. Josh and his mother chose a spot under a towering acacia tree. It didn't take long for her to praise her son. She said, 'I hope you know that I'm very proud of you for what you did. I was afraid to say it in front of the others. You know how cruel King Tiber can be.'

"Josh replied, 'Thanks, Mom. It means a lot coming from you. I just wanted to do one small thing today to make their day a little bit easier. I know Dad would've done the same thing. I sure wish he was still here.' Josh clearly missed his father, and his mother knew the difficulty that his departure placed on her son. She only drew Josh closer to her. They were all each other had outside of the other lions in the pride.

"'I know, my son. I know,' she said as she embraced him.

"The two continued reminiscing and resting in the comfort of the shade until the king came over to speak to Josh.

"'Josh, a word.'

"Josh and his mother knew this was bound to happen again. Josh had more subtly defied the king's wishes before, but not in front of the entire pride like what had happened today. The king came to confront Josh about his open defiance of his orders during mealtime.

"With a small, quick flip of the head, Josh followed the king away from his mother and the rest of the pride. Now alone and face-to-face, King Tiber began.

"'Why did you allow Tatianna and little Nelly to trade places with you?'

"Josh replied, 'I thought it'd be nice to let them have some of the best meat to enjoy. They don't get that opportunity, so I wanted to provide that for them.'

"The king casually responded, 'I see—and what made you think that you were allowed to change my directive?'

"Josh didn't take long to respond. 'It was the right thing to do. I thought about it, and I decided that they deserved it. I didn't think I deserved any better meal than them.'

"King Tiber didn't take well to Josh's explanation.

"'You see, Josh, that train of thought is problematic. I am the king, so I make the rules. For instance, I decide who eats on any given day and in which order. I decide who gets this or that. I decide what's charitable and kind, and what isn't. I decide, not you.'

"'King, I—' Josh was cut off midsentence.

"'I would think that you, being a leading contender in succeeding me as king one day, would understand that. If you want to be a king, you had better stop acting like this and quit doing these silly little things that you think are so wonderful. If I were you, I would try really hard to get this guilt out of your head and get back to the front of the line where you belong.' Josh finally got a word in.

"'With all due respect, sir, when I am king I will give up my crown and let the pride have a voice. If I am given the honor of representing the pride, then I will gladly remain in an elected position. If the pride's voice speaks another name, then I will let him or her assume the responsibility. Regardless, I will ensure that there are safeguards in place to keep any one lion from having too much power again. And yes, that would mean limiting my own power as well. That is what I think would be best for the pride—'

"The king lost it, 'No, no, no! I will not allow it! As of this moment you are cast out of my pride! Get out!' The king snarled and showed his razor sharp teeth. His two trusted bodyguards knew what the king meant when he ordered Josh out. They quickly and forcefully escorted Josh out to the limits of the pride's territory—out where hyenas and leopards warred for land with several other lion factions. On his own, Josh wouldn't last long. The king and his henchlions knew full well that Josh carried a death sentence."

Ryland jumped in again, "Let me get this straight, Josh was willing to give up his power?"

"That's right," Peter replied. "Josh knew that the pride still needed leadership, but he thought it would be fair to have the consent of the other lions in the pride for him to hold that position of power. He wanted to include each lion in his decision making. The king wanted to rule absolutely and completely, regardless of what any other lion thought."

"That sounds reasonable," Ryland weighed the two styles of governing. "I mean what Josh wanted to do as opposed to the way the king ruled. Letting the people have a voice seems like a good thing."

Peter noticed Ryland's thought process, which naturally brought him to a relevant question, "Ryland, which of these two styles of governing best describes the Commonwealth?"

"Hmm. I've never thought of it like this, but I would have to say King Tiber's way." Peter hoped that Ryland would come to an important realization.

"Would you prefer Josh's way?"

"Peter, I gotta say, you are putting some very interesting ideas in my head. How about we continue?" Ryland managed to deflect his answer to Peter's excellent question.

"I'm glad to be of service. Sure, let's do that," Peter replied with his usual smirk, which reflected some degree of intellectual victory.

"As the king's bodyguards forced Josh farther and farther away from the pride's center, they jabbed and jeered at him.

"'You're lucky he didn't have us kill you,' one guard said.

"The other followed up with another respectable remark, 'Yeah, at least you'll still be alive for a while.'

"Josh wasn't too troubled by what the burly bodyguards contemptuously uttered, but more so by the apparent apathy that the other lions seemed to hold on to for the moment."

Ryland interjected again. "Peter, I've noticed this about you over and over since the first time I met you. How'd you learn to talk the way you do?" He seemed to voice some sincere, nonjocular admiration, which was a rarity.

Peter was somewhat flattered by his friend's compliment. "I've had some great teachers, friends, and of course, my family has helped more than I can say. I'm sorry if I'm difficult to understand. I can try and simplify things a bit. Would that help you follow me more easily?"

"No, it's fine. I can understand what you're saying for the most part, but there's no way I can talk like that for long. Please go on."

"All right."

"With their teeth clenched into Josh's fur, the king's enforcers continued to pull him away. The king sat idly, relishing the moment and snickering to himself about his decision that he knew would lead to a great deal of suffering for his newly confirmed philosophical rival. All the others stayed in their small groups and noticed what was going on. None stood up, except for one.

"Josh's mother slowly stood, favoring one of her hind legs to address the rest of the pride gathered nearby.

"'Don't you see what's happening? Do any of you care? Are you all afraid?' The dozen or so lions sat silently. They looked to see whether any others would muster a response. The king noticed and further basked in his glory since he knew there would be no one else to voice their support for Josh or his mother. At least he thought he knew.

"Despite being very introverted, Tatianna spoke, 'Josh did the nicest thing for my little Nelly and me that we have experienced since she was born six months ago. Not one of you stood up to help improve my baby girl's life, knowing full well that King Tiber made her eat after everyone else. We all know that Nelly was born with some defects, and for this reason King Tiber hoped that over time, Nelly would starve to death. You all know that to be true, yet none of you did a thing. Josh was the only one who had the courage to help today. You should all be ashamed of yourselves.'

"The others were absolutely astounded. Tatianna hadn't spoken much since Nelly's birth, so her voice was an unlikely one to hear. Equally astounding was the way that her decisive claims sank right into the hearts of the others.

"She continued after a long pause, 'If none of you have anything to say, then Nelly and I will follow Josh. You can stay if you wish to be ruled by your king, but we will go and follow our real leader. It's like he has wings. The way he speaks to us, the way he treats us. His ways are elevated above the ways most lions behave. I can see it clear as day. I hope that you all realize it.' Tatianna picked up Nelly by the nape of her neck and followed after Josh.

"The statement cut to the bone. One by one, two by two the others came. About a third stayed, content with their relative stability under King Tiber's rule and readily sacrificing their chance at freedom.

"The king noticed but didn't seem to care much. His arrogance told him they'd all be back to continue their existence under his rule. He was wrong, very wrong. Even his two ruthless guards that were pulling Josh away, stopped in their tracks to witness the commotion that was taking place and the members of the pride that had made their way toward them. King Tiber observed the loss of his two most trusted allies and called out to retrieve them, but they never looked back.

"When all was said and done, King Tiber remained the king of only his most loyal subjects, at least until he came across another band of lions to ingratiate, entice, and promise an everlasting equality under his rule. Only at that point in time would he be again capable of ruling over a larger pride.

"Josh, on the other hand, was allowed to represent the members of the newly established pride after they held an election and voted in his favor. He served his constituents with charity, kindness, justice, honor, and mercy. Josh's example, when contrasted to King Tiber's, must be understood or there will always be more suffering to come for those that ignore or refuse to learn the lessons of their history."

Peter transitioned from the end of his story to ask Ryland a direct question. "Have you even been around a 'Josh' or a 'King Tiber'?"

"I gotta say, that was pretty interesting, Peter. Really gets the mind moving. I suppose that I've come across both kinds of people. You were really told this when you were growing up?"

"Well, my parents didn't use this same sort of language when I was younger, but the underlying lessons were the same."

"Very cool. I've never heard any story like that. I can definitely see how you'd learn lessons from it. Hey, how'd your parents get to spend so much time with you anyway?"

Peter didn't answer the question right away. He had to think about his response very carefully. After a pause, he figured out the best answer that he could muster at this hour of the night. "I'll tell you sometime. I'm just really tired right now. Good night, Ryland."

"Night, Peter."

Ryland lay awake for another hour pondering some of the things he heard in Peter's story of "The Winged Lion." The dichotomy between King Tiber and Josh resonated with Ryland in a truly profound way. Maybe he needed to expand his own understanding of the world?

Chapter 11

Home Is Where the Heart Is

"It's great to see you," Peter's uncle, Jim, warmly said as he wrapped his arms around his dear nephew. He hadn't seen or spoken to Peter in nearly four months.

"Same here, Uncle Jim. And you, too, Aunt Missy." Melissa Wilby stepped forward to claim Peter's embrace.

"So nice to hug my sweet nephew, my Peter," Melissa said with her usual serene and cheery demeanor.

The three held each other for a little while, taking advantage of the opportunity. They had to savor the familial bond, which according to current world law, was almost completely forbidden to kin and reserved for government officials.

"Hey, Peter!" Ryland yelled from across the processing and transference center on campus.

Peter looked through the narrow gap between his aunt's and uncle's shoulders, barely visible because of the proximity of the three. Ryland was guiding his parents over to introduce them to Peter and his family.

"Mom. Dad. This is Peter. He's my newest roommate and my newest friend at school."

"It's nice to finally meet you, Mrs. and Mr. Ayzers. Ryland has spoken very highly of the two of you," Peter formally responded. "This is my aunt, Melissa, and uncle, Jim."

Jim Wilby reached his hand out to Ryland.

"It's so kind of you to be so inviting to Peter. I know it's been difficult for him to get adjusted to his new school. You should know that my wife and I are incredibly grateful that you are such a great friend to him," Jim earnestly acknowledged Ryland.

"We've had a good time. Peter is something else. I couldn't imagine having a better friend," Ryland replied.

"Jim Wilby." Jim introduced himself as he extended his hand out to meet Ryland's parents.

"Great to meet you, Jim. I'm Hank and this is my wife, Sabrina."

Jim then shook Sabrina's hand, giving it a gentle squeeze.

"It's nice to meet you Hank, Sabrina, and Ryland." Melissa Wilby took her turn to shake the Ayzers's hands.

"Well, we should probably get going. We've got a full day ahead," Peter said to Ryland and his parents.

"Yeah, we should too. It was so nice to meet you Mr. and Mrs. Wilby. And Peter, I'll see you tomorrow morning when you come back. Have a nice time with your family," Ryland said as the Wilby's and Peter began walking toward the exit.

"You, too, Ryland," Jim and Melissa said nearly simultaneously.

"Bye bye now," Hank said to the departing trio.

Peter, Jim, and Melissa walked toward the final checkout near the door. Peter's bag had to be thoroughly sifted through by campus security before exiting for parental visitation and upon arrival back to school after the twenty-four hour time period.

Nearly at the security checkout, Peter saw Londyn with her father standing nearby.

"Londyn, I just thought I'd wish you a good day with your father. My family and I are just about to head out, so I thought we could introduce ourselves."

"Sure. Thanks for stopping, Peter. This is my dad, Tanner."

"It's nice to meet you, Mr. Farrows."

"Same here, Peter. Londyn was just telling me how she's gotten to know you some in the past week or so. She says that you're pretty new to this school."

"Yes, we've recently become acquainted. It's been good. You have a wonderful daughter, sir. She has certainly been helpful in making me feel more welcome here."

"Well, thanks, Peter. That's very kind of you to say. She is something, isn't she? I don't know what I'd do without her," Tanner answered.

"Hello, Tanner and Londyn. I'm Melissa, and this is my husband, Jim. It's so nice to meet the two of you."

"Same here, ma'am. Jim, it's nice to meet you too," Tanner replied with a warm smile and handshake for each of them.

"Peter, have a good day. It was nice meeting you, Jim and Melissa."

"Same here, Mr. Farrows. Bye, Londyn. Have a good day."

Londyn's eyes twinkled, and her smile glowed as she watched Peter, and his aunt and uncle continue moving toward the security checkout. Peter smirked in his awkwardly playful way.

She never dreamt this friendship could possibly happen—not in her wildest dreams. Londyn, who was once a harsh critic of the new and unusual student, was now intrigued that she befriended the same boy from whom she once wished to remain distanced. How could she not want to get to know him since he was willing to share his unbelievable gift and knowledge with her?

The Wilbys brought Peter to their northeastern suburban apartment in Wilmette by a metro transit hoverbus similar to the one that Peter rode to and from Central Stadium. No private vehicular ownership was permitted any longer, except for those that could find the means to influence government officials. The same written and unwritten rules pertained to land and home ownership.

"It's so good to be back, Jim and Melissa. Thank you again for graciously hosting me. I know there is a certain level of risk to you with me being here. I've been eagerly waiting for the past few months to go by, so I can check in to see if there's been any update from my dad. May I?" Peter politely asked his uncle and aunt as he walked through the front door with a bag slung over his shoulder and looked out a back window from their single level apartment.

The window faced the North Shore Channel, which was about fifty yards behind their residence. Water from Lake Michigan flowed through Wilmette Harbor into the North Shore Channel, which then confluenced with the North Branch Chicago River. The river then flowed into downtown Chicago, which provide a fluvial view for the myriad people crossing the many bridges above. The Wilbys lived on Itasca Avenue at the quiet end of the street. Often, the suburban life was more normal than the inner city life, at least in the sense that the overarching Commonwealth rule was less noticeable. The Commonwealth didn't have skyscrapers out in the "burbs" on which to hang their giant flags. The size of the flags was often proportionate to the proximity to the offices of the members of the Provincial Political Affairs Council.

"Peter, you just feel free to let us know if you need anything. We know you need to get to work. We'll honor that," Jim commented to Peter as he finished looking out the back window at the verdant foliage just in front of the channel.

"Thanks, Uncle Jim. Thanks again."

"We're just trying to do the best we can. We have had an increase in foot traffic recently, so I hope things are going according to plan," Jim responded with somewhat of a disappointed tone. He seemed disappointed for not being able to do enough, at least in his mind.

Peter went to his room in the back of the two bedroom apartment. The view out his window was very similar to the view he had when he first arrived. The primary difference was a large bur oak tree within perfect view from his room.

He closed the door, drew the blinds on his window, and then began to move his bed. Being sure to slowly and carefully pull the bed away from the wall nearest the window, Peter reached down and separated two pieces of the hardwood floor. The fissure between the two seemed normal to the naked eye; however, Peter was able to identify and separate them. Once pulled out of their formally jigsawed position, Peter pulled a thin, flexible microfilm strip from each. He put the microfilm strips underneath his windowsill. As the sensor below the window detected the microfilms, it glowed a dim blue and opened two small slots. Peter inserted the microfilms and took a step back toward the middle of the room. He wanted to get out of the way before the transformation happened.

The top layer of hardwood slid one way while the second layer slid the opposite way. Then a third layer, then a forth. The now exposed foundation of the ranch-style home moved away in all four directions to create a three-by-three foot opening. Peter walked to the uncovered entrance and climbed down the twenty foot ladder below.

He carefully lowered one foot at a time down the steel rungs encased within the brightly lit columnar space below the mundane and seemingly inconspicuous home. Peter eventually made his way down to the source of the white light. It hadn't been on this whole time, but only once the identity verification process ended and the two correct filaments were correctly positioned. From that point, the inner workings of the tunnel came to life.

This particular vault was only accessible by Peter and a number of others in the area. Peter looked behind the base of the ladder and saw that the room containing all the sensitive communication equipment was in working order. He put on a special helmet that would allow him to relay messages and perceive incoming transmissions without relying on a particular device. It was a way of telepathy, but the sensitivity of the helmet really made it an augmented telepathy. This allowed for top secret communications between himself and others. Peter initiated contact with other members of the group operating in Chicago and elsewhere.

"Peter, we're down to the final week until mission launch. How's school?" a curious, and familiar voice echoed out from Peter's receiving earpiece.

"It's going well, Dad. I've made a couple friends so far. I just don't understand how they can teach kids the way they do here. There's no discussion, no teaching, only indoctrination," Peter responded.

"They only care about telling you what they want you to know, rather than how to think for yourself. Sadly, that trend started long ago, son."

"That's too bad. It's so damaging to the students here. They're brainwashed. I can tell by talking to some of them."

"It's a terrible thing to distort a mind like that. Don't worry, son, we'll come get you pretty soon," Peter's father attempted to assuage. "Chicago's one of the most important targets that we'll take first, so we'll need to get you out sooner than later."

"I'm glad you guys ended up letting me go to school here for the experience, but it'll be nice to see you and Mom again," Peter optimistically replied.

"Same here, son. We can't wait to see you too. Just remember, you're safer down there than you would be up here. Otherwise, we never would have let you go."

"I know, Dad. I understand, but it doesn't mean it's easy."

"Oh, of course not, Peter. It was probably one of the most difficult decisions your mother and I made. In fact, your mom is worried sick about you. She is pretty sad she couldn't be part of this conversation. I'm sure you remember how busy she is with her political life."

"Yep, I remember."

"Say, son, I need to get going soon. Do you know where your cousin, Jayk, is by chance? Did Uncle Jim or Aunt Melissa say anything?"

"As a matter of fact, they did mention where he is. I mean, they didn't know exactly where, of course, but they said somewhere near New Zealand."

"Wonderful. I'm not sure if you know, but Jayk has intimate knowledge of advanced Commonwealth robotics forces. His parents are completely committed to helping us, so they can certainly help us change Jayk's mind as to whom he should be fighting for."

"Uncle Jim and Aunt Melissa did mention that he is training with a Robotics Corps unit."

"Do you think you could take a Grebe down to meet with Champion Backstrom aboard a Sparrowhawk near there? I think you can help turn your cousin to our side."

"Sure, I can do that. Like the last time?"

"Yes, Peter. Just like the way you did it before. Thank you, son. I'll see you soon. I love you."

"Love you, too, Dad." The communication went static shortly after Peter's goodbye.

Peter checked some scanners nearby to make sure there were no intelligence gathering threats in the immediate vicinity. He sorted through some equipment and came across some memorabilia from several years ago. A mechanical watch. A printed book. Most were antiques by present day standards; however, there was a more recent addition. It was a patch dedicated to the cause that his parents led.

"Oh, this is where you went," Peter quipped to the winged lion patch, which he still had to put on his uniform when the time was right. Looking over it and feeling the corners of the diamond shaped patch brought Peter back to his years growing up—of what it meant to be a winged lion, just like the story his parents had told him in the past. The inverted chevrons with white feathers facing up and outward sat below the image of a powerful winged lion. Peter put the patch in his pocket to bring it to school so he could attached it to his uniform. The metacognitive sidestep ended and Peter continued with his checklist of items to verify before he went back upstairs to enjoy lunch with his aunt and uncle.

Sitting at the plastic composite table, Peter sat eating his roast beef and horseradish sandwich with Jim and Melissa. Agricultural, manufacturing, and dietary restrictions severely limited the ability to enjoy the sandwiches enjoyed by prior generations, so additional fixings were not commonplace. A side helping of fresh broccoli and carrots were a healthy complement though.

"So, Peter, how is everything going down there?" Melissa asked as she tilted toward Peter's room.

"Oh, pretty well. We're right on schedule. My dad said the time is near."

"We will do exactly as we've been instructed, but how will we know when to carry out our next task?" Melissa asked Peter.

"You'll know. It'll be a very apparent moment. You'll just know," Peter said in his typical, unexcitable manner.

Peter continued to eat his lunch, taking chomp after chomp. He always seemed to be contemplating something, never having a mental moment's rest.

"Is Jayk still away at training? You said he'd be going near New Zealand, right?" Peter asked.

"Yes, he's on his final phases of Robotics Corps training with SouthCom down there. I think he'll be doing some live fire missions soon. It's a dangerous thing to trust machines with the ability to decide who lives and who dies. He had better be careful, since he should be close to being in charge of his own company of WAMs [Warfighter-integrated Autonomous Machines] by now," Jim reflected with a faint degree of regret.

"I sure hope he stays safe," Peter responded.

"I hope so," Melissa reiterated. "Soldiers die training with those things all the time. He's always wanted to serve, so this is his chance to do what he's dreamed of doing." Melissa followed up with an optimistic conclusion. "I just wish he had more of your mindset, Peter. Jayk's just so hardheaded."

Peter continued eating his lunch with his loving and loyal hosts. Despite Jim and Melissa being Peter's uncle and aunt, they showed him the kind of affection and guidance they would have given to their own son.

Jayk didn't know what to think when his parents told him they would be hosting Peter on occasion. As an only child, there was a sense of resentment initially. As time went on though, he was able to come to grips with the reality that his parents shared their love with another child.

"Well, Aunt Melissa and Uncle Jim, thank you for the lovely meal. I know times have been difficult for you. It's been a tough struggle for so many. I'm so thankful for all you've done for me. I'm sorry, but I must be heading back to my room to get back to work. I have a meeting to attend at two o'clock and I should be back by about eight."

"Peter."

"Yes, sir," he respectfully replied.

"You said you have a meeting?"

"That's correct. It's about eight thousand two hundred miles away."

Melissa decided to speak up and complete her husband's thought.

"What Jim is trying to say is—how are you going to get to this meeting, and excuse me, you said eight thousand two hundred miles?"

"That's a great question. I can see why you asked. Yes, it is quite a distance from here. All I can say is to look out your kitchen window in about fifteen minutes. You know, the one with the big red maple at the end of the property due east from the kitchen. Find the top of the tree and look just above it, and you'll know. It'll happen quickly, so stay tuned and you'll see."

Melissa and Jim struggled to understand what Peter nonchalantly told them. Jim could only think of a one question, "Why are you going wherever it is you're going?"

"I'm going to pay a little visit to Jayk."

"Jayk?" Melissa was absolutely flabbergasted.

"How can that be?" Jim inquired.

"My dad and some others are in the process of arranging the meeting. They are searching for Jayk as we speak. Don't worry, they won't hurt him."

"Oh my—they had better be careful. I hope they know that our Jayk is a trained soldier now," Melissa advised Peter.

"Don't worry, Champion Backstrom's men will find him. They're highly trained too."

"Very well. Stay safe, Peter." Jim didn't quite understand how this could all be happening, but he nonetheless accepted it. "Say hello to Jayk for us, will you?"

"We'll see you later, Peter," Melissa acknowledged.

"Thanks, Uncle Jim—I will. See you, Aunt Melissa," Peter said as he withdrew from the table to take his plate to the old and tarnished stainless steel kitchen sink.

Peter hurriedly walked back to his room. Again, he readied the secret hatch into the ground, although the teenager seemed more agitated than usual. He was rubbing his fingers anxiously together while he waited for the floor to metamorphose.

Once the transformation was complete, Peter climbed down the ladder to the lower level and changed into a sleek white suit. The suit had a matching symbol in the center of the chest and on the back between the shoulder blades. The symbol looked like a Roman numeral three. The pictorial fence was contained within an equilateral triangle. The suit looked more like a uniform, but certainly not like the one he wore at school. This one looked like an anachronism, clearly not belonging to this day and age. Peter's uniform manifested the hallmarks of something else—something unexplainable in Commonwealth society.

He continued walking into a dimly lit horizontal tunnel. His white boots quietly scrunched with each step on the damp concrete below. An alcove at the end of the fifty foot tunnel contained several black, metallic objects. They were about twice the size of a full-size refrigerator—at least what used to be a full-size one, before the Commonwealth regulations made them about the size of a large microwave to stave energy consumption. Peter selected one and opened a hatch to climb in.

There was just enough room inside for his five foot, six inch, one-hundred thirty pound frame. It contained a solid floor with little headroom and no visible windows of any sort. The only discernible item in the room was a flight chair lined with shock absorbing material, six safety harnesses, and a V-shaped headrest. Oddly, there didn't seem to be any sensors, gauges, or controls within the cockpit.

Peter stepped into his capsule and buckled himself in with the half dozen straps clicking into place. He then put his hands on the glazed black armrests of the chair and rested his head back. He closed his eyes and began to speak.

"Champion Backstrom, this is Peter Barclay. My Grebe is ready for launch. I should be at your Sparrowhawk in about ninety minutes."

"Sounds good, Peter. We have some good news—Deputy Lumis and his team are tracking our VIP. I hope they return with their target by the time you arrive."

"Very well, sir. I'll see you soon," Peter said as the holographic visual and vocal receiver went blank.

The claustrophobic cockpit came to life when Peter engaged the hellium-3 and mercury-based engine by using his mind. It also activated the previously dim and unadorned environment into a space teeming with light and spectacular three dimensional panels, which projected in front of and to the sides of the teenager turned professional pilot.

The entire ship's outer hull became translucent from Peter's vantage point, but looking at it from the outside, it still showed the reflective black exterior. The enhanced visibility allowed Peter to see three hundred sixty degrees around as well as up and down through the craft. The pilot's mobile chair permitted quick swiveling to view anything exterior to the craft at a second's notice.

Peter sealed the cockpit and activated a water containment system, which flooded the room with lake water. Shortly after the deliberate inundation, an eight-by-eight foot aperture began to gradually appear as the forged steel and concrete door slowly slid from right to left. By the time the opening was passable, Peter's pilot's chair had automatically reconfigured so he was now lying in a prone position. He directed the waterborne craft forward. Its engines were completely silent and the ship's outer coal color changed to match its surroundings, making detection extremely difficult.

Peter thought to himself, "I sure hope this goes as planned like it has the last few times," as he looked through the ship's outer surface and above the water within the channel that he navigated. Heading toward Wilmette Harbor, Peter made sure not to make any sudden directional or accelerational changes. His concentration was absolutely critical in order to avoid being discovered by security sentinels.

Gliding past the harbor into the deepening blue depths of Lake Michigan, Peter skimmed the sandy bottom and occasionally had to elude a large boulder. He precisely identified the path with months of research and surveillance gathering, so he could avoid not only human and drone eyes, but also radar, sonar, and space-based sensors. He guided the Grebe along a serpentine trail that weaved and waved for nearly three miles from the western lakeshore. The end point due east from Jim and Melissa's home was a detection desert—a gap where all known Commonwealth means of identification were discontinuous. It was his best chance of rendezvousing with Champion Backstrom and hopefully, Jayk Wilby.

One final navigation check revealed that the time was right. The sensors were all saying the area was clear. Peter changed the cockpit configuration back to its original, upright position. Looking up and hoping for success, Peter closed his eyes for a moment of calm, then opened them again as he accelerated his Grebe through the water toward the surface. Shortly after its ascent, the ship breached the white-capped waves moving about the immense lake's surface. Peter was airborne and climbing vertically at an incredible rate. Just as was true below the water, the Grebe's onboard engine produced no noise and no exhaust trail. The sleek, tubular shaped craft leveled out its trajectory and accelerated at hypersonic speed toward the southwest.

"This is Peter Barclay. I'm at cruising altitude and should arrive in about seventy-five minutes. I'll let you know when I am ready to board."

"Copy that, Barclay. Have a safe flight," the radio operator replied.

"Thanks. Over and out."

Melissa and Jim were standing side by side with their arms cozily around each other. They stared into each other's eyes after they watched the shimmering craft rocket through the line of sight, just above the red maple tree as Peter predicted.

"I'm surprised he wanted us to see the spectacle since he had been pretty hush-hush with his business here. I wonder what the difference was today?" Melissa asked her husband.

"I'm not sure, but we should trust him. The same kind, gentle boy who appeared on our doorstep asking for help just flew a high-powered aircraft out of the dark depths of Lake Michigan. What's not to trust?"

Chapter 12

The Auckland Raid

"Junior Assault Leader, our new landing zone is west of downtown Auckland, near the coast on the Tasman Sea. The terrain is mountainous with groves of dense foliage and interspersed grassy fields. We should be there in approximately four minutes."

"Thanks, Sator. I hope this is as quick and easy as we planned it in the staging room," Junior Assault Leader Jayk M. Wilby acknowledged his fireteam's second in command.

"I agree, sir. I do hope it goes according to plan. Although, intel does seem to indicate a relatively heavy presence of noncons operating in the near vicinity."

"I heard, Sator—damn—I'm trying to keep my head on straight here. It's my first combat mission and I'm trying to keep things in perspective."

"My apologies, sir. I cannot fully empathize with your meaning, and the manufacturing plant ensured that my head was on completely, as you like to say, *'straight,'* when I was assembled," Sator updated his direct commander with the utmost sincerity.

"I should have known that was coming. I guess I need to save my idioms for humans," Wilby mentioned as he shook his head.

"Timmins, Werster, Hedge, Ellis. Do your Sator units have just as little awareness of figurative speech as mine? I thought the Sator's were designed to interpret more human emotion than the others? I mean, my Tommy, Lister, Ranger, and Fil units are about as personable as a twentieth-century toaster."

"I completely understand, Wilby. Good luck talking to them about women too," Werster confided.

"Hey, Werster. Did you or Hedge ever figure out how to trick your fireteam into thinking Timmins was a noncon spy sent to destroy our whole company?" Ellis mentioned with a sarcastic tone.

"I don't think so. I guess we still need to mess around with our neurocomms that transmit our thoughts to the bots in the field," Hedge replied.

The five men and their brothers-in-arms belong to what is known as the Raptor Group. This unit is formally known as the First Company, First Battalion of the Second Expeditionary Combat Regiment, Second Robotics Corps of the United People's Commonwealth Land Forces. It is comprised of one Head Assault Leader, one Senior Assault Leader, ten Junior Assault Leaders, plus five WAMs (Warfighter-integrated Autonomous Machines) per human officer, totaling seventy-two combatants in the company.

Each officer travels in his own armored vehicle crewed by his squad of five WAMs. The multi-purpose combat vehicle, or MCV, serves as a short-range jet-propelled flying machine, to low-elevation hovercraft, and also as an amphibious vessel for aquatic warfare operations and land engagements. The mode of operation being performed by the MCV is determined by its human commander and the WAMs adjust their combat functions depending on that mode of operation.

When the WAM teams dismount and deploy under the command of their human officers, they operate in tactical phalanxes. The six-unit, man-machine fireteam can move into a variety of formations while utilizing various weapons platforms.

Each of the five WAMs has a nickname, identifying its role in the fireteam. A Tommy is the Automatic Railgunner that wields a heavy rail gun for suppressive, automatic fire for the fireteam. The Lister is the Indirect Fire Specialist that uses smart mortar and hypervelocity missile fire to rain down ordnance on enemies and protect against airborne threats. Ranger is the Extended Range Railgunner that employs a precision rail rifle for long distance sniper protection and capability. The Defilade and Countermeasure Unit, also known as Fil, uses the latest in electronic warfare and has the ability to provide the fireteam protection with a ballistic repulsion shield. The fifth unit in the WAM fireteam is the Sator, which stands for Fire Support Integrator. The Sator specializes in medical and mechanical repair, communications and reconnaissance, including the use of micro drone swarms. The Sator has more advanced capabilities than the others and is the closest with the human commanding the fireteam.

In addition to specialty weapons and instruments, all WAMs have their basic electromagnetic rail rifle (RR-85), which uses electromagnetic propulsion instead of gunpowder to fire large volumes of 6.2 millimeter kinetic rounds. The muzzle energy force nears eight thousand foot pounds because of the hyperkinetic speeds reached by such propulsion in the weapon. The coaxial laser has a much slower firing rate, but can be used to penetrate thick armor, advanced combat vehicles, and fortified positions. Together, the use of laser and hyperkinetic munitions gives the land warfighter an unprecedented advantage in battle.

Matching their human counterparts, WAMs espouse the same Land Forces Combat Uniforms that use a fluid camouflage system that adapts to its surrounding. The combat suit composition is liquid armor with some capacity for active protection, and has a facemask-enclosed helmet with features similar to a first-century Roman Gallic helmet.

Raptor Group's twelve MCVs rapidly approached the craggy mountains which overlooked the blue waves pounding the western coast of Auckland. In two columns, the MCVs flew just over the water—so low that their exhaust distorted the liquid surface below as they moved along their approach. Head Assault Leader Navarro's MCV led the way as the company's cardinal vehicle. His WAMs, as well as his MCV, contained more advanced communications and intelligence capacities than the others, so they were well served at the front of the assault force.

"Sator, do you have any satellite or drone uplink confirming noncons on the other side of this mountain ahead?" Navarro asked.

"Yes, sir. It looks like there are about two scores of people present near a large congregation of animals."

"Perfect. Fil, bring down the MCV near that ravine so we can dismount and gather actionable intelligence."

"Roger that, Head Assault Leader."

"This is Head Assault Leader Navarro speaking. Men, we have about forty people on the other side of the mountain directly ahead. My MCV is en route to land at ravine B23 for dismount to gather intel. Main assault force, land at hill G27 one hundred clicks from my landing zone."

"Copy that, Head Assault Leader," Junior Assault Leader Wilby responded.

With Wilby, the other Junior Assault Leaders, and the Senior Assault Leader landing their MCVs on the hill, Head Assault Leader Navarro's fireteam exited the MCV and took cover in a crouched position, looking for enemy forces in all directions. Navarro ordered his Ranger to move up another hill to surveil for counterintelligence via their neural correspondence integration channel communication, abbreviated as neurocomm. Again, by way of Navarro's neurocomm, he directed his Sator to get micro drone eyes on the targets located on the other side of the mountain.

"Sator, I want you to get me real-time intel using your scanners to search for weapons, IDs, and other information before we make contact."

"Roger that, sir," Sator relayed back internally as it had received the command.

Navarro's Sator determined that the path was clear for it to scope out the suspected noncons toward the edge of an overhanging plateau. Engaging its various visual receptors from its right shoulder and overlaying its eyes, it identified thirty-eight humans in several rows sitting on the plush green grass in the middle of a pasture. In front of the main body of people sitting, there was a man standing at what looked like a table with a long white cloth hanging off of it on two sides. The thirty-nine people were among nearly a hundred sheep, including some lambs that were grazing the land.

Ranger and Sator transmitted their findings thus far by way of neurocomm to Navarro.

"Thirty-nine people. No weapons verified. Unauthorized congregation in progress and of unknown intent. Also noteworthy, there are about one hundred illegal agricultural livestock present—no discernible identification markers of any kind seen on their ears or hides."

"Perfect, Sator. I don't see any evidence of a scheduled congregation at this location today in the Auckland meetings manifest, thus deeming this meeting illegal. The nonlicensed agriculture is another bonus for us," Head Assault Leader Navarro chuckled.

As Ranger and Sator continued their reconnaissance, they noticed the man in front of the table with an item in each hand. One looked like a piece of bread and the other, a cup or goblet. After using infrared, ultraviolet and zoomed color scanners, Sator used a prototypical sensor to investigate what the man was doing. As he activated the highly theoretically engineered interdimensional lens, he saw a clear and intense beam of light coming down from the sky and into the two items that the man had in his hands. The others knelt in the green grass with their heads bowed and their hands together, and Sator noticed unidentified luminosities accompanying each of the people and surrounding the table. Sator could hardly make sense of it. There was no such data that had been uploaded to its artificial intelligence processor—no record of any kind to interpret what it was seeing. Upon taking away its interdimensional lens and back to the normal visual spectrum, it noticed that it couldn't see the radiant beam from above or the light emitting entities among the people gathered. As with all WAMs, Sator's programming destroyed any evidence that would reveal the supernatural to their human commanders or up the chain of command. This is a policy from the top echelons of the Commonwealth government.

"Any additional intel, Sator?" Head Navarro asked.

"No, sir. Nothing. No weapons evident. Illegal congregation still ongoing along with the presence of black market agricultural commodities."

"Okay, that's all we need."

Over the intercom, the head assault leader instructed his men and their fireteams.

"Men, it's time to roll. The targets are unarmed, so we won't be needing our MCVs for fire support or protection. Dismount and assume fireteam level skirmishing groups. We can autopilot the MCVs for extraction after we're done with the mission."

"Yes, sir!" Junior Wilby fervently responded. "You heard the man. Dismount and form fireteam level skirmishing groups."

All the junior assault leaders replied in their own way.

Hedge replied, "Roger that, Head."

"Lock and load," Werster uttered.

Each human ordered his fireteam via neurocomm to dismount from their battle positions within the MCV and assume their diamond patrol formation, with three WAMs in front, human in the center, and two WAMs tapered to the rear. Each WAM looked down its line of fire and scanned for enemies. The human officers observed the field with their own eyes to coordinate the fireteams and maintain their distance from one another.

"Junior Timmins, any visual from the left flank?"

"No, sir," he replied to the Head Assault Leader's inquiry.

"Junior Hedge, any visual on the right flank?"

"Nothing, sir."

"Junior Wilby, take the company up over the hill directly in front of you and commence with frontal engagement. It should be great tactical assault training for you and your machines, as well as the others in the company. Raptor Group, what do we do?"

All units responded, "Dictate and decimate!"

"Booyah, men! I'll be at your six for the assault and will report our progress to Assault Unit Leader Conrad as we go."

Head Assault Leader Navarro brought his fireteam behind the rest of the company as they moved up the hill.

Junior Assault Leader's Wilby, Werster, and Hedge moved within their formations in the center of the skirmish line.

"All units, form four-by-two assault phalanxes with Fils deploying ballistic repulsion shields for cover," Wilby ordered.

"You heard the man," Wilby's Sator replied as it moved next to Wilby while Tommy, Lister, Ranger, and Fil WAMs positioned themselves in front. Each of the four WAMs in front held their weapons around the shield that Fil held for cover.

"All units ready for frontal assault, sir," Junior Assault Leader Wilby relayed to Head Assault Leader Navarro, as well as the Senior Assault Leader.

"Excellent, men. Move out."

"Yes, sir," the company collectively replied.

Junior Wilby's Sator reported, "My micro UAVs have a visual on illegal agricultural animals, and behind them is the unlawful assembly."

"Still no weapons, Sator?"

"Correct, sir. No weapons visible."

Wilby sounded, "Engage and approximate!"

The line of eleven tactical fireteams several feet apart all opened up their firepower onto the sheep and people in the field. With all types of firepower being utilized by the company, within less than five seconds, all people and animals were eliminated.

"That's it, men. They're all wasted," Head Navarro reported to the group while observing through visual magnifiers. "Ceasefire! Junior Wilby, lead the company down to inspect the personnel and any property that might be valuable to us. We might be able to root out more of them today."

"Copy that, Head," Wilby responded. "Company, five-by-one formations. No need to have shields deployed. Forward march."

Raptor Group proceeded down the mountainside toward the site of the massacre with all WAMs side by side and their human counterparts directly behind the center WAM from each fireteam. None had their guard down, but it was difficult to see the reason why they couldn't as they approached the aftermath of what they had done.

"Fireteams, spread out and investigate all persons and items here. WAMs, form a defensive perimeter around all officers," Head Assault Leader Navarro ordered. "All Junior Assault Leaders and Senior Assault Leader, relay to your fireteams. I don't think it's worth enacting emergency WAM control in this situation. If we were under fire, then maybe, but it's a cleanup party, so I don't think it's necessary."

All assault leaders used their neurocomms to order all WAMs to the periphery in order to defend them. No questions asked, they followed orders without hesitation.

Junior's Timmins and Ellis walked side by side, observing the carnage. Of course, they weren't observing with their own eyes since everything was seen through their eye ports within their combat helmets. Seeing the bodies torn to pieces, torsos shredded, faces unrecognizable—those were things that no man should have to see without a barrier between him and the horror.

"Hey, Timmins," the diminutive Ellis uttered.

"Yeah."

"What do you make of that?"

"Of what?"

"Well, look at this table. It doesn't look like any table I've ever seen."

"What'd you mean?"

"It's not made of wood or metal. It's made of slabs of stone."

"Is that some old New Zealander custom for eating meals on?"

Timmins replied, "I don't think so. I've never heard of that before. I had a cousin from here and he never mentioned eating on a stone table in the middle of a pasture."

"All right, let's go see what's in that lady's purse," Ellis suggested.

"Sounds good."

Junior Assault Leader Wilby walked around, looking through pants pockets that were intact, and picking up pieces of jewelry that were strewn across the field and in the cratered ground.

"Nothing remarkable, sir," Wilby told Head Assault Leader Navarro.

"We have to look in every nook and cranny. Southern Command thinks there may be a major noncon presence in these mountains. If they're here we will find 'em and destroy 'em, along with their failed ideas of the past."

"Help. Help. Can anybody hear me?"

Wilby turned his head to make out what he heard. "What was that?" he thought to himself. While slowly creeping among a half dozen bodies, he heard something again.

"Hello. Can anyone hear me? I need help."

Wilby signaled Hedge to come over to where he stood.

"What is it, Wilby?"

"Shhh. I heard something twice now. Listen closely. There's someone nearby that's still alive."

This time, both of them heard it. It wasn't vocal, but it was something rustling down by their feet. Hedge bent down, pulled a man's body off of a pile of corpses, and found a woman underneath.

"Help me. I'm bleeding badly and don't think I'll make it. Can you help me?"

The two soldiers looked down, then back at each other, and down once more.

"Why should I help you? You're a noncon—you're the enemy. I should kill you right here on the spot," Junior Assault Leader Wilby sternly responded.

"Whom am I an enemy of? Whom was my daughter an enemy of?"

"I don't need to answer you. Just shut up. Die already, die."

"Why did you do this to us?"

"I'm a soldier for the Commonwealth. We find enemies and destroy them."

The woman's voice had even less breath within it than before. She was going down fast. "You are a soldier, but are you not also a person? Do you have a mind? Do you have beliefs of your own?"

"It doesn't matter what my beliefs are when I'm killing enemies. I'm ordered to do so, regardless. I follow what I am told to do by my superiors."

"And whom do you listen to?"

Wilby looked over the wounds on the woman's legs and abdomen. He also saw that part of her scalp was torn off. He could only stare with cold, heartless eyes—she wasn't a human to him. He had been trained to dehumanize her since he began his schooling as a small child.

"My superiors are my Senior Assault Leader, Head Assault Leader, then higher-ranking commanders up from them. Out here I listen to them. Ultimately, I follow the Premier and High Council, and the Commonwealth controls what I think and say."

Hedge nodded his head in agreement, but did not want to say anything to the dying woman.

"You can follow men—go right ahead. They will bring you suffering and disappointment. It will happen time and time again—it's part of our nature. I will follow the Shepherd of shepherds. He is the only one that can truly end suffering for us all, including you."

Putting his rifle to her head, Wilby was stricken with rage, "I told you to shut up! I'm going to finish you off right now if you don't shut up!"

"You can kill my body, but you can never kill the rest of me."

Frustrated and sick of talking, Wilby stormed off to let the woman die. Hedge followed promptly behind him.

Head Navarro neurcomm'd his chief WAM, "Sator, my DNA analyzer isn't showing the entire global registry. Can you come down and sample DNA from each of the bodies? I can't tell the lambs's blood from human blood. It's just a bloody mess down here."

"Right away, sir. I'm on my way."

Navarro's Sator trotted down several hundred feet from its position in the defensive perimeter. It grabbed its DNA sampling kit from a compartment in its torso that also housed mechanical repair parts for its WAMs-in-arms, as well as first aid supplies for human combatants.

"Start over there, Sator, and work your way around until you've sampled everybody. This way we'll know if any of these people were known noncon members or wanted persons."

"At once, sir," his Sator responded.

As Navarro's Sator sampled body after body, each DNA was unique and registered to known Commonwealth denizens. None belonged to wanted or suspicious persons. The lambs's blood was clearly identifiable and easily differentiated. As the Sator kept moving from one person to the next, it saw the table it had seen from afar before the onset of the attack. It remembered what it had seen through its interdimensional lens. The unspeakable occurrences and observations were still very much a secret. The Sator noticed the two items the man at the table had in his hands before he was killed.

Puzzled, it wondered, "Why would this group of people share one small piece of unlevened bread like this? It's not even a cleanly cut piece from a local bakery. It doesn't seem calorically sufficient to make it worthwhile for these people to travel here to consume it."

The bread was intact and was spared from any damage or debris from the violence that had consumed the group of people in front of the Sator. It looked at the cup that had been knocked over. The cup hadn't been struck by a bullet or fragmentation, so there was no damage to its bronze surface.

"What is this that spilled out of the cup? It looks less dark than blood—probably wine. A cup that was full of a few ounces of wine? Why would this many people share so little wine?" the Sator thought to itself.

Since this was the same location where it had seen the beam of light with its special sensor equipment from on the mountain, it wanted to see if the beaming radiance was still present. It put down the interdimensional lens over its right eye, looked down at the bread and cup not only to see that the beam of light was gone, but that the two items had changed form.

Looking down at the bread, it had clearly changed into a piece of flesh. It would have been normal at this scene to find pieces of flesh, but not flesh that had come from a piece of bread. Upon examination, it appeared to be heart tissue—specifically from the myocardium of the left ventricle of the heart.

The wine before had a translucent appearance, but had now become thicker and had a more robust redness to it. Under this special lens, the wine had transformed into blood.

With its interdimensional lens still donned, the Sator took small samples of the flesh and blood to analyze.

"This can't be. It must be a mistake. Both samples contained human blood. AB positive, to be exact, and both had identical DNA. How can there be no record of this DNA on the entire planet? Genealogically speaking, there should have been some path to find the origin, but it came up empty."

The sensor indicated that there was no known record to match the sample or verify its origin. The Sator WAM, once again, found itself facing facts that contradicted its decision-making algorithm. It couldn't tell Head Navarro. It couldn't tell anyone. The truth only resided in its memory until it was erased for political reasons.

"Almost done with the sampling, Sator?" Head Assault Leader Navarro asked.

"Yes, sir. I'm just finishing up now. No known operatives present. No wanted persons of any kind."

"Very good, Sator. Once you're done, send your final report to SouthCom headquarters."

"Very well, sir."

Chapter 13

CONTACT

"Do you guys hear that? It sounds really close. That's got to be at least six squads worth of gunfire. Maybe ten. I hear at least four kinds of weapons. Wait—it stopped."

"Colonel Maddox, what do you think that was about?" Lieutenant Hoover asked.

"Not sure, Hoover. Could be a Commonwealth training exercise? Commonwealth Land Forces don't usually venture out this far without reason. Captain Tannis, can you get a team together to get some eyes on what happened out there?"

"Yes, sir. Right away."

"Thanks, Captain."

Underground, the three officers from the Federated Anti-Colonial Front (FAF), also known as Tricorns or Liberators, assembled to discuss their local outreach to infiltrate and subvert United People's Commonwealth political objectives. To Commonwealth entities, the Tricorns were known as noncons because of their "nonconformist" beliefs and behaviors in relation to Commonwealth mandates.

Rural Auckland, New Zealand served as an excellent place to create underground fortifications to house soldiers and supplies, as well as provide vital intelligence from the southern hemisphere to global operations. Its location on the west side of the island made it easy for surreptitious soldiers to travel in small numbers and at irregular times after getting done with their civilian jobs downtown. In all, about three hundred Tricorns could be garrisoned there at once, but most had the week off guard duty, so at the moment, the total force was about thirty. The number would have been closer to fifty, but several recent engagements resulted in some fatalities and prisoners being taken away for processing.

"Sergeant Deems, take two other men out about a thousand meters south to see what the gunfire and explosions were about. Be discreet. We don't want to draw attention to our position, especially with our current garrison being so low on fighters. Keep in close contact with me. If force is necessary, we'll be ready."

"Very good, sir," Deems replied to Captain Tannis as he stood at attention and saluted him.

"Dismissed."

Sergeant Deems hustled down the hall and after making several turns, made it to a common room where privates Gary Yalu and Forstner Bex were playing card games.

"Hey, guys! Scouting party! Gear up! We have orders to recon a bunch of shots fired and explosions heard nearby. Saddle up!"

"Seriously, Deems?" Bex questioned.

"You're damn right, I'm serious. You're my best friends and also happen to be the best shots in our platoon."

"But Deems, I haven't had a chance to take all of Yalu's money yet. Can we play one more hand before we go?"

"This is urgent. Colonel had a bad look on his face when he first heard the shots. He's been through this sort of thing for years now, he knows what he's doing. I'll meet you at exit nine in three minutes. Now go and gear up. We don't have time to waste, we may have civilians to save."

The three men were dressed in their dark blue with red lined uniforms, which had settings that could allow for the soldier to pick the camouflage pattern needed for missions in different climates and terrains. The grassy plains setting seemed appropriate for this mission, so the men chose that setting and the uniforms instantly turned to that pattern. Their scouting uniforms also included digitized textural elements to maximize concealment within their environment. Despite the black market availability of advanced military technology to the Tricorns, the Commonwealth Land Forces still possessed superior combat uniforms that changed camouflage patterns as they moved throughout their environment, much like a chameleon does.

Finally ready to exit their subterranean citadel, the sentries looked up to the top of the ladder that led to the outside. There was a death sentence for anyone caught wearing a rebel uniform outside of the fortification.

"All right, men, helmets on. Yalu, you take point. Then Bex. I'll take rear."

One distinct and identifiable part of the tricorn uniform was the combat tricorn helmet, meant to represent the tricorn hat used during the American Revolutionary War in the late eighteenth century. Though symbolic in nature, the small tricorn affixed to the fully enclosed combat helmet provided radar and electronic support for enemy detection and acquisition.

"Captain Tannis, this is Sergeant Deems. I picked Privates Bex and Yalu for the mission. The three of us are just leaving headquarters now. We're heading southwest toward Jenkins Road. No signs of enemies yet."

"Sounds like a good scouting party. Keep in touch, Sergeant. We're all on standby if you need us."

"Roger that, sir."

Slowly moving along a thick tree line, the trio listened to every sound of the forest fauna as well as the wind rustling downed leaves. Also apparent, was the sound of the wind riding the tops of the tall grassy plains that was intermittently interrupted by the sound of ocean waves crashing into the shoreline. No gunfire or explosions heard. No indications of any distress detected.

Yalu put his left hand up to signal the squad to freeze and be alert. He proceeded to crouch and then point to a reflective spot near the base of a hill, a couple hundred meters away.

Bex looked back at Deems to relay the message, but Deems responded to Yalu and acknowledged the hand signal before Bex could signal his relay sign. Yalu communicated silently to follow the tree line toward the suspicious item.

* * *

"Head Assault Leader Navarro, my Sator's analysis indicates that a few of the PI2s belong to several members of the congregation that live a couple clicks from here, near the outskirts of the small town of Muriwai. Last year, there was an investigation looking into possible ties with noncon activity there. Can we proceed to look for suspicious persons and intelligence?"

"That sounds like a good plan, Wilby. I like your initiative today. Your first combat operation is one hundred percent successful so far. Keep up the great work."

"Thank you, sir. I hope this is the first of many successful missions to finally end this pointless insurrection by the noncons and their sympathizers."

"Be sure you don't underestimate your enemy. These noncons have managed to recruit from our ranks within all branches of the military and other governmental agencies, so they might have some very good intelligence and training. We have had some recent successes in Australia, New Zealand, and elsewhere, but we can't get too cocky. They have also had victories against us. Luckily, no immense losses to our forces, but they still pose a threat to us."

"Understood, sir."

"I'm going to take my fireteam back to my MCV to report our progress to Assault Unit Leader Conrad. Take the company out on foot to pursue your leads. It'll do the men some good not get too used to being driven everywhere. We still do have legs after all."

"Will do, sir."

"Oh, and Wilby, you and the company can change your uniforms from combat camo to civil patrol coloration. At this point, we won't likely have any confrontation with the populace. I think that after our shooting gallery fun, any noncon with an illicit weapon would have dropped it and headed for the hills by now. We may as well serve as a visible show of force with our dark red uniforms. Kind of a nice contrast to all the green."

"Very well, sir," Junior Assault Leader Wilby acknowledged.

By audible command, Wilby ordered, "Men and WAMs change your uniform setting from combat camo to civil patrol coloration."

"Wilby, keep your eyes moving and be mindful of your surroundings," Head Navarro intently relayed.

* * *

Deems, Yalu, and Bex continued their careful and deliberate pursuit of the lustrous object in the ever decreasing distance. Now, within a stone's throw away and coming around the base of a small hill, the men were in shock.

"Are you seeing what I'm seeing, Sarge?" Bex terrifyingly asked.

"Yep."

"Everyone, down," Sergeant Deems whispered.

"Shit, Sarge, did they see us?" Yalu asked.

"I don't see anybody there. No sign of humans or WAMs. They do have sensors on their MCVs though. I hope they didn't pick up on us or we're in trouble." Deems decided to relay the message to headquarters. "Captain Tannis, we have a visual on approximately ten to twelve MCVs that seem to be unoccupied. We are unable to locate the infantry that are presumably dismounted."

"Geeze. What'd you guys walk into? I'll tell Colonel Maddox right now. We'll probably be coming out to assist very shortly. Just don't start a firefight if you don't have to."

With Colonel Maddox fully informed by Captain Tannis, the remaining garrison at the base briefed for a mission to locate the Commonwealth group, evade detection, and then find Deems and his men.

"Deems, it's Tannis. We're on our way now. We'll split up into three squads of nine or ten each. We have to find the Commonwealth infantry first, then we'll try to find you. Prepare to fight. It might be inevitable when we've got three blind mice chasing a cat."

"Sounds good, sir. We'll lie low and gather intel. Let us know if you make contact."

"Very good. Tannis, out."

* * *

Wilby led the company of men and machines through a small gorge en route to Muriwai. In their patrol formation, the units tried not to lose their footing on the uneven terrain at the base of the mountains' sides. Their red civil patrol uniform color scheme displayed a harsh juxtaposition to the verdant flora abound.

"Wilby! I caught of glimpse of a possible noncon on the hillside. Maybe a scout," Hedge relayed.

"Check out the area with your bio rangefinder with infrared detection wavelength. That'll show it if it's organic. Noncons don't use WAMs, so it should show up."

"Right away, sir."

Hedge ordered his fireteam to surveil the ridge line where he thought he saw the scout. His Sator and Fil units used their various sensors to look for the combatant lifeform.

"No indication of a noncon, sir."

"Okay, Hedge. Before you lost sight of it, what'd it look like?"

"It appeared to be a human in all white armor. I could tell it was armor because of the way its silhouette seemed to be exaggerated for its height and shape. Too big of a profile not to have armor on. Like I said, I just caught a glimpse of it, but it appeared to have some sort of metallic design on its sides. They almost looked like wings. They didn't stick out like a bird's wings, but they looked like a picture of a metallic bird's wings. I know it sounds crazy, but that's what I saw."

"Sounds like whatever it is, it's more like an animal than a person, Hedge. Company, prepare to meet more of these creatures that can apparently fly," Wilby sounded with a sardonic tone to his men.

"I know what I saw, Wilby. It was looking at me—not moving, just looking. I couldn't tell if it had a weapon or not. All I know is I've never seen anything like it before."

"If you saw it once, we may see it again, Hedge. We'll just have to wait and see," Wilby responded with a slight level of annoyance.

Timmins chimed in, "Don't worry, Hedge. If our MCVs break down, then maybe it can fly us back to base."

"I'll bet it'll bring you back to its home for a romantic dinner," Hedge quipped.

"Only after you, buddy."

"Okay, we're done with the topic of conversation. Just keep marching soldiers," Wilby ordered.

* * *

Captain Tannis led a squad around from the west and then back north toward the initial area of gunfire that he heard at headquarters. The ten men had their rifles at the ready as they were anticipating running into upward of twelve fireteams of Robotics Corps soldiers. They would most certainly be outgunned, but with the right tactics, they could try to make it feasible to engage and live to tell about it.

Lieutenant Hoover took a squad straight north and Colonel Maddox took his squad east, until they turned north toward the rendezvous point. Each of the officers knew it could be his last mission. They had not deployed downrange with this many Commonwealth forces in the vicinity and with so little reconnaissance. The risks were high and the probability of success, low. The FAF forces globally were not averse to risk. In fact, they were the primary ones on each continent that stood up to tyranny. Without their willingness to fight, the world's masses were without hope for any sense of liberty that had been commonplace to the fortunate in years past.

"Colonel, I've located the source of the sounds we heard at base. I'm looking at thirty-nine mutilated bodies in a valley. It looks like they were having a church service when they were killed. I see Father Briar dead near the altar. I'm pretty sure I see Hoover's wife and daughter down there—it's pretty ugly, sir. We'll probably want to tell him after this is over. We need his focus on the mission right now. Afterward, we can go identify the bodies and notify their families.

"Dammit, this is a tough one, Tannis. Hoover's a twenty-five-year-old widower and father of a murdered six-year-old child. We'll need to protect the civilians from repercussions by the Commonwealth for holding forbidden religious burial services."

"Sounds like a plan, sir."

"We'll come up with a plan to notify the townspeople when this is all done. Man, this is going to be difficult. Land Forces don't normally target this many people in one spot, so the magnitude isn't typically this extreme. But thirty-nine men, women, and children—now that is a massacre. What were they doing to deserve this? They were destroyed while trying to save their souls."

"Colonel, whatever the reason was, they did this without mercy. I'll record footage of this for our records and then you can see for yourself before we go back to identify the people there. It's the bloodiest site I've ever seen. I'm still in shock that those barbarians did this to our neighbors. In fact, Jack Biggins, one of my friends, is also down there. It looks like he tried to shield his wife, Abby, and their young son, Kenny."

"Tannis, this is why we fight. We're not meant to accept this as normal. When this becomes normal, then we've surrendered. The Commonwealth colonized the earth by selling vulnerable people ideas of equality, prosperity, and security, but at the cost of expending liberties and replacing it with control. This is why we fight, this is why we sacrifice. I'm sorry for your loss as well as LT's immense familial losses. In part, we honor them by continuing our fight."

"Colonel, this is Hoover. We think we found fresh impressions that are probably Robotics Corps tracks. Two-by-two WAM tracks, followed by one WAM and one human. They can't be far."

"Very good, Hoover. Excellent news. Captain Tannis and I will converge our squads to your position now. Keep tracking them, but keep your distance. We definitely want to have all units in place if we're going to fight. If they get too far down that valley we'll have to engage them sooner than later. We can ill afford to allow Commonwealth forces to disrupt our fortifications, and intelligence gathering capabilities."

"Will do, Colonel. Out."

* * *

As Wilby and his company continued their march through the valley, Wilby's Ranger noticed several small houses several hundred meters ahead.

"Let's head there first. Hopefully, we'll find some more fish to fry, or at least find some lures for the next catch. Keep moving, men. We're almost out in the open."

* * *

Sergeant Deems, Private Bex, and Private Yalu remained in their concealed positions to avoid detection as they kept their eyes on the MCVs.

"Colonel, any new orders for us?"

"Deems, things have changed. We have multiple civilian casualties in the area. Captain Tannis and his men found the bodies as well as ammo, tracks, and explosives that match Commonwealth Land Forces signatures. We're going to end this fight. We're about to end innocent bloodshed on this island for today.

"I'd like you and your two men to destroy all the MCVs that you see. Rig them all with plastic explosives and wait for my command. We have to blow the MCVs at the exact same time that I order our ambush of the main force. It's absolutely paramount that we're on the same page. After you destroy their means of escape, haul ass to my position because we will probably be in an intense firefight and need more firepower. Any questions?"

"We'll get right on it, sir. What if we come across any targets before we blow the MCVs?"

"If they threaten you, your men or civilians, and make no attempt to surrender, engage them and then neutralize them. Clear?"

"Yes, sir. Crystal, sir."

"Wait for my command. Out."

"Roger that."

* * *

Head Assault Leader Navarro and his fireteam continued to march toward their MCV, which was parked next to the eleven others. Now within sight, he certainly was looking forward to returning to the safety of the MCV and the comforts of his commander's seat within the armored craft.

"Sator, prepare your comms to link with Assault Unit Leader Conrad," Head Navarro ordered.

"Right away, sir."

"Thank you. I'm sure Unit Leader Conrad will be pleased with our mission's success so far."

As Navarro's Sator neared the principle MCV, it noticed an anomalous wire out of place in the cockpit.

"Sir, you should—"

A massive explosion erupted in Navarro's MCV, then the next one, and the next, and the next until all twelve vehicles were destroyed almost simultaneously. With Navarro's fireteam so close to the MCVs, they were destroyed by the explosions. Head Assault Navarro's body was shielded by his Ranger and Tommy WAMs, so despite being knocked to the ground and injured, he was conscious and tried to stand up.

"Freeze! Don't move!" Sergeant Deems shouted. "Move a muscle and you're dead. Say a word to your buddies and you're dead."

Head Navarro, still kneeling on one knee, didn't say a word.

"Okay, soldier, put your hands on your head nice and slowly," Deems ordered.

Navarro followed the instruction promptly, but also let out a code by mouth as he hastily pulled a small railpistol out of a compartment on the left side of his breastplate.

"Gun! Gun! Drop him!"

Bex and Yalu fired first, then Deems, once he finally reacted. Navarro dropped to the ground face first. Blood poured out of wounds in his thorax and abdomen onto the plush green grass.

"Shit—why'd he have to go and do that? We wouldn't have done anything to him if he would have cooperated," Yalu sounded off to his compadres.

"We'll never know. It was his choice and he made it," Bex reassured Yalu.

At the same time as the first explosion at the MCV docking position rang out, Colonel Maddox also ordered the onset of the engagement in the valley with the company of Robotics Corps infantry.

"Hoover, do it!" Maddox ordered.

Hoover touched the red button located on a popup digital screen that opened prepositioned trap doors in several locations within the column of the Robotics Corps company. The valley was a natural choke point that served as an excellent location to preposition booby traps for enemy forces. The first and last fireteams were mostly lost to the trapdoors, which fell into pits nearly sixty feet deep. The bottoms of the pits had a forest of razor sharp tungsten pointed pikes within a powerful electrical field to fry people and destroy WAMs.

The middle trapdoor consumed Werster and half of his fireteam as they fell into a diverted lava tube that melted them on contact.

"Ambush! Deploy shields and engage!" Junior Assault Leader Wilby screamed as he took cover behind his only remaining two WAMs.

The three squads of Tricorns began to fire their anti-personnel rockets from a few positions on the hillsides, which were covered by rocks and fallen trees. The other men began firing their rifles. The rifles they used had served in the previous century and into the beginning of the twenty-first century until most were confiscated by Commonwealth authorities and their antecedents. Once the two primary weapons of adversarial armies, the rifles united in common purpose to defend the collective from the new world governing body's cruel practices. The M16s/M4s and AK-47s/AK-74s that the FAF managed to find and manufacture were fitted with new barrels and components to fire the same caliber, gunpowderless, kinetic projectiles that the Commonwealth military forces used.

The bullets being fired were numbering in the thousands by now, as each soldier on both sides of the equation could carry nearly two thousand rounds of ammo because of their decreased weight and overall size.

The zooms, plinks, and zips of near fatal shots, as well as ricochets, and explosions ripped the valley and overlooking hillsides. Several Tricorns were killed instantly. Commonwealth WAMs were notoriously good shots and Commonwealth soldiers weren't far behind.

"Colonel, most of my squad is gone. We've taken out some of them, but they've got us pinned with their heavy weapons and indirect fire," Captain Tannis urgently reported.

"We've got to pull through, Tannis. We don't have any choice. Keep pushing." A Ranger WAM's laser bolt narrowly missed his head and impacted the boulder to his ten.

Lieutenant Hoover updated Colonel Maddox, "Colonel, only Corporal Pharis and I are left. We can't hold on much longer."

"Hang in there, Hoover!"

Colonel called Deems for support.

"Deems! We are getting our asses kicked! Bring your men now!"

"On our way, sir! Hold on!"

As Deems, Bex, and Yalu ran to where they easily heard the gunfire, they saw a pair of dark aircraft fly through the sky toward the same place they were heading.

"Colonel, you've got two helidrone hunters coming your way. They're nearing your position now. Looks like their weapons bays just opened."

Just after the distressing message was relayed to the colonel, Deems saw a flash streak down through the atmosphere, then curved below the cloud line toward the two helidrones.

Two beams of light shot out of the streaking object and destroyed the helidrones in the blink of an eye. Within quick succession, four pods jettisoned from the vessel at a high rate of speed. The cigar-shaped aircraft accelerated forward and then banked almost straight up and out of sight.

"Colonel, there's something else up there and it just annihilated the helidrones! It also just dropped some unknown objects down on your position."

"Deems, what the hell is going on up there? What happened to the helidrones? Whatever it is, I'm glad it's on our side!"

"I have no idea, Colonel. There is some crazy shit going on."

"Hurry, Deems! Hurry!"

"We're coming as fast as we can, sir. I can see your position."

The three men were nearing a dead sprint as they watched the four objects heading toward the ground come to a stop in the air, several feet above the grassy valley. Once at a standstill, a circular elevator telescoped down from each pod at the same time. The elevators touched the ground, then quickly retracted back into the pods. The pods then accelerated upward into the blue depths of the sky at a high rate of speed. The pods were gone, but they each left three unknown figures in their place.

The Robotics Corps troops continued engaging FAF forces as if nothing had happened, until the three beings that came out of each of the four pods began targeting them from both sides of their battle line. The beings were dressed completely in white, except for a shimmering metallic design on their side and around their backs. They lifted their right arms and without hesitation, fired weapons from their forearms. They struck the WAMs before they could be targeted. The pulsed laser beams tore the WAMs apart with one or two shots each. Next, the beings targeted the Commonwealth soldiers as they moved closer and closer to the valley floor.

One of them spoke, "Put down your weapons and you'll live!"

The soldiers stopped firing and listened.

"Aim your weapons at any one of my men or the others here and we'll shoot."

The voice spoke in English and did not sound artificial in any way.

Wilby, Hedge, and Timmins were the only ones left. All WAMs were eliminated, as well as the other eight humans with them on the mission. Unbeknownst to them, Head Assault Leader Navarro was also dead.

"Okay, okay—woah there. We'll put our weapons down—we surrender," Wilby acquiesced and was shocked to be in the presence of a superior group of soldiers.

Wilby and the two other men proceeded to put their weapons on the ground. Swallowing their pride, the men knelt before the few remaining Tricorns and their newly found celestial allies.

"Accendia, converge," the unknown commando said.

The mysterious combatants approached the three Commonwealth officers with their weapons fixed on them, in case of any suspicious behavior.

"Bind 'em," the mysterious being ordered his apparent subordinates.

"You three, stay there. No funny business. Since you willingly surrendered, you will all live. We need to transport you for detainment and questioning."

The leader of the twelve called on his communications device for immediate evacuation.

"This is Deputy Lumis. The mission is a success. FAF facilities remain intact. We have three prisoners and six allies in need of immediate retrieval; however, we did not make it down in time to save the several dozen civilians that we saw on the way in."

"Roger that, Deputy, I'll bring down the Sparrowhawk. Over and out," said the deputy's superior officer, Champion Backstrom.

Colonel Maddox, Captain Tannis, Lieutenant Hoover, Sergeant Deems, Private Yalu, and Private Bex were formed in a line according to rank. When they heard Deputy Lumis call for a retrieval transport and mentioned that allies needed retrieval as well, the Tricorn battle survivors could only look at each other with disbelief.

"Um, Colonel, what's he talking about?" Lieutenant Hoover asked.

"I thought this might happen. I didn't know how or when, but here it is," Colonel Maddox said, explaining himself no further.

"What do you mean, Colonel?" Captain Tannis chimed.

"Men, this could be a very, very long conversation. Only senior people on a need to know list in the FAF know about the grand scale of what's going on here. The main reason for our drill this weekend was to inform you men of a powerful ally we have. It will be very difficult to comprehend what I am about to say to you now, but please believe me, this is one hundred percent true.

"The Accendia, the ones in the white combat suits—they are a highly advanced and very intelligent group that know much more than we could hope to know. Their weaponry is superior to any known assets that we or the Commonwealth have for that matter. Their technology includes capabilities that you and I can only dream of. That unequaled technology is what allows them to be here in the first place."

"What do ya mean, Colonel?" Sergeant Deems asked.

"Well, this is one of the most unbelievable parts of this whole ordeal. Gentlemen, these Accendia are human. They have the same DNA, the same everything as us, but they are not from now. These men and women, the Accendia, are from the future. They discovered the ability to traverse the space-time continuum and have come to assist us in our fight against the Commonwealth. They have been here for about eight years already, but now they are becoming more active among us."

"But why now and not before the Commonwealth existed? Or why not before the last world war that paved the way for the Commonwealth?" Tannis asked vigorously.

"Those are great questions that I cannot answer. I don't know. I do know that none in the FAF command know those answers either. The Accendia don't even know. From the ones I've heard from in the past few months on the intercom, they just knew it had to be this time. There are some things that we are not meant to know, or cannot possibly understand. All I do know is that for whatever reason, we have help beyond our wildest imagination. We already have the major pieces in place to begin a major assault on North America. After we can liberate our armies there, we will then invade Europe to take the Commonwealth capital at Trier. Once the capital falls, the other provinces around the world will fall. Operation Cloudburst is set to begin within a couple weeks. The details are beyond top secret, so that is as much as I can tell you. We have some details to hash out, but we will proceed on schedule. I know that I speak for many of the

FAF leaders, as well as Accendia commanders, when I say that the human race is not meant to live this way. People deserve their undeniable rights to freedom. To deny the basic intellectual, spiritual, and physical rights of humans is to deny their existence in their totality."

Deputy Lumis walked over to the FAF soldiers and informed them their retrieval ship would arrive momentarily. The Commonwealth soldiers were still kneeling in front of the Accendia forces.

"Here it comes—the Sparrowhawk, gentlemen," Deputy Lumis announced. "Squad, get the prisoners up and give them each a conscious-abrupter pulse, so they'll have no idea what's going on until we deem it necessary. Then, escort them onboard for detention."

"Yes, sir," said Lumis's squad leader.

"FAF soldiers, please follow my men behind the prisoners. Once aboard, they will bring you to a room for rest and refreshments to your liking. Colonel Maddox, please accompany me to the bridge for debriefing."

"Of course, Deputy," Colonel Maddox replied.

The aircraft landed soon after the deputy's commands. This retrieval and command craft, called a Sparrowhawk, was shaped like a large V—different than the cigar-shaped Tanager aircraft that quickly arrived and disappeared earlier. Each wing extended roughly two hundred and fifty feet from the center of the aircraft. Several floors of windows were clearly noticed along with interspersed weapons among them, as well as larger turret-like weapons on the top and bottom.

"Okay, men, we have clearance to board. Up the ramp and to your previously established destinations," Deputy Lumis said.

"Here we go, men. No need to fear—these people are on our side. I'll see you once I'm debriefed by Deputy Lumis and the other commanders onboard," Colonel Maddox placated the remnants of his war-torn cohort.

"Here we go, Bex," Sergeant Deems said.

"Well, Yalu, I wouldn't have guessed we'd be going up in a spaceship with a bunch of people that are apparently our distant descendants. See, I thought hitting a royal flush was the least likely event today," Bex remarked while walking up the ramp with his friends.

Once all were inside the ship, it lifted up from the ground and jetted into the sky.

Chapter 14

ABOARD THE SPARROWHAWK

"Colonel Maddox, this is Champion Backstrom. He is the champion of our First Air Infantry Group," Deputy Lumis introduced his commanding officer while standing at attention in the conference room, within the ship's bridge.

"Champion, it's a great honor to meet you," the colonel said as he accepted the champion's firm handshake and then followed with a mutual salute.

The burly, redheaded champion replied, "It's nice that I can finally meet some of your men, although I understand that many are on leave this weekend. We will reach them in the coming days to prepare for the upcoming mission."

"Yes, and unfortunately, we had a number of losses during our latest contacts. Your men saved us down there, and I thank you for that."

"It's our duty. I just wish we had acted sooner so we could have saved your men in the valley and the civilians at the shepherd's field." Champion Backstrom lowered his head as low as his voice sank with regret. "We couldn't afford to act that quickly. We didn't want to draw much attention since we were trying to secretly track that specific company of Robotics Corps troops. Also, since the area of contact was so close to numerous subterranean munitions and supply depots, not to mention your own men, we couldn't use larger aerial weapons systems."

"This fight has cost us so much already, Champion—we can take it. I just ask that you help retrieve the remains of the family members of one of my men. They were slaughtered along with the others among the slain lambs on the shepherd's field."

"I will send a detachment right away, Colonel." Champion Backstrom made eye contact with and nodded toward Deputy Foxworth. "See to it, Deputy. Oh, and bring the others as well. They all deserve a proper burial."

"Right way, sir," Foxworth replied as he saluted prior to exiting the room to gather his team for their mission.

"Thank you, Champion," Maddox graciously remarked.

"Of course, Colonel. It's the least we can do."

"When I said we were after that specific company of men that attacked you and your men, we were after one specific man—Jayk Wilby. He is an up-and-coming Junior Assault Leader within the Robotics Corps of the Commonwealth Land Forces. Raptor Group is a group of especially zealous officers that command their WAMs without mercy. We've been following them for several weeks and have come to the conclusion that Wilby can provide critical information to us in our operation. We'll be able to convince him to join us—I can assure you of that. He won't have a choice."

"What can he offer us, Champion? If you don't mind me asking, sir?"

"The Robotics Corps are elite forces that use both human and automated soldiers, which are neurologically integrated into an effective fighting force. They are a fireteam-based fighting force that tend to deploy and operate in companies. The further up the chain of command one goes, the more control one conceivably has over more autonomous units. There must be a limitation to this, though. Otherwise, the highest in command could effectively take control over every autonomous unit in the Robotics Corps. That would mean a massive army at one person's disposal, especially since—in essence, one general could command every unit by his or her thoughts. We will find out whether one or several individuals are capable of controlling the entire autonomous contingent of the Corps. Our intelligence estimates that the autonomous forces within the Corps are about a million units worldwide. Their ratio is five WAMs per human, so the entire Corps doesn't take very many human fighters away from the larger Commonwealth Land Forces.

"If our forces or yours were able to intercept, infiltrate, or decode their neurological communications, we could in theory, take control of one million robotic warfighters. Jayk Wilby might be the piece that we need to unravel their man-machine integration."

"I see." Maddox pondered the idea.

"Now, that number would make even Julius Caesar blush if he could imagine the day when he'd be crossing the Rubicon with a horde of metal warriors of that magnitude."

"Champion, that would give us a massive boost to our ranks. I know that finding fighters these days isn't exactly easy—the best luck seems to be in North America. At one point, freedom was in their DNA, and thankfully, some have continued to covertly pass it on to their posterity."

"Exactly, Colonel. That's why our mission begins there. Our operatives on the ground estimate that of the fighting aged civilian men and women in the heart of North America, about five to ten percent are willing to rise up against the Commonwealth if the right catalysts occur. That means between six and twelve million potential fighters or at the very least, supporters. Our underground resistance has been training roughly three million in collusion with separate, but allied militias that include another million men and women. In total, this force can be used to liberate the world."

"Champion, what about the forces needed to liberate North America?"

"Excellent question. That'll require more discussion time than what we have available now since I need to discuss updates with upper command. Let me just say that you and your men will serve as an important part of that force. Most of the others are already training together in a safe place, far away from any enemy eyes. Colonel, it's where your men here and the rest in Auckland will go by the end of the day."

"That sounds good to me, sir. We will do our best. I trust that you'll be able to get the rest of my unit to the location?"

"Yes, Colonel. I already have another detachment working on retrieving the rest of your unit for departure to our secret base of operations. Do you have any other questions for the time being?"

"No, Champion. Thank you for the debriefing. I'll inform my men."

"There's one more thing I should mention—there is someone else aboard. He's one of our young ones being hidden in the Chicago area and he happens to be Junior Assault Leader Wilby's cousin. He has a way of influencing others—his name is Peter Barclay. He'll be the one to turn the hardhearted Jayk Wilby to our side. He's already helped to rescue General Marion from one of those hideous extermination arenas, so I have great confidence in him."

"I'm sorry, sir—did you say he rescued General Marion?" Colonel replied with a small degree of curiosity and uncertainty.

"Yes, Colonel, that's right."

"I had no idea. I thought we lost him. I hate to say that I gave up on him, but he'd been captured so many months ago, I had little expectation that he would make it out alive."

"We might have had a role in his escape plans. Peter was just the one to execute it. We needed the general back for the North American liberation."

"That's excellent news, sir." Colonel Maddox could hardly contain his enthusiasm or his growing optimism in their mission. His smile was so wide his face could barely support it.

"Indeed. Colonel, I must be going. It's been a pleasure meeting you." Champion Backstrom stood at attention and saluted Colonel Maddox.

The colonel saluted back and was escorted out of the bridge by Deputy Lumis, who walked him back to the guest quarters where his still stunned and dazed compatriots awaited his return.

"Prisoner. Prisoner. Prisoner! You with me?" Sergeant Delgado desperately snapped his fingers, trying to get a response from the groggy Jayk Wilby.

"Yeah, yeah—I'm here. Wow, what a headache," Wilby acknowledged.

"Get up. You're going with us for questioning." Delgado pointed to the other three Accendia men in their sparkling white combat suits.

"All right. I don't suppose I have any choice in this?"

"You sure don't. Remember, you're a prisoner now."

Wilby stood up, needing to use the wall in his detention cell to help support his body weight. He was still feeling the side effects of the consciousness-altering drug used to disable him prior to boarding the Sparrowhawk. Once he finally found his balance, he came to the door where the four Accendia men stood.

"Put your hands behind your back," one of them ordered.

Without any thought of noncompliance, Wilby slowly put his hands in position. He certainly did not want to have to contend with Accendia weaponry again.

"Good—let's move, people," Sergeant Delgado said to his squad as they begin to escort Wilby to an interrogation room.

Down the hall and several turns later, the men led Wilby into a bright room that was empty except for a table and two chairs. Nothing seemed out of place or particularity intimidating. It was ordinary, for an average interrogation room.

"Take a seat." Delgado pulled a chair out and guided Wilby into it. "I'm not going to regret taking your restraints off, am I?"

"No, of course not. I know what'll happen if I try something."

"Okay, glad we have an understanding. You play nice, we play nice. Stay in your chair, the interrogator will be in soon. See these walls?"

After looking around at the four suspiciously indistinguishable walls, Wilby turned and said, "Yeah—what about 'em?"

"We'll be watching you. Like you said, you know what'll happen if you try something," Delgado reminded the rather diminutive soldier without his combat armor as he pointed to his stowed weapon on his right forearm.

Delgado and the other Accendia left the room, leaving their nervous prisoner's mind to race. Wilby wasn't sure how much he'd be tortured—worst of all, he was thinking about how much pain might be coming his way. He thought to himself, "I'm gonna be able to walk again, right?" Sitting in his titanium chair, Jayk was debating which arm he would lend to the interrogator for maiming. He was left handed after all, so he could spare losing some function in his right arm.

The room suddenly went dark. Jayk's already increased respiratory rate continued to climb. Each breath carried with it a more sinister idea of how he might be physically harmed. Mercilessly abused to obtain intelligence, injuring his body to gain access to his mind—the scenarios were endless. His mind had not been tormented like this since he was not used to being the one without control. He let out a sigh as he heard the door opposite him unlock and quickly slide open into the wall. A shadowy figure walked in from the brightly lit anteroom with no feature but its silhouette—a defined and illuminated outline around the being—only inducing more questions than answers.

The ostensible interrogator walked to the chair opposite Wilby, pulled it out with a screeching grind across the alloyed ceramic floor and sat. The lights flickered on. Jayk's eyes had to adjust for a second to see who was sitting across from him.

"Peter! Peter? What are you doing here?" Jayk yelled out. He couldn't tell if he was happy to see Peter or if he was happy to find out it wasn't a menacing interrogator with torture devices beyond his wildest imagination.

"I know this comes as a complete surprise to you, Jayk—I know that. I also know that this isn't what you envisioned when we spent that week together before my school transfer went through while you were home on leave. We had just met and eventually you took me in as kind of your own little brother. I learned about you and you learned about me. It wasn't that long of a time, but I had a good idea of what was important to you and what you wanted in life. I hope you had a similar experience. Everything that I ever told you about me was absolutely true. I just kept a few important things to myself—this being one of them."

"I don't get it. How are you involved in this? Please, Peter—tell me. I need to know why you betrayed me."

"It's pretty easy for me to say. It's quite simple, actually. You need to believe me when I tell you that I did not betray you. I helped you, I promise you that. Things are not as they seem in this world. It's not your fault. You were created by your parents only to be confiscated and raised by the government. Everything you have been taught has been carefully crafted. Everything you learned in school from pre-K through post-secondary school, continuing into basic training and officer candidate school—all of it has molded you into an individual created by and for the government. All you know has been introduced by and reinforced by them. My job is to tell you what you have been taught is wrong. What you think is justice, is actually unjust. What you think is love, is actually hate. You've been taught to see the world not as it is, but as a powerful few would like it to be."

"I just don't understand."

"It'll take time to open your mind. I know you can, and in time—you will. It's very disturbing to find out that much of what you believe each and every day is either partially true or a complete lie. You've only been taught to view the world through once specific looking glass. Unfortunately, that has drastically limited your ability to think reasonably. Your knowledge of the past and the present is greatly inadequate and distorted. Your looking glass cannot see what truly goes on in this world and what happens after you leave it."

"What do you mean when I leave this world? Like leaving with the Commonwealth Space Forces?"

"No, not at all. I mean when you die—when you leave your physical body."

"How is that possible? When you die, you just die. That's it. There is nothing after death."

"See, that is a critically important aspect of life you have not been taught. Your soul moves on to the afterlife. Where it goes is dependent upon the way that you lived your physical life on earth and the beliefs that you held. If you have no notion of the afterlife, then your sole purpose is to live this life. Unfortunately, powerful forces of evil on earth know that too. For that reason and many others, they want you to be completely dedicated to their causes on earth."

"Okay—so I'm someone's pawn?"

"Many entities are pulling the strings. There are legions of them, both natural and supernatural."

"Supernatural?"

"This will be terrifying to you, but you have to see what accompanies you in your life."

Peter stood up from his chair and walked over to Jayk.

"Give me your hands. I promise you won't be harmed, but you will be afraid—very afraid. Just remember, I will be with you this whole time."

Jayk extended his hands and met Peter's hands in the middle. Jayk's eyes were awestruck. He had to look around in front toward Peter, then back behind his own right shoulder, then his left.

"Geeze! What's going on? What is this? Peter! Help me!" Jayk yelled at the top of his lungs and lunged out of his chair to squeeze Peter for protection.

"It's all right, they won't hurt you," Peter said as he tried to calm Jayk from the spiritual entities in the room with them.

"Most of the beings you see are here to help you and help others with you. But you need to be very, very careful with the other one."

"What should I do, Peter?"

"You don't have to do anything right now. I just want you to look at all four of the beings in this room with us. Look at their faces and tell me what you see."

Jayk, still trembling with fear and on the verge of a psychological breakdown, began to look around the room with more deliberate eyes. He looked at the first being behind Peter. Adrio, Peter's guardian angel, stood with a beautiful, glowing smile—a smile that was one of the most inviting signs he'd ever seen.

Adrio enunciated the words, "You'll be okay." Jayk took the message to heart from the radiant being dressed in all white.

Jayk moved his head to the left, over Peter's right shoulder, and saw, very clearly, a luminous being dressed differently than Adrio. This being appeared to be wearing armor, and a belt that had a large sword sheathed. This being looked like a warrior angel.

Dressed in gleaming white and silver, the being introduced himself to Jayk, "I am called Michael, Michael the Archangel. Fight with me, fight with us—we need your help."

Jayk's eyes grew so wide that you could have set dinner plates between his eyelids. He couldn't believe what was happening—he just communicated with two spiritual beings that he was always taught could never exist. He didn't know they were angels because the concept was foreign, although Michael did introduce himself as an archangel. Jayk nodded at Michael, who put his hand over his breastplate and acknowledged Jayk's response.

Jayk continued scanning the room and over his left shoulder, he saw another being covered in white. He looked like Adrio, Peter's guardian angel, but with a slightly different head shape and facial structure.

"I am your guardian angel," the angel, with shoulder-length hair and slightly wider-set eyes, said to Jayk. "What would you like to call me?"

"Um—I don't know. Uh, how about Sam?"

"Fine by me. You may call me, Sam. It's so nice to formally meet you."

Jayk noticed that Sam didn't seem as joyful as Adrio did. He wasn't sure why, but there was a clear distinction between the two.

Continuing to turn to the left, he noticed a being much different than the others. This one was not quite as bright. It certainly wore no smile, and its face looked somewhat distorted and less approachable.

"I have been pleased with your training, and so has my master," the dimly lit being said with a disheartening grin.

"Jayk, that is a demon that's been influencing you. It's latched on to you because of the way you've been living. Luckily, I have an antidote here with me," Peter said with his accompanying warm smirk.

"Michael, will you please help him?"

"Of course, Peter."

Michael flashed forward and struck the demon in the chest with his sword, unleashing a radiant beam of light that forced the demon into oblivion.

"That'll free you from its clutches for now, but it isn't a permanent solution. A change of heart and a rooting in faith can help you resist them."

"I've got to sit down, I don't feel so good," Jayk said as he reached back for his chair, on the verge of vomiting.

"This is a new beginning for you, my cousin. You'll learn more in the coming days. Will you help me? More importantly, will you help us?"

Jayk, still clutching his stomach with queasiness, looked up at Peter and said, "Of course I will. I just don't even know what to think anymore." Peter placed his hand on Jayk's back, consoling and providing reassurance. Jayk looked around to see if the beings were still there in his presence. He couldn't see any, so Peter must have discontinued the capability of his supernatural sight. Jayk knew that Peter did it for his own good.

Sergeant Delgado and his two men-at-arms reentered the interrogation room as Peter exited.

"We've got to get you back to your holding cell for transport. Our Sparrowhawk is going to uplink with the nearest Condor. General Marion is aboard it and is requesting your presence."

"What's a Condor and who is General Marion?" Jayk asked, trying to learn more about his captors turned allies.

"It's a host ship for ones like this. If you think this ship's big. Just wait till you see one of our Condors—those things are a couple miles long. They're our command ships for all FAF operations. We're going to General Marion's flagship, the *Lexington*. Our leaders have allowed him to utilize it for the pending invasion. The general is your new commander. You will report to him and his subordinates."

Jayk thought to himself while being walked back to his holding cell, "And I thought I was a tough guy commanding my own MCV with a bunch of metal-bodied meatheads." A question popped into his head.

"Hey, Sergeant, where are we going to meet this general?"

"I can't tell you exactly where, but you'll soon find out."

Jayk knew he had much to learn, and a great deal of trust to be gained, but he did feel some satisfaction with his choice. Hopefully, he could convince his fellow Robotics Corps prisoners to find their hearts too.

Chapter 15

One's Duty

"Man, I wish we had more than twenty-four hours to get away from this place. It just gets old, you know. Plus, why does it have to be every trimester? Why not, like—uh, say, every month? Don't they trust our parents?" Ryland unloaded his feelings and rhetorical ruminations into vocal onslaughts that rained down on Peter as they unpacked their things after returning to school.

"That would make things a lot better, wouldn't it," Peter answered, despite not being entirely sure if Ryland was speaking rhetorically.

"It sure would be better, Peter. Better to get our heads out of this hole and see our families. It would be better to enjoy hanging out and doing things without having to write a report about it for class. At least we didn't have to do that last assignment—you know, because there was that—that should I call it—situation that we were sworn to never talk about. Pretty coincidental that the first time you ever go to a Tri Annum, you get picked as an operator. Then, you happen to be the only operator in history whose offender escapes after he turned your harvester into a spaceship. I'm glad we didn't have to write those stupid papers, but geez, Peter—what are the odds?"

"It's a pretty complicated world out there. There were lots of things that played into those events," Peter explained, reexamining his thoughts after saying them.

"That's one way to put it. No kidding, it's complicated. It had to have been an inside job. I mean, Nathaniel was a tough dude, but he had to have had lots of allies in his corner. I'm sure the right people were put in place to get him out—there had to have been a bigger plot."

"I think you're right. We shouldn't talk about it though—remember, it never happened," Peter said while smiling with his back turned toward Ryland, moving clothes back into his dresser. Then, he went to the communal bathroom down the hall.

Peter nonchalantly opened the door as he came back to his and Ryland's room. He went right back to unpack the last of his belongings from his auburn-colored vinyl suitcase, which seemed to have had plenty of traveling experience.

Ryland then asked a question with an unusual level of brevity, one that starkly contrasted his previous ramblings.

"What are these?" the alarmed fourteen-year-old asked him while holding one patch from Peter's suitcase in each hand.

Peter quickly turned, realizing the seriousness of Ryland's question. How could he possibly explain this? Peter was fairly sure that Ryland knew what one of them was, but mostly definitely not the other.

"Those are my patches?"

"I can see that. Why do you have them?"

"They're mine. I found them at home, so I thought I'd bring them to school."

"Why do you have them in the first place? I'm not sure about this one, but I definitely know this one here is an illegal symbol to have, draw, or even mention by name without a good reason."

"I have both of them because they're important to me."

"Peter, you do know that they'll put you in prison for a long, long time for having this?" Ryland angrily chastised his friend while holding the three and one-half inch by two and one-quarter inch patch of fabric with the American flag on it. "This flag and what it stood for are dead. Weren't you ever taught that? I first heard about it in, like the second grade. It stood for injustice and inequality, so it's been phased out. Its history has been erased from the records. What were you thinking?"

"That is not what the American flag stood for, Ryland. It stood for justice, liberty for all under the law, and guaranteed freedoms that no other nation in the history of mankind ever had. Its government provided more freedom, rights, and privileges to the largest number of people ever allowed. Some of those people rose to power by utilizing the benefits embedded within its founding: liberty, the pursuit of happiness, civic virtue, and individual responsibility. Those very same people that benefited so much, were the ones that took away those same opportunities for others. Of course it was never perfect—there is no such thing as long as we humans are in charge. It was the best option in a fallen world and its life was systematically smothered out of existence."

"It doesn't matter. How dare you? I have to report you. I would say that I'm sorry, but I can't. It's my duty to report you."

"Well, it's my duty to stand up for what's right. What you are doing is completely acceptable, based on what you've been taught. I understand that, but you're wrong. This system—the Commonwealth's system—is completely wrong. It's backward. It's warped. Its view of the world is the exact opposite of what is true. Instead of focusing on its own depravities and its own level of oppression, it projects policies and propaganda in order to destroy a past way of life that was superior—otherwise, people would wonder what they were missing. People like you, Ryland, would wonder why we lost it and became this way. Instead of that inevitable outcome, you've been taught to mock, hate, and persecute those who differ from you, and despise a nation that was the greatest experiment in human governance that the world had even seen."

"Whatever. I can't even listen to you. You don't make any sense. I should have known this all along. I don't even want to know what this other patch stands for."

Peter, still keeping his cool, responded.

"You couldn't point out truth if it hit you in the forehead. You've been taught to forget or deny truth, and accept lies in order to create a different worldview. That other patch you're holding, that patch represents a movement beyond myself that will rise up and help to restore the promises held within the stars and stripes of the first patch. The winged lion symbolizes forces of good around this world, meant to lift others into a higher domain of existence—an existence of faith, fellowship, honor, respect, individual responsibility, and so many other values that have been arbitrarily deemed offensive and irrelevant."

"Before I turn you in, I have to know why you got involved in this mess."

"I volunteered. It's my duty. To any end, my commitment is to help others. If I die for my actions, but primarily because of my beliefs, then so be it. I would not have chosen a different path—I would do the same thing again."

"But why? Why would you give up your life for others that you don't even know?"

"Doing things for others whom one doesn't know is what truly sets one apart from the wicked. Ryland, if you're willing to pave the way for my imprisonment and possibly, my death, then I know you would not hesitate for one second to do the same to a stranger—that is what truly saddens me. You have no respect for human life. None, except for your own and those whose worth you justify by a false sense of moral superiority. My friend, I am so sorry to tell you that you have been molded into a machine designed to know nothing and feel nothing except that which has been deemed appropriate by elitists who run the world. These people see nothing in you but only a way of solidifying and maintaining their own power. You are a pawn in their game to rule over every person on this planet."

"It sure sounds like you're a pawn, too, mister righteous one."

"I'm doing this voluntarily to help others. You're being forced into your position by laws and edicts. I have a choice. Your only choice is to obey or be locked away—that is the difference. I hope you'll understand one day."

"Peter, you're a traitor. I have to tell Ms. Danvers, right now!" Ryland ran out of their room to notify his teacher in the educator's quarters.

As Ryland bolted out the door, Peter spoke, fully aware his friend wouldn't hear him, "A traitor to what this society has become—I gladly accept that notion."

It didn't take long for Peter to be taken into custody and whisked away to a secret location for interrogation and internment. He didn't fight. He didn't question the reasons for his detainment. He knew he had been betrayed by the person closest to him at school. It was how Ryland and others like him had been taught. It wasn't necessarily their fault since their morality was almost exclusively contingent on what they learned from government officials or from government sponsored platforms of influence. In that sense, the way Ryland reacted to hearing Peter's point of view was natural.

Those controlling the opinion of the global citizens maintained their distance within their contained lives of opulence and grandeur. The splendor of the rulers's palaces and mansions provided the layers necessary to insulate them from the real suffering and injustice felt across the world. The exact suffering and injustice they claimed to eliminate was primarily in existence because of them and their oppressive ideology.

Meanwhile, Ms. Danvers thought she should take the opportunity to debrief Ryland.

"Ryland, you did the right thing. I know he was your friend. It's not even worth mentioning his name at this point, not after what he did. I'm proud that you stood up to maintain the integrity of our way of life, instead of letting your friend continue on his ill-advised path. There may be some ignorant students at our school who will tell you that what you did was wrong—don't listen to them. One day, they'll realize the value in what you did. It's impossible to know what you might have prevented. You might have saved lives. You might very well have saved our way of life. Who knows?"

Ms. Danvers attempted to justify Ryland's decision to report Peter to the authorities, knowing full well their close relationship. Ryland still wasn't convinced that he did the right thing. During the interchange with Peter and as he brought the guards back to his room to arrest him, he was certain of his decision. Now, just thirty minutes later, he began to doubt himself.

"But, Ms. Danvers. What will they do to him? Are they going to kill him?"

"Oh, I see what's happening to you, Ryland. You have remorse. Is that what your struggling with?" Ms. Danvers was eager to help Ryland get through his uneasiness about what had happened. As every Commonwealth educated was sworn to do, Ms. Danvers had to do her part to preserve the unyielding unanimity of thoughts and expressions of all her students.

"Yeah, that's part of it—" before Ryland could continue his sentence, Ms. Danvers proceeded to intervene.

"I knew it, Ryland. That's normal—completely normal. It's a normal thing to feel after the courageous deed that you did. It'll pass—I promise you it will. Over the years, I've had to do things that I knew were the right things to do, and then I second guessed myself afterward. Luckily, it's a temporary feeling because when I consider all the knowledge I've gained, especially Commonwealth doctrine and the Commonwealth curriculum that I teach my students, it always leads me to affirm my actions. I'm sure that if you look through some of the class material about perfidious and intolerant activities, you'll come to the conclusion that you were right and completely justified in turning your friend over. Like I said, Ryland, you have to remember that you probably prevented further damage to others in our class, possibly beyond that. It's almost impossible to overstate the extent of negativity that your friend's ideas could have created." Ms. Danvers knew her explanation would surely get through to the still young and impressionable student in her midst.

"I just don't know. I wish I could see it your way, I really do. I'm sorry to disappoint you, Ms. Danvers." Ryland felt bad about his continued uncertainty. He could tell she was trying really hard to make him feel better, but it had little impact.

"Oh, Ryland," Ms. Danvers maternally sounded as she went in to hug her student. She typically wouldn't show any sort of warmth to her students like that, but given the circumstances, she felt the need to allow for an exception.

"You just need some more time. I know it was the first time you've had to defend your values like that. It gets easier the more you have to do it, I promise you. Just remember, you ended something that has no place in our society." She let go of Ryland with the hope that she might have tipped the balance in favor of her persuasive comments. She eagerly waited to hear what she thought would be a remark of confirmation from Ryland about his change of heart.

"I don't think I've ended anything," Ryland replied as Ms. Danvers stood with a look of astonishment that she still hadn't influenced her young pupil. Ryland added a chilling thought before Ms. Danvers could respond, "I have a feeling that this is the beginning of something else."

Ms. Danvers just stared. She wasn't quite sure what to say next. Ryland had a level of certainty in his face that gave her a slight worry, but at the same time, she knew that a teenage boy couldn't have much influence. Could he?

Chapter 16

SHINAR

Trier, the capital of the United People's Commonwealth and center of the First Province, is nestled along the Moselle River in what used to be southwestern Germany. The rolling hills in the surrounding vicinity contain myriad groves of dense, mature trees and sprawling meadows. Despite the continuous expansion of communal housing and consequently, the destruction of the surrounding environment, the outer city limits teem with life. Deer, small mammals, birds, fish within the ponds and brooks, all manage to survive and thrive. Looking away from the city at the surrounding natural beauty, you can find complete peace and serenity; however, turn the other way and you'll find something else—an unnatural structure unlike anything in human history. Certainly, an anachronism, but updated with modern technologies and modern materials, Shinar Palace stands at the center of Trier and towers over all the surrounding government buildings. Its stepwise, structural pattern on each of its four sides are reminiscent of an ancient Mesopotamian ziggurat. The palace stands six thousand feet high, including its elevation of four hundred and sixty-three feet above sea level. This behemoth—the tallest structure on earth—is a fitting symbol of the premier's preeminence over the world, including the subordinate members of his high council.

The bureaucracies that run the world's affairs share dozens of smaller buildings in concentric rings around Shinar Palance. None are close to its equal in size or grandeur. Even if combined, the mass would still equal only a fraction of the building which houses the premier and his most loyal associates. The lower half of the palace is occupied during government working hours by administrative personnel and other anonymous officials.

Premier Kerioth and his high council were gathered and about to convene.

"Ladies and gentleman, I was just informed of an interesting occurrence that happened in the Eighteenth Province. It's the reason why I called this emergency meeting, at which I am pleased you all so urgently made sure to attend."

The seven council members, all sitting in their designated seats in the surveillance-proof conference room, looked at their leader with anxiety as to the reason for their presence. Several of them looked at each other, hoping that another purge would be avoided tonight. One late councilman met his end after a capricious change of heart by the premier several months ago. Ever since, the council has been much more nervous attending meetings, especially unscheduled ones.

"We have a new lead in General Marion's escape," Premier Dormin S. Kerioth irritatingly told his still worried council members as most of them avoided eye contact, and instead, looked over his spotless black suit.

"I am so glad to hear that, Premier. I know there has been much frustration over the lack of sufficient leads," Councilman Berough replied.

"Indeed, Councilman. I, too, am glad that we now know who, but I am not glad to finally know what we are dealing with. General Marion was allowed to escape by an orchestrated plan carried out by a number of suspects."

"How many suspects?" Councilwoman Rendal asked.

"At least ten, as of now. Some from a defense firm—Dynamo Robotics. Two from the detention center where General Marion was being held, and several from Central Stadium—where the general escaped."

"How are these suspects all linked?" Councilman Morris inquired with an eyebrow raised with a degree of suspicion.

"It seems that the FAF rebels are behind this."

"That sounds easy. How about we get rid of all the conspirators as soon we get every last bit of intelligence out of them?" Morris questioned.

"That sounds like a simple answer, Councilman Morris. The only problem is they are almost certainly not alone. We don't have confirmatory evidence of this yet, but we have some evidence of others helping FAF forces. These others are people from the future that have come to this time in order to restore their vision for humanity, or some nonsense like that. All we know is that their vision for humanity is completely opposed to our vision."

"They're from the future? How can that be?" Morris looked completely puzzled and a little distressed.

"We still don't know how they did it, but it seems that they were somehow able to manipulate the space-time continuum and come back to our time period. They are undoubtedly more advanced than us, which certainly leaves us at a tactical disadvantage. Despite being from the future, we don't know how far into the future they're from. We don't yet know their capabilities since we haven't seen their military equipment or systems platforms. My hope is that they aren't from too far ahead, and that some of our top secret systems can compete with whatever they have—we shall see. I hope that I am right for all our sakes."

"What kind of people are these individuals, Premier? I mean, what do they believe?" Councilwoman Gains asked with contempt for the notion.

"We are dealing with a group of people that look to God as the ultimate authority, so man is futile in establishing dominance as we have done. An enemy which does not view governmental authority as absolute is a very dangerous entity to us. No law that we create is valid unless it is confirmed by their God's laws. Even more dangerous is if these ideas spread around our planet once again. Without complete allegiance to the Commonwealth, our rule will be short lived. Do you think it is any coincidence that we abolished all religion on earth?"

"I see, Most High, Premier," Councilman Morris worriedly remarked.

"My greatest fear is that the military branch of these unknown people manages to coordinate and combine forces with our well-known FAF, Tricorn, idiots—I mean, zealots. Freudian slip. Ladies and gentlemen, we will be facing a global rebellion."

"This is very disturbing information. Should I have provincial affairs leadership notified to increase our efforts to weed out these separatists?" Councilwoman Gains added.

"No, this global effort being undertaken cannot be made public, not even to them. This has to remain completely compartmentalized. Military and intelligence command are the only ones that need to know right now. They will deal with these threats. They will report to me as they learn more, then I will report to you as necessary."

"Of course," several council members recited at the same time, reinforcing their predilection for sycophantic mannerisms.

"There is also one more anomaly with all this. The commanding officer of the Omega 21 Detention Center in Chicago informed me of a new offender in his custody. He's a fourteen-year-old boy named Peter Barclay. Apparently, Peter's roommate discovered an old American flag patch in Peter's suitcase, and I guess Peter rambled on about his defense of the old American way of life. From the officer's report, Peter sounded like the brightest boy he'd ever met."

"How fascinating," Councilwoman Gains remarked. "How did he know how to even muster a defense of America? I thought that content is explicitly forbidden in our schools."

"Exactly. I have no idea how he came across those ideas. It certainly wasn't something he learned in school, so it had to have been learned elsewhere. It's very concerning, nonetheless. The thought of finding one American flag in one of our Commonwealth-run schools is something that I will not tolerate. He must pay dearly for doing that. I personally believe he should be put to death for committing the offense. We cannot afford to have any students like Peter Barclay in our public institutions—just think of the influence a kid like this could have on other impressionable minds."

"I concur, Premier. Excellent points, indeed," Councilman Morris affirmed.

"That is why I told the commander of the detention center to process him as quickly as possible after harshly interrogating him." The premier chuckled and grinned. "I do find it intriguing that Peter Barclay was also the operator who was controlling the harvester with which General Marion flew out of Central Stadium. I wonder if he was involved or not? We shall see what the interrogators can get out of him and put him down, regardless." He put his hands together and looked out at his high council. "This meeting is concluded."

The premier exited the emergency council meeting conference room within the secretive depths of the enormous palace with a snarky smirk of satisfaction and vainglory in anticipation of Peter's hasty demise. As these meetings and others like them often transpired, the high council felt as low as many of the commoners of the Commonwealth empire. Despite their selection for various reasons to the council, their place was well known to be far beneath the throne of the premiership.

Walking back to his living quarters, which amounted to an amazing twenty floors of Shinar Palace and its two-hundred thousand square feet of living space, the premier turned his giddy stride into an angry stomp among a group of his heavily armed and highly trained Varangian Guard. The premier's rumination regarding the situation with Peter Barclay was wearing his patience down to its breaking point.

Carrying on through the passage of the reconstructed artifacts of the Processional Way and finally to the completed replica of the Ishtar Gate, the group continued. Adoring the pictorial menagerie illustrated in blue and gold along the resounding walls, the still angered Premier managed to gain some emotional distraction. The detailed imagery of the ancient lions, aurochs, and dragons reminded him of a time that he wished to bring back to the present day to a certain extent.

The acknowledgment of difficulties within his system of governance was the most intellectually distressing topic for him. The inner tug-of-war was the very sort of dispute that was worthy of his wife,

Mira—his most trusted advisor. She was Premier Kerioth's closest ally and confidant. Unlike the sycophantic tendencies of the council members that are employed in order to ensure their own survival, Mira held nothing back. She could speak freely. Her husband valued what she had to say.

"Mira!" the premier shouted as he entered his palatial suite through the sliding magnetic door. The door automatically closed and was then blocked by his personal guards, who were standing at attention.

"What is it, Dormin?" she answered while brushing her hair, standing in front of the master bathroom's full-length mirror, which was part of her evening routine. She had the distinct opportunity of addressing the premier by his first name—a privilege that was forbidden to anyone else.

"I have a problem that I'd like to run by you."

"What is it this time? It's not about General Marion, is it?"

"No, it's not about him this time. Although, it's very possible this is related to his escape," the premier said.

"Really? You mean collaborators?"

"It seems so, but one of the collaborators is a teenage boy."

"A boy, you say? How could one boy be bothering you so much, sweetheart?"

"He's not just any boy, Mira. Peter Barclay is a prodigious one. It seems that he has more wisdom than almost the entire population of the Eighteenth Province combined—he is not to be underestimated. Intelligence units seem to think he may have played a role in General Marion's escape. We know he operated the harvester which allowed for Marion's escape, but we don't know if he was complicit in the planning or execution of the plot or not."

"So, he's a genius who's somehow involved with the FAF—how does that change anything?"

"I'm not sure if he is or not. It would seem so since he was arrested for having an American flag in his possession, and trying to proselytize his roommate with American values."

"My, my. He is an interesting boy, isn't he?" Mira asked with a high level of incredulity.

"It sure seems that way. I just can't understand why he would do that and where he would learn those things."

The premier's presentiment wasn't that unusual. A man so powerful always feared losing his authority and control, especially in light of a new example that illustrated a breach in information control and dissemination.

"Well, it's not like he's a physical threat, right?" Mira inquired.

"What kind of threat would you assume a boy that can see angels and demons poses?"

"Excuse me?" she skeptically replied.

"You heard it. This boy can see and interact with spiritual beings. He told one of the guards when he was asked what he was looking at. Can you imagine the impact on minds if he was able to show others?"

"Oh, Dormin, you and I both know those are just fairy tales. How can that be?"

"My dear, these are things that we choose to ignore, but we cannot pretend like there is no possibility that they might actually exist. We're aware of the volumes of literature and accounts. Unlike the others obeying the laws on this planet, we know but do not believe. We don't let the commoners know, so they aren't able to believe."

"If he was somehow able to demonstrate these abilities to others, it would destroy any credibility we have. Everything we have been trying to do over these decades to degrade those beliefs would be completely reversed overnight."

"Exactly, my dear."

"You can't let that happen. He must lead you to others if there are any and then he must die."

"That's what I had in mind. I'm a lucky man to have you to lean on," the premier said as he walked over to Mira and held her from behind, then kissed her on the cheek.

She grabbed onto his forearms, turned her head, and looked into his eyes as they stared at each other in front of the mirror that extended from floor to ceiling, and wall to wall.

The premier conceded "I just hope we're not too late. After so many years of our ways finally coming together, it only takes one cataclysm to crumble its entire foundation. I fear this boy is a harbinger we have been hoping to avoid."

"Hope can only get us so far. We need to be fierce and merciless. Will they show us mercy? If they're anything like us, they most definitely will not."

"I hope they're like us. If they're like us, at least we'll know what motivates them. If they're different—now that is what scares me," Premier Kerioth said with a minor note of trepidation as he closed his eyes to seek the comfort of his wife's warmth.

The two walked hand in hand out to the grand staircase outside the master suite and gazed at the fully recreated and refurbished area below. There sat the Altar of Zeus, exactly as it was erected in Pergamum in ancient Asia Minor. It made its way from Berlin, piece by piece until its full completion several weeks ago. Dormin and Mira's new exhibit seemed to be a fitting attraction since it was also known as "Satan's Throne." The irony of its new location could not be overstated. The same location where Shinar Palance stood, began a philosophy in the nineteenth century that led to the deaths of many millions. Not just physical death, but also—spiritual death.

Chapter 17

THE LONG JOURNEY

"Is this Champion Backstrom?" an unfamiliar and faint voice called out.

"Yes, this is he. Who's speaking?" the champion said with a degree of uncertainty and his left eyebrow partially raised out of curiosity.

"I'm so sorry, Champion. There was no one else that I could contact. My husband, Jim, and I didn't know what else to do. This is Melissa—Melissa Wilby. Jim and I have been hosting Peter since he arrived in Chicago."

"Ah, now I see. To what do I owe this unexpected conversation, Mrs. Wilby?"

"Something's happened to Peter. I'm not sure what exactly, but we are being summoned to go to a detention center downtown for questioning. They told us that Peter is being held there. We're not sure what happened, but Peter told us to use the device that he left with us shortly after we first met. He directed us to notify you if something should happen to him. He gave us a very specific list of things that you should be made aware of."

"I'm glad you contacted me. I'll need some more information, including your list, so I can assess the situation."

"Of course, Champion. I'll do my best to help—anything to help Peter."

"Champion, this is Jim. I can certainly help out too. Melissa and I are both available to you. Whatever you need."

"Excellent, Mr. Wilby. Thanks. My team and I will be part of this conversation. Do you have some time and a safe place to speak?"

"Yeah, sure. We're here at home. We've got some time."

"Excellent. Mr. and Mrs. Wilby, we will do our very best to find Peter and bring him back. That is a priority now."

The conversation went on for nearly twenty-five minutes. Every possible detail about the location, the timeline, with whom the Wilbys spoke, as well as any other pertinent information was obtained by Champion Backstrom and other Accendia soldiers listening in on the interchange. Shortly thereafter, a solution was devised. Champion Backstrom called his recently emancipated friend to discuss the matter. He knew if there was one man he could trust to get Peter Barclay back, it would be General Nathaniel Marion.

"All right, folks, we have a new situation," General Marion said to a room full of dozens of high ranking FAF commanders from around the world, as well as a few commanders from the Accendia contingent. "Peter Barclay, one of our youngsters in Chicago, has been captured. His importance cannot be overstated. We all know who his parents are and what their roles are for the cause—we can't let them down. We also know that Chicago is one of the most important strategic locations for our upcoming assault, so our intelligence assets there are extensive."

The general pointed to a three-dimensional projection of the prison in its downtown Chicago location. Time elapsed intelligence also provided exterior patrols and defensive outposts. "He is most likely at this Omega 21 Detention Center, and undergoing barbaric torture as we speak. I can only imagine what they are doing to him to obtain the vital information that he has—poor kid," the general said with his volume trailing off and eyes looking down at the floor out of sadness. "Our intelligence specialists in the region suspect that his execution is imminent and probably scheduled to take place within the next couple days, depending on how long he can hold out. We need to act quickly in order to save him. I will personally lead a quick reaction force to rescue him. We all know I would not be standing here right now if it wasn't for him. I will not allow him to die at the hands of those monsters—the same monsters that did this to me while I was being held captive." General Marion pointed to a pale pink scar with jagged edges that ran from his left ear down nearly to his mouth, then tilted his head back to reveal the uppermost edges of a deep burn, still healing, along his neck underneath the jawline.

"I need two platoons of your best men for this mission. I already have assurances that Champion Backstrom will provide four of his FITs (Fast-attack Interdiction Teams). Colonel Maddox, you and your men have faced the most direct action to date, so I would like your remaining squad to go because of their experience. We'll need others to supplement your group, but I know the men you have can fight. I've read the reports."

"We'd be honored, General," Colonel Maddox responded.

"We leave for Chicago in ninety minutes. We'll be going with a squadron of Accendia ships. We will all ride in one of three Waxwing transport and close air support craft, and will be accompanied by eight Merlin fighter and attack craft, six Thrasher air defense and electronic warfare craft, and four Skylark psychological operations and ISR (intelligence, surveillance, and reconnaissance) craft. We'll move quickly to the target. We will strike surgically, get Peter, and leave. If he's already gone, it's just as vital to retrieve his body. Dead or alive, he comes back with us. After we've found him, we'll rendezvous at one of or both of these exfiltration locations. If other opportunities present themselves, we will act on them as appropriate. It all happens in under fifteen minutes. We do not want to get bogged down and end up fighting the entire city's defense force. Brief your men with these—study them well. We cannot afford mistakes. Dismissed." General Marion handed out handheld projector microchips which contained structural details of the detention center, as well as potential secondary and tertiary targets, street layouts, and exfiltration spots.

FAF leaders have been carefully preparing for the invasion of North America, specifically its heart. With the assistance of the Accendia, FAF fighters, as well as the indigenous resistance, the nation that once declared its independence in the year 1776 will re-emerge as a bastion of liberty from which the world's oppressive government will meet its end. The operation will begin after Peter's rescue mission.

"James, you sure you're ready for this one?" Captain Tannis asked Lieutenant Hoover with a gentle hand on his shoulder to see if he was emotionally capable of going on the new mission. Hoover brought his own calloused hand to his cheek, rested his head on his fist, and contemplated the decision. His eyes began to well with tears as he thought about his family members who were murdered a couple of days ago. The thoughts were crippling at times and still gave him stabbing bouts of despair.

"I have to do this, Kieren. I just have to. I need something to lift me up. I know that sitting around here thinking about my wife and little girl will drive me down more and more. I need to do some good. If we can save this kid, it might make me feel a little better. It might help take away some of the guilt I have—the guilt that has messed with my sleep and left me crying in the middle of the night. The same guilt that weighs me down, and blames me for letting my family get killed by those savages and their murderous machines."

"Aw, brother, it wasn't your fault. You gotta know that. The colonel felt the same way you do after his family, well—you know. I just wanted to see what your thoughts were. Either way's fine by me."

"I'm ready, Captain. I'm coming. Let's go get 'em."

"You got it, LT."

They shook hands and briefly hugged one another.

"Sarge, what do you think about all this?" Private Bex asked Sergeant Deems.

"'Bout what? Oh, you mean the spaceship that we're on. Or did you mean our Supreme FAF Commander coming back from the dead to lead us? Or perhaps, that we'll be fighting side by side with men and women from some time warp?"

"Smart ass. You know what I mean, 'bout this mission?"

"It sounds pretty dangerous since we'll be part of a small team of fighters going into the heart of devilry and death. Chicago is the quintessential representation of the Commonwealth and all its injustices. We're going along for a joyride downtown to rescue some kid that we never met, for some reason that we don't know. Not sure how many troops and security guards this prison has. It could get pretty ugly, if ya ask me."

"Fair enough. That's what I thought. See Yalu, I knew that Sarge'd tell us what his thoughts were after his reflexive crap spewing."

"Yep, you called it, Deems," Private Yalu said as he was partially laughing.

"Come on you idiots, get your heads in it. This is serious stuff. You wanna make it back?" Deems chided his two pals.

Deputy Champion Mullen gathered with his subordinates, including Deputy Lumis. The five of them are the officers that will command the FITs deploying with FAF forces to rescue Peter.

"We will not deploy from our Tanagers like we typically do. We will disembark from the Waxwing craft together with our accompanying FAF forces. We need to look after them. Commonwealth forces are able to disrupt most of their armor with a direct hit from their weapons," Mullen explained to the other officers.

"I've seen how Colonel Maddox and his men fought a couple days ago, they're fierce. I think they could be some help to us in the field," Lumis defended his new friends.

"Very well then. Just keep your teams on edge—we can't afford any hiccups. It's obvious we don't have very many troops to spare, so take caution into consideration here. Deputy Lumis, your FIT will take your own Waxwing to extricate another target. Review your mission specifics while onboard and make sure you know every detail since there will be numerous civilians present. You three and myself are on the other Waxwings. Dismissed."

The FITs and FAF forces were anxiously waiting aboard the three Waxwing aircraft. The pilots and co-pilots were conducting their last systems check before liftoff. Tensions mounted as they knew they were going into a heavily populated and hostile city.

Deems looked out the window next to him and saw the other accompanying aircraft lifting off within the holding bay in the belly of the massive Condor-class ship. The Merlins, Thrashers, and Skylarks, all smaller than the medium sized transport Waxwing ship, had different shapes and different weapons configurations. Each had its own purpose, but were designed to achieve the same objective—to win.

General Marion's flagship, the *Lexington*, was safely located behind the far side of the Moon to conceal its position from Commonwealth forces. The massive armored door to holding bay number five opened to allow the squadron to exit its host ship and head toward earth. As the flying formation of ships continued to accelerate to within a few thousand miles of the moon, a huge blast of energy came shooting overhead.

"Wooh!" Captain Tannis shouted as the blue light emanating from the blast bounced off the whites of his eyes. As his eyes tracked the lopsided beam of blue light, they quickly backtracked to follow another blast after the first one.

The two giant blue fireballs hit a Commonwealth communications and surveillance outpost. The base, as well as its high tech equipment and the power supply plant nearby were completely destroyed the moment the blue bombarding beams hit. The blasts left two large explosions and several smaller, secondary explosions from munitions and power cells igniting.

"Would ya look at that, Colonel?" Lieutenant Hoover was enamored by the mystifying blue flames and technicolored explosions as he looked out the nearest window to his flight chair within the fast-moving Waxwing aircraft.

"Quite a sight, isn't it, son?" the equally mesmerized officer replied.

General Marion, sitting next to Colonel Maddox, added to the commentary, "You haven't seen anything yet—just wait."

The squadron of aircraft continued their journey toward earth, increasing their velocity by the second, it seemed. The Thrashers and Skylarks disabled Commonwealth satellite feeds and on-board weapons systems in the vicinity, leaving the fast approaching flock invisible as they encroached well within Commonwealth territory. Once the speeding squadron screamed through the stratosphere and into the Windy City's airspace, the rescue mission truly began.

* * *

Ms. Danvers and her students sat in their tenth floor classroom silently anticipating a special event that they were instructed to watch. Apparently, all students within two time zones in either direction from Chicago were ordered to watch it. Only the most senior administrators knew who ordered the viewing. The educators knew what was to come, but the students didn't—at least all but one student didn't know.

The visual monitor came to life, front and center in the barren, top floor classroom.

"Today is a special day for the Commonwealth. Now that all of you are watching, I'd like to extend a big thank you to the brave student whose actions managed to avert a threat to our national security. Without your quick thinking and prompt action, it's unclear how much damage might have come to our society. I am pleased to announce that shortly, we will be showing the execution of a criminal who is likely part of a larger criminal ring that is trying to destabilize our way of life. To those who have successfully declared their allegiance to the Commonwealth, this will be a treat. To those who are against our way of life, implicitly or explicitly, may this serve as a warning." The stern and threatening voice trailed off as the picture switched to Peter being strapped to the titanium execution table.

Londyn, with a look of complete horror on her smooth and unblemished face, whispered to Zameera, "Oh my gosh, it's Peter."

Zameera didn't know what else to say. She was equally shocked that they were going to watch their own classmate be put to death, especially Peter. He was the nicest kid you could possibly meet. Charming, always courteous, and always kind. He never spoke ill of anyone. He never did anything to hurt anyone.

"Ryland sold him out and now he'll be murdered in front of all of us," Zameera quietly replied.

"What do we do, Zameera?" Londyn eagerly sought her advice.

"There's nothing we can do right now. We have to sit tight. Peter knew this might happen."

"How can that be?"

"There's more going on than meets the eye, Londyn. You just have to trust me. We both have to suffer here while we watch our friend die for his beliefs. We can use the pain from his sacrifice to fuel our drive for action. Believe me, Londyn, this is something worth fighting for."

Londyn pondered the immensity of that thought and turned back to the visual monitor to lay witness to the unconscionable act of cruelty about to commence. Overwhelmed with compassion for Peter, Zameera began to cry. Ms. Danvers, Slade and his toadies, even Ryland seemed satisfied by the events transpiring before their eyes. To them, and to others easily ingesting the values of the carefully constructed system, it was normal and a necessary action meant to help guarantee the continuity of the global system of totalitarian governance.

Ms. Danvers's class, other classes in the school, as well as additional schools across North America, continued to watch the preparation of the execution of one of their own. The procedures commenced as a warning to all Commonwealth students watching.

Peter's aunt and uncle said their final remarks, enveloped in sorrow and anguish. Their son, Jayk, to their knowledge, had been trained to kill people like Peter, so in a remote way, they felt responsible for Peter's murder. The executioner, also known by the poisonous name and distinct title, Venenum, had another set of emotions. He expressed joy and a sense of accomplishment, a fulfillment of duty—not the normal human experience when one is about to put a child to death. This can only be the sentiment of a truly warped and wicked individual. His feelings were encouraged and nurtured by the partial and unjust way of jurisprudence in the Commonwealth. Unfortunately, he is one of hundreds of millions that felt the same way. That is how the Commonwealth managed to maintain its power—by turning person against person, belief against belief, community against community. Of course, the authorities take one side and thus, the other side inevitably loses. How could an individual or a group of people possibly overcome such insurmountable structural bias and inculcated opposition to liberty? A worthy answer could be found in the depths of history in order to see a possible glimpse of what the future might entail.

As the theft of Peter's innocent life was fully complete, Londyn noticed something strange—something she hadn't noticed in several days. Her face quickly turned from a quivering frown to a composed and ebullient smile. The tears continued, but for a different reason.

She thought to herself at a deep and profound level of introspection, "There you go Peter. Thank you. Thank you from the bottom of my heart. You were the one who made me realize that I still had a heart. You helped me remember that I should still have hope. Thank you."

Her tears didn't let up. In fact, they intensified as she watched Peter's soul being led by his guardian angel, Adrio, and Michael the Archangel. There was an unexpected serenade following. Walking two by two until lifting off toward their heavenly destination, were representatives from all nine choirs of angels. There were twelve from each choir present to escort the persecuted boy's soul to heaven's gate. The brilliance of light brought an indescribable sense of peace to Londyn. She could only gaze in complete awe. Wait, she had to let her friend know. She could trust Zameera, right? Londyn knew that Peter told her not to tell anyone else, but she had a feeling that this was the right decision. She turned and whispered, "Zameera, Zameera. You'll never guess what I just saw?"

"What do you mean?" she asked.

"You'll never believe it, but I saw Peter's soul and a bunch of angels with him."

"I was hoping you would. Isn't it miraculous?"

"Wait, what? How do you know?"

"Peter and I have the same gift. He wanted me to guide you if something was to happen to him."

Londyn nearly shouted in excitement, but had to refrain since she could end with the same fate as Peter. She had to hold back.

"This is so crazy," she vehemently whispered.

"You don't know half of it. Just wait," Zameera carefully answered.

Ms. Danvers stood up from her desk to make an announcement. She walked over to the center and asked, "Well, class, what did we all learn today?"

Maksim was quick to respond. "We all need to think the same way. Otherwise, we'll end up the same way Peter did."

"Very good. Yes, we all need to be inclusive." She smiled with delight while holding the class hedgehog, Reno.

"Who else wants to express a lesson learned from the special event that we just had the privilege of viewing?"

The class fell silent. The students were waiting for somebody else to raise their hand and continue the morbid discussion, which seemed to lack the level of sympathy that would typically be warranted. No one seemed to want to speak. Some were still crying inconspicuously. The silence grew greater as time elapsed.

Malaya slowly raised her hand as others sitting behind her noticed. They were impressed by her courage.

"Ms. Danvers, why did Peter start bleeding after he died?"

Ms. Danvers was hoping she wouldn't have to explain the answer to that question. She gathered her thoughts with the hope of finding the perfect answer, but it never came.

"Can you be a little more specific, Malaya? Sometimes at the moment of death, the body can do some strange things—things that don't make sense to us because we're alive, but seem perfectly ordinary at the time of death."

"Of course I can be more specific, Ms. Danvers. I want to know why Peter started bleeding from his wrists, his feet, and his right side. It looked like he had circular wounds on his wrists and feet, and a gash on his side, all which appeared and started to bleed after he died."

Ms. Danvers began to get a little warm and uncomfortable. She couldn't say what her real thoughts were, not about such a sensitive topic. She thought her best chance to avoid answering would be to discredit Malaya.

"Who else saw what Malaya just described? Raise your hands if you did."

At first, nobody had the courage to admit to seeing the impossible. Ms. Danvers was glad her plan to isolate Malaya may actually be working. Then she noticed movement. Zameera began to raise her hand. Then Londyn. Then Briley. Then Slade. Then Maksim.

Then Kamren. Every single student raised his and her right hand to acknowledge what they had seen.

Malaya looked around and noticed that all her classmates seemed to corroborate what she saw. She was overcome by an immense feeling of relief to know that she wasn't alone.

"Ms. Danvers, it seems that we all saw the same thing. Didn't you see it?"

The cornered teacher didn't know what else to make of the situation. She lowered herself down against the teaching board and sat on the floor.

"Yes, Malaya, I saw it too. This sort of thing is incredibly rare. I cannot tell you what it is."

"What do you mean you can't tell us?"

"It is illegal for me to mention what I think it is, so I will not. I am an educator. I educate you all based on what we are supposed to teach. There is no room for anything else."

Zameera couldn't take it any longer. "Fine. If Ms. Danvers won't tell the class, then I will. It's called stigmata."

"What are you talking about, Zameera?" Ms. Danvers scolded.

Londyn decided to speak her mind, "Ms. Danvers, what we just saw was a miracle, and the most you can do is say that we can't talk about it?"

"Londyn Farrows. What did you say? Who told you what a miracle was?"

The palpable tension rose. Ms. Danvers stood up, put Reno back in his cage, and took an authoritative stance as she prepared to discipline Londyn for raising the question. Not a single sound could be heard, just the heartbeats of the terrified students not knowing what was going to happen to Londyn or Zameera. Could they be next?

Without warning, a part of the ceiling blew off the classroom in a loud, forceful blast. All the students in the classroom buried themselves under their desks and chairs the best they could while a cloud of dust rained down on them. Ryland managed to crawl over to Reno's cage and retrieve him, thus ensuring the safety of the beloved class pet. Ms. Danvers crumbled back down to the floor in shock.

Six FIT soldiers rapidly descended into the classroom on a fibroin-derived cable apparatus. The Waxwing above anchored the cables for their infiltration and extraction, and stowed reinforcements if needed. Several Thrashers, Merlins, and Skylarks patrolled the surrounding airspace to neutralize threats and prepare an evacuation route.

"Nobody move!" Deputy Lumis yelled as the other Accendia soldiers cleared the room for hostiles.

Ms. Danvers slowly raised her head to comprehend what was happening. She discreetly moved to avoid any attention.

"I'm glad to see that you're okay, Zameera. We weren't sure if they'd come to take you away, so we thought this was our best time to get you while on mission to get Peter as well," Lumis remarked.

"Thanks, Deputy. I'm glad you dropped in. You haven't heard?"

"About what?"

"It's Peter. They just broadcast his execution on live stream about ten minutes ago."

"What? The other teams are making their way inside the detention center as we speak."

"I'm sorry. You were just a little too late." Her eyes began to well up again after mentioning the horror she had just witnessed.

Deputy Lumis didn't know what else to say. His mission was to ensure Zameera's safe return, but he couldn't help but think about Peter and his family. He went down on one knee and put a hand on Zameera's shoulder.

"I'm sorry, Zameera, but we need to go. It's not safe here."

"I have to bring someone with me. She has the gift, but just needs more training. Peter started it. He would have wanted it this way. I know she'll be helpful to us," Zameera pleaded.

"Okay, fine."

"Londyn, you heard the man. Let's get out of here."

Londyn couldn't believe what was happening to her. She gave Zameera a big smile and began to hurry over to her, but she stopped mid-step. She forgot one important thing.

"Give him to me. I always wanted him and here's my chance," Londyn demanded of Ryland as she pried Reno out of his fear-struck, limp hands. Ryland was so terrified of the entire ordeal that he had no choice but to acquiesce. After all, he played a part in Peter's death since he was the one who turned him over to the authorities. Deep down, he wasn't sure if these mysterious super soldiers came looking for him to avenge Peter's death. He just stayed down and kept quiet.

Zameera put a hand on Londyn's back, guiding her toward Deputy Lumis's squad so they could evacuate. Malaya shouted out, "Zameera, what about me?"

She had another decision to make. Londyn, yes, but what about another? Malaya has potential, especially after the way she stood up to Ms. Danvers and demanded the truth. That took courage, especially in an age of institutionalized deception.

"All right, Malaya, come on," Zameera said as she turned to look for Lumis's approval.

"She comes too," Lumis acknowledged.

After quickly harnessing in, the girls lifted up with the soldiers back to the Waxwing transport aircraft. Londyn, clutching the hedgehog with all her might, looked down into her classroom. All the remaining students, still hiding under their desks and chairs, stared up in absolute wonder. Ms. Danvers looked up with astonishment. She had finally lost control of the situation. It certainly was not something she had been well accustomed to. Malaya saw that look on Ms. Danvers's face and could only smile—the whole scenario had worked out just right.

Deputy Lumis's group of men and their escort aircraft made their way back to the Condor as they rapidly accelerated back out of the atmosphere, leaving a large sonic boom and glowing white streaks in the bold blue sky.

"Objective completed, Deputy Champion Mullen. Zameera has been extracted along with two of her classmates."

"Very good, Lumis. We're descending to the designated floor as we speak. We've met some resistance, but they were dealt with. Luckily, we've had some help from the inside, so it seems. It appears that some of these security doors were intentionally left wide open for us."

"Sounds like a trap, sir."

"Could be. Hopefully not. We can hope it's just a kind gesture. Not to say that we won't be ready for a fight."

Deputy Lumis continued listening, all the meanwhile knowing that Peter was dead. It was a difficult call to make. He wasn't sure if he should let Mullen know or not, especially since the group was already so close to finding out for themselves.

"Sir, I received news that Peter has already been executed. Zameera said she watched it live in her class."

"I sure hope that isn't the case. It's so hard to tell what's propaganda and what's real with these Commonwealth streaming networks. We'll verify. Thanks though, Lumis. When you get back to the *Lexington*, please debrief your men and find suitable quarters for the girls."

"Yes, sir. Will do. Are you sure you won't be needing my squad?"

"I think we've got plenty of men. Our Skylarks are barely picking up much of a response being mobilized at this point, so we should be long gone by the time ground forces or additional security forces arrive. Any air forces will be dealt with by our squadron waiting for them." Deputy Champion Mullen continued. "Keep up the good work, Deputy. Over and out."

Chapter 18

THE RECOVERY MISSION

The three joint squads of FAF and Accendia forces made their way down two different utility shafts. The larger force, including General Marion and Deputy Champion Mullen, went down one shaft, and the smaller group went in the other shaft. Their advanced equipment allowed them to repel floor after floor within the relatively small passages of the fifteen-story prison in a short amount of time. Timing was an absolutely critical aspect of the operation, so speed was paramount. Without a quick entry and exit, the forty or so men risked fighting several thousand troops that could be mobilized and sent to quell the incursion within about twenty to thirty minutes. Realistically, Commonwealth security forces could mobilize and respond to meet the threat within ten to fifteen minutes. Despite being a paramilitary organization, the security forces still conducted themselves fairly well in combat scenarios.

"General, we're approaching the fifth subfloor," an Accendia soldier reported as they continued their belay below the fourth subfloor.

"Let's get off here on the fifth sublevel and come down to the sixth sublevel from above. I don't want to be too predictable. The longer we're in here, the more likely they'll know which way we're coming," the general ordered.

"Very well, General," Colonel Maddox replied.

Deputy Champion Mullen didn't have any reason to disagree with the general. It was still a work in progress to decide the chain of command between the FAF and Accendia. For Mullen, this instance was no different than many other situations in which he and other mid-ranking Accendia officers have unquestionably followed the general's command. General Marion has a real way about him. Aside from his exemplary military schooling, he has a way of knowing an enemy and knowing his own forces—an impalpable way of playing out mental war games, if you will. During the Fifth World War, his division knew him as General Savo. Savo, short for savoir-faire, which is what the French Legionnaires embedded within his unit called him. The man that knew what to do in any situation, even situations that training couldn't possibly prepare one for. His experience, unparalleled knowledge of military history and strategy, and ingenuity made him a commander like no other. The FAF knew almost immediately after the rise of the Commonwealth that General Marion was exactly the man needed to lead the world back to liberty. The Commonwealth knew this, too, and began their witch hunt early on in order to eliminate him.

Captain Tannis and Sergeant Deems slowly entered as the door to the sixth subfloor corridor opened. Private Yalu followed, then Private Bex. Lieutenant Hoover and Colonel Maddox closely came next. Each pair of men tactically trailed the pair in front of them, never knowing if they may soon be looking down the barrel of an armed guard's rifle, or find Peter alive and eager to leave with them to safety.

Continuing their tortuous journey along the serpentine hallway, Captain Tannis raised his right hand, telling his squad of New Zealand–based men, General Marion, and the two FIT units led by Deputy Champion Mullen and Deputy Greyson, to stop. All stopped immediately, disobeying any obligatory inertia. Tannis signaled again using only his right hand, indicating that two targets were down and there is an unknown left corner ahead.

Tannis, Hoover, Deems, Yalu, and Bex stood in a staircase formation to clear the corner with the man to the left being one step ahead of the next. Tannis signaled, one, two, three. The formation crept around the corner, rifles pointing downrange for target acquisition.

"Down on the ground! Down on the ground! Hands up! Hands up!" Captain Tannis yelled at the lone guard in his gray combat uniform sitting behind a large metal desk that had a trail of deep gouges in the stone floor's surface in front of it. The guard, without hesitation, dropped his weapon and knelt to the ground as commanded. His helmet was already removed, so the rescue group could see the face of the enemy instead of an empty, expressionless mask.

The mentally broken guard, with his hands behind his head, spoke.

"I did it. I did it."

"Did what, guard?" Colonel Maddox asked while standing behind Captain Tannis with his rifle pointing at the eerily hysterical guard.

"You killed these men?" Maddox followed up in quick succession.

"Yes, I killed them."

"Why?" Maddox asked with a high level of incredulity.

"We set up this spot to ambush the first group of enemies that came by. It looks like it would have been your group. Just looking at your force strength, we might have been able to get a few of you guys before being cut down. I didn't want to see any of your men get hurt."

After being searched for other weapons, intelligence, and communications equipment, the traitorous guard continued talking to Colonel Maddox, until General Marion stepped forward.

"Colonel, I'll take it from here."

"Of course, General."

Maddox stepped aside as General Marion walked up to the guard and took a knee.

"Why'd you kill your two buddies?"

"I didn't want your men to get hurt."

"I heard you say that before. You know, I just don't buy it. I think that maybe you decided that you didn't want to die, so you'd rather kill your unsuspecting friends and surrender to the presumed enemy that would have most certainly taken you down."

The guard looked frustrated that his message was not being received the way that he hoped.

"Why did you really kill your own men?" General Marion asked with much more persistence.

"I wanted to make sure you found the one whom you came for."

"What's that supposed to mean?"

"I know you're here for Peter—that's no secret. I can show you where to find his body."

The general looked a bit puzzled. He was having a difficult time ascertaining how this guard could possibly know they were there for Peter.

"You said his body?" Marion replied with a surprised tone. He couldn't believe what he had just heard.

"Yes, his body. I'm sorry to tell you, but Peter is dead. Sir, I'm Officer Tanner Farrows. I'm assigned to the juvenile dispatching block at this facility. I was one of the men charged with escorting Peter to his execution. I also helped strap him down just before he was killed." The subject was too much for him to handle again. He began to cry as he thought about the last words that Peter said to him.

General Marion grabbed Officer Farrows by the bottom of his chest plate, lifting him up off the ground as he yelled, "Do you have any idea what kind of a kid you just killed? Do you? Answer me you sick son of a bitch!" The general threw Tanner down to the floor and his crying became more inconsolable. After twenty seconds or so, Tanner was able to gather himself enough to speak again.

"I remembered him from last week. I met him while picking up my daughter from school for visitation. She and Peter were classmates. She said he was great, but I figured that if he ended up here he had to have done something terrible."

"You have absolutely no clue what he did to end up here. He was one of the brightest and most gifted human beings I have ever met. He made everyone around him better. Don't you dare think for one second that he deserved to die."

"I realized how special he was when I was strapping him down on the table before his execution and he didn't seem concerned about himself. He seemed concerned about me. He looked at me in a way that felt like he was looking right through me. It seemed like he knew my past. Like he, like he knew how lifeless and cold I'd become after leading kid after kid to their death."

"He had a profound affect while interacting with most people he met," General Marion added.

"After he told me he knew I'd do great things in the future, I knew I had to change. I knew I couldn't go on like the way I had been. Whether he knew it or not, he was the one who made me realize what a monster I've become."

"Oh, I think he knew. He knew lots of things that you wouldn't suspect."

Officer Farrows couldn't get Peter's face out of his mind. The discussion brought him back to the moment before Peter's end. How could he forgive himself?

"All right, Tanner. Bring us to him. We're running out of time."

"Of course, General," Tanner said while looking at General Marion for any sign of mercy toward him.

"Very good. Let's go."

General Marion stood up to address the cadre of men, who had been eagerly awaiting orders. If they didn't get Peter and find an egress route, exfiltration would be almost impossible. The three FIT squads and their accompanying FAF forces could ill afford to get bogged down in a battle with hundreds, if not thousands of mobilizing Commonwealth units converging on their location at this very moment.

"Men, this is now a recovery mission. Unfortunately, we didn't make it in time. This man knows where Peter's body is, so we'll follow him. Let's keep it tight people. We'll get through this if we stick together."

Despite the already determined and professional demeanor of the men, they still managed to become more sullen after hearing the unfortunate news that Peter was dead. They carried on with their mission, following the apparently duplicitous guard, who had found a new way of walking through his life. With each step came one more uncertainty. Could they really trust a guard who made a living off of keeping children imprisoned, and then leading them to their deaths? If Peter was executed there, then what did the others do to deserve the same fate? More unimaginable to consider was what kind of person could supervise and partake in that kind of barbarity, and look his own child in the eyes when allowed the opportunity?

"It's just beyond that door." Officer Farrows pointed ahead as the group kept moving toward the execution chamber.

"Bandore Team, follow my signal. We need to converge on the execution chamber. Accloy Team will be arriving in thirty seconds," Deputy Champion Mullen ordered as the time of reckoning drew near.

"I sure hope this is it, Colonel. With Hoover and Bex wounded, I'm not sure how many more hits we can take and make it out alive," Captain Tannis uttered while on the move.

"Don't worry, Tannis. This should be it. We don't have any reason to doubt this guard."

The group breached the door with explosives, and met no resistance. Half went to the right, and the other half went to the left. The Commonwealth flag hung in the background, and served as a reminder of what the fight was about to each of the men. The anti-liberty, anti-humanity, and anti-life triumvirate represented the quintessence of why the flag must fall.

"There he is!" a FIT soldier cried out as the rest of his squad cleared the execution chamber and the postmortem examination room. "There are a lot of guards on the ground in here! Oh, man!"

Then there was a brief moment of silence. Deputy Champion Mullen urgently demanded a response.

"Sergeant Brees, what's happening in there? Answer me!"

"Sorry, Deputy Champion, we've got two civilians in here. They were apparently guarding Peter's body, and waiting for us. They took out a bunch of guards in here. I'll bet the guards were sent to get rid of Peter's body before we could find him. Too bad for them they didn't anticipate being sedated with these micro darts that the civis must have used."

"Good to hear. Prep Peter's body for transport. Bring the civilians with too."

"Yes, sir."

Brees's group of six FIT soldiers came out with Peter's body on an automated lift stretcher that followed the command of the soldier in charge of its operation. This improvement in technology allowed for transport on a stretcher without having to occupy the two soldiers that would typically need to carry it.

Jim and Melissa Wilby stayed between two of the soldiers for protection, keeping their heads down and bodies crouched the best they could.

"General Marion!" Melissa broke her previously tacit and cautious behavior. She ran over to the general with Jim trailing behind to catch up.

"Mr. and Mrs. Wilby, it's great to see you. I'm so sorry about all that's happened to Peter. I'll never forgive myself, and will be always indebted to him for saving me. I only wished I could have returned the favor."

"General, with all due respect, Peter knew this could have been the end for him. He dedicated his heart, his soul, and his short life to changing others for the better. I'm sure we will all see some good come out of this." Melissa hoped to provide some comfort to the lamentable circumstance.

"I'm sure you're right, of course. You knew him pretty well before he went off to school. And, Mr. Wilby, you too. I know Peter respected the two of you very much. You were the best people to look after him that he could have hoped to have. I'm sure his parents will be completely devastated because of what's happened. It's going to be really tough."

"Yeah, I'm sure it will be," Jim Wilby responded.

"Well, folks, since you helped our cause, you know you can't go back home. You can come with us. You should know that we have your son, Jayk. He's opted to fight on our side. I must say, he will probably be a tremendous asset to us."

"You have Jayk? I'm glad you were able to turn him. How'd you manage to do that?" Melissa Wilby questioned.

"Peter came to do that job. It worked just like we had hoped."

"Sounds good. We're ready to help too," Jim Wilby replied.

"Let's go. We've got to get to the Waxwings. We only have two minutes to get to the rooftop. Officer Farrows, get us up to the roof. Accloy and Bandore Teams, let's move."

The general's transmission made it to Accendia and FAF command, as well as the squadron designated to provide air support and transport.

"General, this is Captain Hopswerk, Commander of the Waxwing craft in Indigo Group. Merlins, Thrashers, and Skylarks are lighting it up out here. There are heavy reinforcements arriving from the west, including five companies of Robotics Corps MCVs. We've taken some hits, but are still operational. What's your egress time?"

"We'll be right on time—twelve twenty-five. We'll be up top in two minutes. Thank you for the update, Captain."

"Hang tight, General. We'll start making our extract approach now. I'll let Jasper Group know the plan."

"Very good. Over and out."

The three teams, now with eight injured, including six FIT soldiers, were barely keeping up the pace necessary to egress as planned. They didn't anticipate a prison to be so heavily fortified with defensive weaponry and gunports. Luckily, no KIAs, but two of the wounded were in serious condition, according to the FIT medics.

"Keep it up, men. Hoover, Deems, hang in there." Colonel Maddox offered his support to his squad of men as they escorted two wounded FAF soldiers on their levitating, autonomous gurneys.

"Captain, I think I liked fighting in rural Auckland better—none of this urban crap," Private Yalu complained.

"Yeah, Captain. At least we had a chance out there," Private Bex naturally chimed in as well.

"Well boo-hoo, babies. Do you remember that all of us nearly got wasted by those hunks of junk and their human leashes if it wasn't for the Accendia guys dropping in?" Captain Tannis reminded them all.

"I guess I was so scared shitless that I didn't know what to think. We usually fared way better than we did that day," Yalu acknowledged.

"Well, that's 'cause we usually fought regular land forces in platoons at most—not Robo Corps companies like the one that whacked us there." Captain Tannis was trying to maintain his composure as they were quickly running through escape routes straight up to the top of the fifteen-story building.

"We're almost there! Keep it up guys!" Deputy Champion Mullen exclaimed.

"Accloy and Bandore Teams breaching roof now," Deputy Greyson informed the aircraft groups.

"Roger that. Stay clear of the center. We're coming down now," a pilot responded.

All the people made it up to the top either on their own two legs or on a stretcher, including Melissa and Jim Wilby, and Officer Farrows. The FIT units provided peripheral security on the rooftop as the Waxwings landed.

"Would ya look at that," Jim said to Melissa as they stood behind General Marion waiting for the transport ships to land. Jim had his head pointing almost straight up as he watched a fierce aerial dogfight. The nearly twenty small and medium-sized attack craft were performing acrobatic chaos with the ill-equipped Commonwealth aircraft. On occasion, Jim saw the Thrashers leave the cloud of swarming aircraft to destroy targets presumably on ground level as a loud boom would immediately be heard after deploying their high powered laser cannons.

"Wow." Melissa couldn't describe what she was seeing in any other way. Or perhaps, she was so distracted by the show that she couldn't think to find more descriptive words.

"Come on, let's go!" a loadmaster ordered as he ran down one of the two deployed ramps from a Waxwing transport craft.

"You heard 'em—move!" General Marion shouted.

Everybody retreated to either of the two Waxwing aircraft. Last were Deputy Greyson and a few of the men in his squad since they were actively fighting a group of land forces that made it to the rooftop. They were tactically shooting and moving toward the ships, when Deputy Greyson was hit with a projectile that pierced his back and burst through his chest. He fell instantly and lay motionless.

"Sniper! Sniper!" one of the FIT soldiers called out as he dove next to an industrial air conditioner unit near Deputy Greyson's body.

"Any aircraft available for close air support? We're pinned down!" a FIT corporal cried out as he hit the deck beside Deputy Greyson's body and checked for signs of life.

"I'm in the area. Confirm target location," a Thrasher pilot responded as he patrolled the evacuation route.

"Do you see my targeter?"

"Roger that, soldier. I've got a visual. I'm out of air-to-ground missiles. Strafe run in T-minus five seconds."

"Okay, thank you!" the relieved soldier replied as he saw the streaking Thrasher attack craft flash down toward the sniper's location.

"Engaging talon," the pilot informed.

The top of an adjacent building, which was several stories higher than the Omega 21 Detention Center, burst into flames after two high speed projectiles were fired toward the sniper's position, and exploded with menacing effectiveness.

"Talon eliminated. Ascending for additional support."

"Thanks, man. You saved us down here."

"My pleasure, gentlemen. Call if you need me again."

"Copy."

The men didn't have time to get their automated stretcher out, so they carried Deputy Greyson's body up a Waxwing ramp. The medics on board went to work, but they knew the moment they saw the deputy that there was no way of bringing him back. He had lost far too much blood from the large exit wound in his chest. He was gone.

The Waxwings began their ascent out of the Chicago area's airspace with their accompanying aircraft. All the military craft made it out except for one Merlin that was lost while providing close air support against armored units of the Commonwealth Land Forces.

Deputy Champion Mullen reported back to his superior officer, Champion Backstrom, while they continued out of the atmosphere. "Champion, this is Deputy Champion Mullen. We are in route to the *Lexington*. We have Peter's body. He didn't make it—we were too late."

"I'm sorry to hear that, Ed. I know his parents had hoped he would have been safe in Chicago. It's a tough one to bear. Did we lose any of our own?"

"Yes, sir. We lost three. One KIA with eight more wounded on the ground, plus the pilot and co-pilot of a Merlin that crashed during the operation were KIA as well. Deputy Greyson was killed just before we took off as we were egressing from the rooftop of the prison."

"Deputy Greyson was KIA?"

"Yes, sir. He was."

"Man. We had such high hopes for him. He was an outstanding leader and an outstanding man. May God grant rest to the souls of the departed today. I'll see you at the *Lexington*, Ed. Nice job today. I know it wasn't an easy mission, especially one with such complexity that was put together on such short notice. We'll have to get the pilot's bodies on another mission."

"It was my duty, sir. I was honored to go. Thank you for the opportunity."

"We'll report this to Chief Champion Barclay and Representative Barclay when you arrive. I know they'll be devastated with the news of their son. We couldn't let them know until we were one hundred percent sure. They'll want to know what happened and determine if it will affect the Operation Cloudburst timeline. Thank you, Deputy Champion. I'll see you soon."

"Very well, sir."

"Over and out."

Chapter 19

On a Razor's Edge

"Are you aware of what just occurred in Chicago? I would advise you to afford me the knowhow that you assured me of having before you were promoted to your current position."

"Yes, Premier. There was an attack on one of our detention centers in the downtown Chicago area. Initial reports from the ground indicate at least a couple hundred military KIAs, several hundred wounded, and apparently, several dozen guards at the detention center were killed as well. It appears there were four groups of a light infantry force which penetrated the Chicago airspace at a rapid speed, and were largely undetected until their arrival. Three of the units converged on the Omega 21 Detention Center and the other went to a school, Secretary General Darius Karlem Primary School."

"I'm impressed so far, Information Officer Thanes. Why were these raiders and their ships undetected prior to entering the Chicago airspace?"

"My apologies for not illuminating that detail, Premier. The groups of aircraft were not detected because one of our lunar outposts was destroyed, and the malfunctioning of our satellites left us effectively blind to their arrival. Once in the atmosphere, even our ground-based systems were jammed by the incoming aircraft."

"Which outpost was hit?"

"The Pontine Ridge, sir. I'm afraid to report there are no survivors and all critical structures have been completely destroyed."

"Geeze. I knew those outposts needed more protection. We'll have to fortify the remaining lunar outposts for possible hostile activities."

"I will make note of that, sir, and advise your council of your request after our meeting."

"Go on, Mr. Thanes."

"Very well, Premier. At the school, a squad of the marauders took three students. We're looking into their identities and backgrounds now. Meanwhile, at the detention center, the larger force took the body of Peter Barclay, a very recently executed inmate. Also taken were his aunt and uncle, who were present for the execution, and apparently the invading soldiers captured one of the guards as well. Surveillance footage review and interviews with surviving guards and employees are being conducted as we speak. It's unclear if the Wilbys and the guard were taken as hostages or what the circumstances were."

"Peter Barclay, you say?"

"Yes, Peter Barclay. Have you heard of him?"

"I sure have. In fact, I have heard his name a lot recently. I personally saw to it that he met a quick death."

"Oh, I see." The ill-prepared information officer didn't know what to say. What could he say?

"And Mr. Thanes, do you happen to know who these individuals were that took Peter Barclay's body and the three others?" the premier asked while gazing in a completely different direction. He did, however, manage to make eye contact with an occasional scoff.

"It sounds like special FAF troops, but I'm not sure why a fourteen-year-old boy would be of any importance to them. Not to mention that the soldiers were escorted by a squadron of highly advanced aircraft that downed nearly fifty of our drones and manned aircraft. It seems like a strange set of circumstances to me."

"I didn't realize you were appointed to your position to give opinions. Your title is *Information Officer*, is it not? I don't recall it saying Pundit Officer or Opinion Officer."

"Yes, of course, Premier. I'm sorry. I don't know what overcame me."

"To answer your question, Mr. Thanes, the reason why these troops were interested in taking the body of a fourteen-year-old boy has nothing to do with the FAF. He is a member of a group that is—how should I say? Visiting us."

"Premier Kerioth, what are you talking about?"

"I'm afraid we are dealing with two enemies. We know plenty about one, very little about the other, and most disturbing to me is that we know nothing about the relationship between them. Thank you for the update, Mr. Thanes. Good day."

Information Officer Thanes looked uneasily at the premier, expecting further explanation. Yet the empty, lifeless eyes of the man who ran the world only looked back at the fawning underling standing before him.

"Good day, Premier Kerioth." Information Officer Thanes walked away with a subtly perplexed countenance. Of course, his expression wasn't apparent until he had turned his back to the premier while walking away from the briefing room. Officer Thanes knew well enough, the predilection of the premier to easily dispose of anyone that displayed any hint of sarcasm, patronization, or anything else deemed personally offensive.

Premier Kerioth knew deep down that the Chicago incident was incredibly disturbing—much more so than he led the junior officer to believe. He couldn't possibly let an underling like him know anything close to the true magnitude of the problems at hand. The once mostly hypothetical notion of trans-temporal humans intervening was now plainly visible during the midday raids in Chicago. What was the premier to say to the people who witnessed it? What was he to do to discredit the rumors swirling about the Commonwealth's inability to protect some of its most vital interests in the heart of a heavily populated provincial capital? How will he deal with this affirmed threat that had managed to devastate numerous defense units in aerial and ground-based combat? Another important question arose. Where will they strike next? Premier Dormin S. Kerioth knew all too well that this was only the beginning of an arduous struggle he hadn't anticipated.

* * *

Ms. Danvers and her class, along with the rest of the students, teachers, and administrators, waited in the auditorium. Commonwealth authorities were interviewing each member of the school for information related to the capture of three of their students during the assault on Chicago. There were a half dozen lines of students, and two lines for staff members waiting to be called next to interview with intelligence and security officials. Nobody really knew what to expect. Would they get arrested if they said the wrong thing?

An announcement tone went out over the school's intercom system with its finely tuned humming sound. Then, an unfamiliar voice spoke. All eyes in the auditorium looked to the nearest visual sensory panel.

"This is Chairman Bagley, the head of the Eighteenth Provincial Political Affairs Council. I am pleased to announce these important messages this afternoon as I know there has been some cause for concern in the downtown area. Rest assured, I completely understand what you must think at this point. The sounds of loud noises in the streets, some of which may have sounded like gunfire. The sightings of military aircraft in the skies and soldiers in our streets. These are all things that were very real to those of you who heard or saw them. Everything that you witnessed or learned of today was part of a military exercise. Therefore, you needn't have any worry of any threat to this city and its inhabitants. The Commonwealth Land Force and Air Force planned this training mission months ago in order to practice their urban warfighting tactics. For those of you in the affected areas and on the street level, you might have noticed the appearance of destruction and battlefield casualties. Engineers used specially designed props and actors to make the city look like it was damaged during this exercise, and to simulate casualties sustained in combat. The troops and vehicles involved were not using live ammunition, so they couldn't have possibly caused damage of any kind. I hope this news will ease your worries. The Commonwealth at all levels of government is most certainly standing behind you by informing you to the very best of our abilities. I know personally, that we take accountability and transparency very seriously, here in Chicago. If there are any new details about today's training exercise, you will receive another announcement transmission. Thank you and good day."

"Can you believe that horse crap, Kamren?" Slade asked incredulously.

"When Chairman Bagley speaks, you can almost always bet that what he's saying is absolute BS."

"I just can't believe he stands up there and tries to tell us all what we saw and how it was part of some kind of exercise. He didn't mention the part of the training mission that involved kidnapping three of our classmates."

"Well, Slade, it seemed like they wanted to go with the soldiers, so I don't think I'd classify it as kidnapping," Kamren retorted.

"Fair enough. Did those soldiers look like Commonwealth Land Forces troops?"

"No, I don't think so. If they were from the Land Forces, they would never wear white. They'd wear red or some camouflage pattern."

"Right, right. I've never heard of Commonwealth troops ever wearing white."

"This whole thing is fishy. I wonder what really happened?" Kamren pondered.

Ryland stood alone, nearly in the front of the line where he'd be called next. He was trying to process what he heard from Chairman Bagley just now and what he could recall from the last time he'd seen Peter in their dorm room. He was also trying to remember any details from Ms. Danvers's classroom during the alleged training mission.

Ms. Danvers already had her interview, so she was sitting down waiting for her students to finish theirs. She thought over her answers in her head, introspecting deeply to find any areas that she might have accidentally left out. She also considered what Chairman Bagley said. His official message seemed far-fetched from what she witnessed firsthand. She didn't see any casualties or gunfire, but she did have part of the roof of her classroom blown off and then invaded by a small number of unknown soldiers, none of whom looked like any soldiers or security forces she'd ever seen. Ms. Danvers was completely dedicated to any official message disseminated from party officials, but this one seemed hard to believe, considering her first-hand account of part of the incident.

* * *

Far away from the sinister Shinar Palace where the premier received his intelligence briefing, and far from the school in Chicago, soared the *Lexington*. It sat about 0.08 astronomical units or over seven point four million miles beyond the far side of the moon. The Condor-class cruiser used by General Marion for space-based command of the FAF forces on earth was shared by the Accendia for the purposes of systems integration and force collaboration. The *Lexington* accompanied one other magnificent marvel of engineering, the *Concord*. The two ships contained an impressive array of systems and manpower. Each of the cruisers housed a garrison of ten thousand service members, including five-hundred FIT unit members, and the families of those in uniform. Some served as pilots, others as defense gunners, but most served in noncombat roles. Many of the Accendia service members were married to one another. For those that are married to civilians or service members, it was wonderful that they were allowed to bring their families with them to live on the ship. The ships acted as mobile bases with schools, shops, housing, recreational activities and facilities, in addition to their military roles.

The Accendia squadron returned to General Marion's flagship, the *Lexington*. The group carried with them the bodies of the dead, including Peter, as well as those brave servicemen that suffered injury during the mission. Deputy Lumis's FIT unit had already returned to the *Lexington* after rescuing Zameera and her two friends from the school. The men changed out of their gear, decompressed, and then were debriefed. Meanwhile, the girls were getting acquainted to their new living quarters, with Zameera providing a rich tour of the incredible ship and all its amenities.

"Captain, what of our wounded?" Colonel Maddox asked Tannis.

"Hoover and Deems are being taken care of in the clinic as we speak. It doesn't sound like either of them are seriously wounded, mostly superficial injuries. They should be good to go for the big show in the coming days."

"Very good. Keep me informed."

"Will do, sir."

"Tannis, go take a break for a while. Get out of that uniform and relax. You deserve it."

"Thanks, Colonel."

The two men parted ways in good favor and took some time to explore the ship and relax.

In the ship's control station, Champion Backstrom walked along the metallic surface with Deputy Champion Mullen. The two men showed no joy while ambulating to debrief Representative and Chief Champion Barclays. Backstrom and Mullen knew full well that Lucile and Peregrine would have a terrible time receiving the grim news.

Trekking along the walkway, the two men were saluted on the left and on the right as they approached subordinates working on systems navigation, intelligence, and communications for the *Lexington.*

"Welcome back to the Top Tier, gentlemen," a lower-ranking officer said as he saluted.

"Thank you, sir," Mullen replied as he and Backstrom saluted.

Meanwhile, General Marion stood watch over the wonders of the cosmos as he anxiously awaited Backstrom and Mullen. He witnessed the brilliant flickers and flashes of unobstructed and unadulterated stars, light years away. He watched an occasional asteroid gracefully streak by as it made its way from one side of the window to the other. The natural beauty that the general observed in the depths of space quickly faded as he turned and realized his two Accendia friends were just steps away. Backstrom, Mullen, and he would soon have to find the grace to tell the Barclays about the death of their precious son. That unthinkable reality squelched all thought of the whimsical dances in the cosmic backyard.

"Well, men, are you ready?" General Marion asked.

"I guess. There's no easy way to do this. I've got some folks in the med clinic ready for assistance, if needed. Mostly bereavement related."

"That sounds like a good idea."

"It's the least we can do for the chief champion and representative. We all knew Peter. He was a great kid."

"He sure was," Mullen added.

"I wish I could've gotten to know him a little more. I wouldn't be here if he hadn't rescued me."

"Very true. Well, gentlemen, we should go see them now. They've been eagerly waiting to hear from us."

"Let's do this," Backstrom said with little enthusiasm to the two others as they began to walk to the chief's office of the Top Tier, where Lucille and Peregrine Barclay waited for their mission debriefing. They were not informed prior to mission launch that the primary objective was to rescue their son, so they had little idea of what was to come.

Champion Backstrom placed his right hand on the wall beside the door for DNA verification. Once confirmation was completed, the door quickly opened upward and revealed Chief Champion Peregrine Barclay and Representative Lucille Barclay sitting at a table in anticipation of their arrival.

"Right on time, gentlemen," Chief Barclay acknowledged.

Marion, Backstrom, and Mullen stopped to salute before they proceeded.

"Of course, sir," Backstrom replied.

"Please take a seat. We're eager to hear about the mission in Chicago."

The men sat down on the polymer-based chairs, which didn't seem to be as comfortable as the plush leather chairs from the old days. Marion and Backstrom exchanged a brief glance, knowing full well what conversation was to come.

"Chief and Representative, I am afraid that I have some terrible news," General Marion began to say before being interrupted.

"It's Peter, isn't it?" Lucille quietly asked. She didn't want to consider it, but she knew deep down that it was likely.

"Yes, ma'am. Peter didn't make it. I am so, so sorry." General Marion brought his hand to his mouth, realizing the magnitude of his words to the now mournfully beleaguered parents.

Lucille and Peregrine Barclay clutched each other as they began to cry. How could they have let their beautiful son get caught up in such a terrible place with such terrible values? How could they let it happen? All the questions of why and if, placements of guilt, and manifestations of despair—so many emotions overcame them. The three harbingers sat with desolate countenances. What else could they say? What else could they do? The highest ranking military leader and the only civilian representative of the Accendia had just lost their only son.

"Where is he?" Lucille inquired. "We need to see him."

"He's down in the med clinic. We can bring you there whenever you're ready," Champion Backstrom said.

"Let's go now. I can't wait another minute," Lucille implored.

"Very well, ma'am."

The Barclays stood, trying to exchange their sobbing for some semblance of composure since they knew they'd inevitably pass by their subordinates and constituents. They needed to maintain their presence of mind. The task seemed impossible, but they did their best.

Leaving the chief's office with their Accendia and FAF companions, as well as a small detachment of security personnel, the Barclays led the way down through the Top Tier toward their son's remains in the med clinic. They were unsure of what shape their son would be in. They had no idea of how recognizable he would be, so they prepared themselves for more pain. With each step came yet another anticipation of dread. Each turn brought with it, an accumulating visceral reaction of anxiety. The walk to Peter's body was the most agonizing thing they had ever experienced. How could it get any worse? It was already horrifying to hear of his death. They only imagined that terrifying hypothetical question. How much worse could things possibly be?

"Where is he, Sergeant?" Chief Barclay demanded of the medic at the front desk of the med clinic, in front of a waiting room full of people.

The sergeant stood at attention and frightfully reported, "Right this way, sir."

The medic came out from around the desk and led the group back to the morgue where Peter's body was being prepared. Peter was covered with a pure white cloth that had blood stains on it near his extremities and on his torso. He was on a gourney away from all the others in the post-mortem room. Two of the technicians approached the Barclays.

"Chief Barclay and Representative Barclay, are you sure that you'd like to proceed? Your son has not been fully prepared yet since we just received him."

"Let us pass, Tech Sergeants," Lucille commanded as she and her husband walked by the two men, barely breaking stride. The two techs didn't have time to respond, so they simply moved out of the way.

"Lucille, no!" Peregrine decried as she began to pull back the linen cloth.

She couldn't stand waiting any longer. She had to see her son, no matter what his condition. She grew more desperate and dramatically yanked the corner of the cloth, pulling it completely off Peter's lifeless body. Already teared up from the moment she entered the med clinic, Representative Barclay gasped at what she saw. She quickly retracted both of her hands to her mouth in disbelief. Peregrine put his hand to his forehead. The rest of the personnel in the room stared with astonishment.

Peter's wounds were still bleeding. He had been dead for several hours and he still had blood flowing from his wrists, feet, and the right side of his thorax—just as they had been since he passed in the execution chamber. Shock, astonishment, and then awe transpired as the seconds ticked by.

Chief Peregrine Barclay put his arm around Representative Lucille Barclay as he began to kneel. Mrs. Barclay followed his lead and also knelt as she clutched his hand that wrapped around her side. It didn't take long until all fifteen people in the room were in absolute astonishment and completely overtaken by wonder. They all knew they were in the presence of a very unique and mysterious occurrence. There was no plausible explanation. No matter what each of the individuals personally believed, everybody knew they were witnessing a miracle—a phenomenon only explainable in a different plane of existence, a supernatural realm beyond human experience and rationality.

Each of the techs, officers, and soldiers in the room showed their respect to Peter and then left, one after the other. Only Lucille and Peregrine remained with Peter. They wanted some time alone with their boy.

* * *

On the other side of the ship, far away from the med clinic, Tanner Farrows was held for testing and questioning. Accendia and FAF leadership needed to know his true motivation since the story he told General Marion in the detention center still had many ambiguities that needed to be explained. He did, however, lead the expeditionary group to Peter's body as he had indicated, so that helped to bolster his story's legitimacy. General Marion was more skeptical than Deputy Champion Mullen, but he was also the one who was betrayed, detained, and tortured for two years, so that certainly seemed justifiable.

"We've already gone through this for the past hour. I don't understand why you think that I would betray you people?" Tanner asked the interrogator. "I don't know who you people are. I don't know where we are. I'm starting to think we're not even on earth at the moment, so that seems a bit odd to me. I just want to help you guys."

"Help us with what?" the interrogator sternly asked.

"I assume you folks want to take down the Commonwealth?"

"Of course we do. That's our purpose here. My question is why would you, a recently former employee of the Commonwealth government, want to suddenly turn around and take down the same institution that provided you with sustenance and a livelihood?"

"I thought I already made myself clear about that, but whatever. Yes, of course I worked for the Commonwealth. How else would the men from here have found me?" Tanner said rhetorically. "I was asked to take my position at the detention center under difficult circumstances."

"What kind of circumstances?"

"Under the worst ones I've had to go through."

"What do you mean?"

"I don't think I told you that I'm a single dad, did I?"

"No, you never said that."

"I didn't think so. But yes, I am. I have a daughter named Londyn—she's my everything. I would do absolutely anything for her and she knows it. The problem I ran into is that my wife got involved in some risky business. She was communicating with rebels—the FAF. I'm sure you're familiar with them. A bunch of them were there when they took me from the detention center, so I know you're involved with them somehow."

"Very well. Proceed."

"My wife got caught red-handed by a few Commonwealth agents who were posing as FAF members. They got her to confess to plotting violent acts against Commonwealth authorities, so they had her fast-tracked through the justice system and before I knew it, she was gone. To this day, I have no idea if she's alive. She's either dead or wishing she was. The authorities questioned Londyn and me. We didn't know anything, but they still wanted to be absolutely sure, so they threatened to kill Londyn right in front of me. I begged and I pleaded, and they told me the only way they would let my girl live was for me to work in the detention center where your men found me. They put me in that position so I would personally lead hundreds of kids—my own daughter's age—to their deaths because of what they did or said that the Commonwealth disagreed with. It was the only way I could keep my baby girl safe."

"I see. And how long ago did they take your wife?"

"Four years ago—the worst four years of my life. The sick part of it is, that over the months, I didn't feel as bad for the kids as I dealt with them. Over time, I actually began to side with the Commonwealth and treat them as if they deserved to die, including Peter."

"You believed it was right for Peter to be put to to death?"

"Yes, I did. It was just moments before his death that he changed me. He was the first person I had encountered who was able to see whom I used to be."

"What'd ya mean by that? What were you like before?"

"What I mean is I used to see the good in people. Even when I was a police officer, seeing the terrible things humans brought upon each other, I could always differentiate evil from goodness. Over the years, especially when carrying out the sentences of minors in that terrible detention center, I only saw evil in them. Every child of every background, no matter what the offense, was evil in my mind. That is how lost I truly was. I forgot how unfair the laws had become and how they punished many that didn't deserve any repercussions."

"What if I were to tell you that your daughter, Londyn, is onboard and waiting to see you?"

"Wait—what'd you say? Londyn's here?"

"That's right. She's on this ship as we speak."

Tanner was very skeptical of what the interrogation officer said. Surely it was just a tactic to get him to talk more, so the Accendia and FAF could get what they wanted out of him. How could she possibly be on this ship? Why? He just couldn't understand how it could possibly be true.

"I don't believe you. You've gotta be lying."

"No, I'm not. You want proof?"

"Yeah, I do."

The interrogator didn't suspect Tanner of being any kind of spy or saboteur. Tanner truly wanted to change, that seemed clear. He would still require plenty of monitoring, but for the time being, his story checked out.

"Open door two."

The door opened, and in walked Londyn. She knew her father was being questioned and was asked to help him cooperate, if needed. This revelation was not meant to generate false information. It was simply a reward for Tanner's veracity and his willingness to save allied lives during their mission. His assistance in locating Peter's body also carried a lot of weight.

"Dad!" Londyn cried out.

Tanner stood up and turned around to find his daughter running toward him with a huge smile on her face. He could only reply with an equally enthusiastic tone.

"Londyn! My sweet girl! I can't believe it's you!"

He met her halfway in the room for a hug that seemed to go on forever. Both of them cried out of sheer joy and held on like it was the first time they had seen each other in ages.

Once they began to come back down from their clouds of ecstasy, Londyn asked her father, "What are you doing here, Dad?"

"My detention center came under attack and I helped the people that attacked us. They were looking for Peter, your classmate."

"I know about Peter. We watched what happened to him at school. They made us—it was awful. I'm still sick to my stomach about what happened."

"I didn't know they still showed that stuff at school. I'm sorry you had to see that."

"You helped them find Peter?"

"Yes, I did."

"How? You're a maintenance man there. How would you know where he was?"

"Well, honey, that's not exactly true. I told you I was a maintenance worker because I didn't want you to know what my real job was."

"I don't get it. Did you even work there?"

"I worked there, but I was a corrections officer. I was involved in Peter's execution today. You probably saw me on the visual monitor at school, but with my suit on you wouldn't have known it was me. I'm sorry, Londyn. I know this must be a tough thing to hear from me. Believe me, I wish I could take it all back. I really do."

"I can't believe a word you're saying—you're a monster! Get away from me!"

Londyn created some distance and began to look for a way out the door she had previously walked through. She couldn't believe her own father was involved in Peter's murder. That's exactly what it was—a murder. That made her father an accomplice in a murder.

"I can't believe I loved you at all. If I would have known what you really were, I never would have seen you again."

"Londyn, I'm sorry. I wish I could change the past, but I can't. You should know that Peter changed me. He affected me in ways you couldn't possibly understand."

"Of course he did, he changed everyone he knew. He changed me too."

"What'd he change about you, honey? You didn't need to change."

"He made me realize about the invisible realm on earth. Angels, our souls—stuff like that. I can never look at people the same way again. There is no way he would have done that for a monster like you."

"Stop right there, Londyn. He made me realize I was a monster for going to work every day, knowing full well I was sending people like him to their deaths nearly every afternoon. He made me realize I still had a heart that could love and still had a heart worth loving."

"I don't believe you."

"You don't have to, at least not right now. I know you're angry with me. I understand that."

"I can't even look at you right now. Someone let me out of here, please."

Door number two opened and Londyn stormed out nearly as swiftly as she had entered. Tanner stood with his head tipped back and his eyes closed, as he tried to take in all the emotions that were swirling around in his mind from the early, cheery beginning with his daughter through the fiery end of their conversation. How could he fix this one?

The interrogator spoke after witnessing the whole ordeal. "It looks like in order for you to return to your old self, you'll have to convince your daughter as well. Welcome to the *Lexington*, the flagship of General Marion, and the heart of the spaceborne command of the FAF. You may leave the room and move about at your leisure. Take this information here and you'll be able to find your living quarters."

"Thanks." Tanner didn't quite know what to say to the man.

"Thank you for your cooperation. Once again, welcome."

Tanner sat in his chair for a moment to take in what had just occurred. The interrogator already left the room, so Tanner had the room to himself. He went through what had happened in his mind. The interrogator had unexpectedly revealed that his daughter was on the same mysterious ship which he was aboard, only to have an impromptu reunion that contained nearly the full spectrum of human emotion, including the temporary dissolution of his and Londyn's typical relationship. Once he was able to more fully appreciate the details of his and Londyn's conversation, he was ready to get up. He stood, approached one of the doors, which promptly opened, and then walked out to find his living quarters. Tanner knew he had quite a journey ahead of him, both literally and figuratively.

* * *

By the end of the day, many members of FAF leadership aboard the *Lexington* that were directly involved in Operation Cloudburst notified their subordinates of an upcoming relocation to a secret base in the Pacific Ocean. The location was only known by those on a very short list. General Marion only had a select number of trusted subordinates who were fully aware of the base's existence. The Horizon Deep was only a myth to most because its role in the global fight against the Commonwealth was so important. Its location had to be safeguarded at almost any cost.

General Marion had always trusted Colonel Maddox, so he was one of a few dozen individuals that he had told of the Horizon Deep's existence. General Marion considered Maddox an exemplary lieutenant colonel, and was certain of his confidence in him.

"All right, guys, we're moving out at 0400 tomorrow morning. I can't say where, but I will say that it is state-of-the-art and at an undisclosed location. We will join tens of thousands of fellow men and women in arms. It is our last staging point before Operation Cloudburst begins."

Captain Tannis wasn't surprised. With so many new revelations in such a short period of time, what more would it mean to learn of a top secret base? Going from a highly advanced spaceship to a highly advanced base—no big deal.

"Sounds good, Colonel," Tannis nonchalantly responded.

Hoover, Deems, Yalu, and Bex didn't seem surprised either.

"I will say this, gentlemen. We will be reunited with the rest of our unit, so we'll be back at our three hundred man company strength. I know we've been through a lot, but Captain Springs, Captain Zed, and the LTs need to know what we've learned. They need to know what we now know, I mean as far as the Land Forces tactics and armaments—that knowledge can save lives."

"Will do, sir," Hoover acknowledged.

"Luckily, we haven't been here long, so packing should be easy. Just remember, 0400. We'll meet at bay seven and ride out together. Dismissed."

The squad members saluted and went their own ways to enjoy the last of the amenities on the *Lexington*, before they would get chow and head back to their quarters to pack. Of course, Yalu and Bex stayed together to explore.

* * *

Back in the chief's office within the Top Tier of the ship, Lucille and Peregrine sat together. They just wanted to stay with each other during this most heart-wrenching day of their lives. The med technicians had to prepare Peter's body, so they only had about twenty minutes with him, which wasn't nearly long enough. In the recesses of the chief's office they had the luxury of departing from their numerous duties for even a small amount of time. They were allowed to give solace to one another as they continued to unravel the shock and agony that had met them less than an hour ago. Lucille and Peregrine tried to veer off topic and talk about something else, something less painful. Their sense of duty to their cause still gave them guilt, despite enduring such a personal tragedy. They almost felt sorry for diverting their attention and energy away from their leadership roles.

"We need to address the people at the Horizon Deep base. You know we have to. We're already going there tomorrow morning. They need to know they have our full and unwavering support as we begin the operation," Representative Barclay explained to Chief Champion Barclay.

"Of course, Lucille. My question is how do we do that when we still need to make arrangements to say goodbye to our son?"

"I know, I know. Obviously, Peter will get a proper funeral. At the very least, he deserves that. It's just such a pivotal moment for the whole movement, we don't have much time to spare. We need to exploit the opportunities while they remain vulnerable."

"How about if we have a mass funeral for Peter, the men that died trying to rescue him, as well as the people massacred in Auckland most recently? We can certainly accommodate that kind of undertaking down there. Each person that has paid the ultimate price deserves to be honored. You and I both know that under Commonwealth law, none of them are eligible for a government authorized burial because of the circumstances of their deaths. We will see to it that they have an audience to honor them and find a final resting place."

"That sounds like a great plan, Peregrine. Let's get it set up. Every one of those people needs to have the same treatment that Peter will have."

"Sounds good, dear. I'll tell Champion Backstrom to get the ball rollin'."

Lucille and Peregrine continued to grieve and be near each other. Their resilience was tested amid the horrendous torment brought upon them by the institutionally sanctioned murder of their son. They had to mourn the loss of Peter, honor the others recently killed, and at the same time, inspire thousands of soldiers in attendance at the funeral for the upcoming operation. This task was certainly within the realm of possibility for the extraordinary couple. The moment would probably epitomize their leadership, perseverance, and humility in front of the many men and women who would die under their command and leadership.

As the day went by, the busy soldiers and civilians who knew of their upcoming relocation were trying to prepare for their journey to the secret base. Nearly three-quarters of those on the *Lexington* will be making the move. Seven thousand five hundred soldiers and thousands more family members meant that about twelve thousand will need to transfer. Numerous craft will be needed to make the dangerous mission to earth and avoid detection when they will plunge through the atmosphere and into the dark depths of the Pacific. The predawn weather conditions will hopefully be perfect for a concealed approach by the aircraft convoy that will be charged with transporting the people and cargo—overcast in the entire region with fog over the water—a perfect duo for avoiding any unwanted attention by Commonwealth forces. Of course, surveillance technologies will be temporarily knocked offline to further disguise their stealthy approach.

The time was here, 0400 arrived with all personnel ready and waiting for launch.

"All craft are a go. All departure bays are ready for launch. Command—confirm launch," the master sergeant loadmaster echoed over the comms units.

"Very good, Master Sergeant. Countdown to launch," Chief Champion Barclay responded while aboard an unspecified craft within one of the departure bays. He and Representative Barclay were aboard different aircraft in case they encountered hostile activity, so that leadership of the mission would still be intact.

"Yes, sir. Ten. Nine. Eight. Seven. Six. Five. Four. Three. Two. One. Launch."

Each pilot of the sixty Turnstone transport ships waited for their bay to launch.

"Bay one, Accloy Turnstone—launch," the first pilot said as his ship descended out of the bottom of the *Lexington.*

"Bay one, Bandore Turnstone—launch," another pilot said.

"Bay one, Crambo Turnstone—launch," by another.

"Bay one, Dogcart Turnstone—launch."

"Bay one, Eskimo Turnstone—launch."

"Bay one, Froghopper Turnstone—launch."

"Bay one, Galaxy Turnstone—launch."

"Bay one, Hornet Turnstone—launch. Bay one cleared."

All eight Turnstones from bay one launched as scheduled. The remaining bays cleared in the same manner—orderly and by the book, with no hiccups whatsoever. After only a few minutes, all ships launched and then traveled to their destination in a tightly packed, linear formation. The configuration of the aircraft reduced the radar and sensory detection profile to further ensure their complete secrecy. They didn't anticipate any resistance along the way, but the Turnstones were equipped with some means of protection. Nothing like the more heavily armed aircraft the *Lexington* had previously launched for the Chicago raid, but they could hold their own against most known threats for some duration of time.

Slamming down at the speed of a slow meteorite, the spaceships blasted through the atmosphere, which changed their appearance to that of shooting stars raining down over the Pacific waters. Any untrained eye would recognize them as meteorites because of their astounding similarities. Within several thousand feet of oceanic impact, the craft all slowed down in complete synchrony. The bows of the aircraft changed slightly to brace for aqueous impact and to minimize tidal wave formation, as well as to allow them to more safely propel themselves through the dark depths of the ocean.

As the craft breached the water one after the other, they displayed their uncanny ability to navigate through liquid nearly as easily as they could through space and the earth's atmosphere. The journey down to the Horizon Deep was nearly over. There was a fairly close call with a humpback whale, but luckily there was no impact. Other than that, the rest of the journey to the undersea world came to a safe close with their arrival at the loading and receiving building at the base in the Tonga Trench. The journey down was over, but the real journey—the journey of rising up against the Commonwealth in force—would take place in a couple of days.

Chapter 20

THE TRENCH

The Federated Anti-Colonial Front's Strategic Training and Operations Command Center (STOpCom), also known as the Trench, was located in a massive undersea complex that was comprised of two dozen domed buildings built with specially designed Accendia technology. Several of the buildings were enormous, while the others were more humble in size. Since training on land was nearly impossible with the worldwide surveillance state watching every possible move, the ocean's innumerably abundant lairs of secrecy provided a much more suitable environment for subversive activities.

In the Pacific Ocean, southwest of the Samoan Islands, was the Tonga Trench—the location of the second deepest point on the face of the earth. Only after the Mariana's Trench, did the Tonga Trench rank in terms of its bone-crushing pressure because of its extreme depth. Its deepest point, the Horizon Deep, was nearly seven thousand feet deeper than Mount Everest was high. The Accendia provided expertise and materials to the FAF engineers to build the base at such a dangerous depth. The pressure per square inch was so great in the Horizon Deep, that pressure reducing technology was absolutely necessary to counteract it, otherwise the entire complex would be crushed like a soda can.

The Tonga Trench also provided a very strategic location for STOpCom. It was located in the Pacific, away from most inhabited islands, which helped to avoid more unwanted attention than necessary. It also had vast amounts of open Pacific Ocean between it and the first target—North America. More specifically, the geographical location of the previous United States of America. The open waters will allow for the armada to easily maneuver eastward for the upcoming operations.

The base took years to build under careful and inconspicuous construction by carefully crafted "companies," so as not to draw attention by Commonwealth authorities. The immense level of precision and constant quality checks assures the safe home for up to two hundred thousand FAF fighters and their families, as well as their Accendia allies.

The newly arrived soldiers began to get acquainted to their new, short lived home, much like the previously experienced brief duration on board the *Lexington.*

"So what do ya think about this place, Hoover?" Captain Tannis asked his still healing comrade in arms.

"Well, there's definitely more to do down here than what we could do on that spaceship, so that's nice. It's usually a treat to have more than one gym on base or maybe an extra shooting range, but to have a few parks at the bottom of the ocean, now that's pretty cool."

"Yeah, this place is definitely the best place I've ever been deployed. It was cool being able to see our solar system from our rooms aboard the *Lexington*, but there is something just as peaceful being down here."

Colonel Maddox walked into the squad's pod as the two were speaking.

"Colonel, what do you think of the new base?"

"Seems charming enough. We won't be down here too long. Just have to get acquainted with our new unit and the new operation. Luckily, we've had more action than most of the men and women training down here, so we're some of the more experienced guys in this army. The rest of our unit is here already, so we'll need to meet them in a little while. It'll be nice for us to be in a company-sized outfit again, instead of a platoon-sized one like that last one in Auckland."

"When's our time, sir?" Hoover asked.

"Two days, son. I know we've been running ragged for the past six months, but we're in this for the long haul now. Once we start Operation Cloudburst, there's no going back. All we can do is push forward."

"We'll be ready, sir."

"We sure will, Colonel," Tannis interjected.

"I know I can count on you men. Always could, always will. Hoover, after my meeting here, come find me by the Combatant Commander's Wing. I should be about twenty minutes."

"You got it, Colonel."

The men carried on. Colonel Maddox went to meet with other commanders in their division. Captain Tannis and Lieutenant Hoover went to see if Deems, Bex, and Yalu were holed up somewhere playing poker or causing trouble.

"Who would've thought there'd be elevators like this under water?" Private Bex turned and asked Lieutenant Hoover as he saw him alongside Captain Tannis.

"I don't even know what to think anymore. My idea of what normal is has been completely destroyed this past week," Hoover responded.

"What are you guys doing out here?" Tannis asked Bex, Yalu, and Deems.

"Oh, nothing, sir. Just taking it all in," Sergeant Deems answered. He wore his newly issued knee brace to help support his tweaked knee from the Chicago incursion. Deems also had a couple of long bandages on his right arm to cover some bullet graze wounds he received while fighting in the detention center.

"It's quite a view, isn't it?" Tannis rhetorically asked as all five of them stood at a railing and looked down into a gigantic atrium shaped like a lemon, and lined with concentric levels, much like the rings within the cross section of a tree trunk. They could see down about fifty floors from their vantage point. The upper levels easily added another fifty or more floors. The forty high speed elevators connected all of the seemingly innumerable floors within the inner lining of the atrium, providing quick transportation to the inhabitants living within the densely populated living quarters.

The people walking in all directions, coming from all over the world, were united by the belief of restoring hope to the world. Not an empty, hollow hope based on superfluous platitudes, but the kind built upon a solid foundation that has been shown to work time and time again. That is what they volunteered for—to restore hope to the world by dismantling that which takes hope away. The Commonwealth was the institution which supplanted every descent and viable institution in the world, and is thus, the primary perpetrator of fear and oppression—two inherent barriers to hope for the human spirit. The Commonwealth must fall.

"How was the meeting, Colonel?" Lieutenant Hoover asked as Colonel Maddox approached him outside the Combatant Commander's Wing.

"Very good, LT. Very good. We've got some great men and women among us. We'll be all right. This'll be a tough fight ahead, but we're in a very good position to win."

"Excellent, sir. So what was it that you wanted to discuss?"

"Well, son, I thought it would be a fitting time to have a little talk about your family and mine. We are more similar that you may realize. I think before we get into some heavy fighting in a couple days, you and I need to let it out in order to help cope with our losses. As painful as it is to discuss, I'd like to do that if you're up for it."

Hoover wasn't expecting the topic of his wife and daughter to come up. He thought that since it was such a recent loss, his teammates would leave it alone for a while as he tried to find his own way through the torment. Hoover was pleasantly surprised by the invitation.

"Of course, Colonel. Where would you like to talk?"

"I saw a bunch of tables out by commissary row, with all the restaurants and shopping. I think it's in one of the next buildings over. We'll have to check, but I'm pretty sure. This place is so big down here, I can hardly figure out where anything is. How about you and I go take a look-see?"

"All right, sure."

The two walked over to one of the massive junction points where the barracks met the commissary. The barracks seemed to be the central hub, and had subsequent linkups in several directions to other structures. One way was the training center along with the armory. Another way was the recreation pod. Commissary row was opposite the direction of the recreation pod. It had dozens of restaurants, shopping for essentials, and several grocery stores. You name it and the odds are it would be there.

Of course, many of the modern luxuries and amenities were absent since it was at the bottom of the ocean after all. Figuring out the logistics of operating the base was a tricky process, and maintaining supplies at such a depth had to be taken into careful consideration since the Commonwealth controlled all surface water commerce. At least the Commonwealth thought they did; however, there were some operating commercial ships that served different purposes than what the nautical authorities may have realized.

Sitting at a small table along one of the major walkways in commissary row, Colonel Maddox and Lieutenant Hoover imbibed some locally manufactured, carbonated beverages.

"So how ya doin'?" Maddox asked.

"I've been better. That's for sure."

"I know you're hurting, James. I know the pain is still raw."

Hoover didn't know what else to say to something so obvious to him, and something that he clearly didn't like to explain to others.

"Of course you're right, Colonel. That sting is still there. It's been less than a week, which I realize isn't very long at all, but I guess I thought I'd have a little more peace by now. At least a little more solace after going back downrange where I have my purpose and the duty to look after the guy next to me. The mission ended and my pain came right back—right back the way it was before going to Chicago."

"A week isn't long at all, especially when your family was murdered. It's something that you'll never completely get past. There will always be pain to some extent. It'll have its ups and downs as time goes on, but there will always be a certain residual level. Focusing on what you had with them while they were with you can help. Using your hurt to do good is something else I've found to be tremendously beneficial."

"How do you know all this, Colonel?" Hoover had no idea how Colonel Maddox could possibly understand what he was going through—losing his wife and little girl. He either had to have had his own misfortune of losing family or he had a lot of gall for pretending to know what to think.

"I, too, have lost my family, James. I know you didn't get much time for grieving on the *Lexington*, but it was the best we could do, given the circumstances. You did choose to come with us to Chicago, right? That's what Captain Tannis told me. Anyway, what I wanted to say was that my wife, Abigail, died during the initial hours of the Fifth World War. My two sons, Juniper and Lenton, died at different times during the same terrible, ugly war. That war took everything from me. It claimed the lives of my wife and my boys, my country, and my way of life. All I had left were the men under my command who managed to make it, and the memories of what life used to be like."

Hoover knew that Colonel Maddox served with distinction as a second lieutenant and worked his way up to major by the end of the three year war.

"I guess I knew some of your story, you know—your history as an officer—your history fighting in some of the big battles, but I didn't know about your personal losses. I'm sorry, sir. So sorry."

"Thank you. It's not something I wear on my sleeve, so to speak—and it isn't the sort of thing I go telling everyone, especially among young soldiers with beautiful families. It's important now that you understand that I wouldn't be half the man I am now, if it weren't for having them in my life. No matter how much time was cut short—it was still enough to change me. They drove me to keep striving, to keep pushing to better myself. I'm sure your wife and daughter did the same to you."

"Oh, of course. They sure did. Luckily, as soldiers we can rely on our brothers to push us as well, but my ladies knew how to improve my vitues like no men could replicate. In fact, Colonel, if it wasn't for them, I know I never would have joined the FAF. Without having a family to protect and to provide a better future for, I am certain I would have sat all this out. The FAF was the only logical way I could get involved and try to fight for them."

"That sounds like a fine enough reason to me—getting involved in all this to help your family. Risking injury, torture, and even death—all on their behalf. I am sure that that provided enough of an example to prove what kind of husband and father you were to them. I'm sure they never forgot that and you should be proud."

"Thanks, Colonel. I sure hope you're right."

"I know I am because I know what kind of man you are. Just remember every time you put on that uniform you're wearing right now, you are continuing to fight for Audrey and Serenity."

"You got it, sir. I will."

"Very good."

The two continued their chat along the busy walkway. As busy as the surrounding was, the heart-to-heart discussion the two grieving men had was completely intimate and without distraction. Their hearts were in a different place, and they were able to tune out all the chaos of the undersea base life. Colonel Maddox hadn't had a discussion like that in a very long time. Lieutenant Hoover hadn't had an interchange of that sort since he found out the terrible news of his family. From two different experiences and two different points on the timeline of loss, the two men's outflowing of joy, sorrow, hope, and other profound emotions allowed them to better prepare themselves for the mission ahead—Operation Cloudburst.

In yet another vast structure at STOpCom was the Soldier Readiness Center. There, the four-thousand acre, thirty level behemoth enabled the training of all units of the FAF that readied themselves for the upcoming mission. Floors were dedicated to simulated offensive and defensive maneuvers in various climates, rural and urban settings, water to ground, ground to water, topographical variations, and other complexities of the battlefield. All exercises conducted used simulation rounds that looked, sounded, and felt exactly like the real rounds would feel in their FAF-issued weapons so that training was as realistic as it could be.

War games that utilized these highly advanced technologies allowed for units of the FAF and Accendia to seamlessly integrate, which will prove to be critical for mission success in the coming fight ahead. Land vehicles of all classes and types were used just as they would be down range. Aircraft training relied on simulator technology to achieve multibranch collaboration in the controlled environment. Just about every feature of training for war in the year 2090 was available there. It was something that Commonwealth officials would never suspect. How could a bunch of freedom fighters from different parts of the world have this kind of leadership, command and control hierarchy, technology, and training at their disposal? Premier Kerioth never really looked highly upon FAF capabilities in the past. When Operation Cloudburst begins—he won't know what hit him.

Within the Soldier Readiness Center, Colonel Maddox, now changed into his FAF Combat Uniform, stood in front of his brigade. He didn't expect to get a promotion out of his role in the Auckland and Chicago missions, but nonetheless his status of full bird colonel was something which he highly valued. General Marion personally issued the recommendation and bestowed the honor to him after returning from Chicago.

The five thousand men and women were part of the First Brigade, Second Infantry Division, First Army Corps, with General Marion at the helm. The First Army Corps consisted of a larger force of one hundred thousand. Their task will be to infiltrate and secure major cities in the Great Lakes region and along the Mississippi River in the heart of the Commonwealth's presence in North America. Colonel Maddox's brigade and the rest of the Second Infantry Division will be responsible for taking Chicago.

"Ladies and Gentlemen, I am Colonel Maddox—the commanding officer of the First Brigade of the Second Infantry Division. It is an honor to be with you all today, here in the Trench. I know that we have all made many sacrifices to be here right now. We have all given up a great deal of security and peace of mind. You and I know that if we are caught fighting for what we believe, we will almost certainly meet our deaths. Therefore, the bravery that you show for just being here is more than most will ever display in their lifetime. We will all need to carry that bravery on a new mission. Tomorrow, we will embark on a several thousand mile journey to fight in North America. Our goal is to liberate Chicago, at the southwestern corner of Lake Michigan. It is the quintessential metropolis which represents the harsh and cruel realities of the Commonwealth's grip on the world. The merciless destruction of liberty, charity, and the value of humanity, are just a few examples of what this deplorable mindset has done to our families, friends, and our very lives. We are going into battle against a hardened and sophisticated enemy—that is a given. More importantly though, we are going into battle in order to uproot a hateful ideology which has strangled the life out of humanity for too long." Maddox looked around the room, gazing from face to face.

"We leave at 0600 tomorrow. We will be using around one hundred Krait subs to bring us to the fight. We'll be accompanied by auxiliary subs that will provide medical and logistics support along with specially modified commercial vessels that will transport vehicles and supplies. The Kraits will transport our brigade and the rest of the division through the Great Lakes, and to the channels and shoreline of Chicago. From there, we will disembark and converge with our vehicles and weapons systems in the downtown area. Critical infrastructure and defensive targets will already be knocked out by FIT teams that will deploy the night of our arrival. We will get air support from Accendia aircraft using their air superiority and strike technologies while we're on the ground. The whole mission to take Chicago should take no longer than forty-eight hours. The operation to liberate Chicago and other major cities along the Great Lakes is all part of Operation Cloudburst. Let us go and be that sword which pierces the heart of the ruthless beast that has overtaken the former bastion of hope and liberty on earth.

"Battalion and company commanders can come to me with questions afterward. Once again, ladies and gentlemen, thank you for being here. The world may never know liberty again, if not for you and your efforts. Thank you. Dismissed."

Each of the brigade combat team's colonels in the Trench addressed his or her soldiers in a similar fashion. Every brigade in every division had a specific target. Chicago. New Orleans. St. Louis. New York. In all, four divisions of twenty-five thousand troops, or twenty brigades of five thousand troops each came out of the numerous rooms. The space in the Trench to accommodate this many soldiers in one location was absolutely astounding to anyone that had the opportunity to lay witness. Those that were new to the base were in sheer amazement at the monstrous size of the place and the way in which such a large force could be successfully mobilized, trained, and deployed.

All units waiting for mission launch were eagerly anticipating the moment when they would all be addressed by General Marion, Chief Champion Barclay, and Representative Barclay at a memorial for the fallen. The occasion had been scheduled for later in the day—1600. In the meantime, each of the units of troops made sure their equipment was in working order and all accounted for. Most men and women prayed for a safe mission, while some were too nervous to do so. Each soldier carried his or her stress in a different way. It was natural to see so many reactions in the face of such an extensive operation that would undoubtedly result in many of them losing their lives. Unbeknownst to all except the upper echelons of command, the estimated casualty rate of the operation is projected to be between thirty and sixty percent. It is certainly a high price to pay, but the targets are invaluable to the greater goal of defeating the Commonwealth, so the rewards outweigh the risks.

Sometime later in the day, approaching 1600, a calm female voice spoke over the base's intercom system.

"The time is 1530. All base personnel, military and civilian, please make your way to the Grand Auditorium for a memorial of the fallen. Thank you."

The Grand Auditorium was the third largest building on base after the barracks, and the Soldier Readiness Center. It could seat the base's entire census of three hundred thousand, which was more than twice the occupancy of the Rungrado First of May Stadium in the formerly hermetic nation of the Democratic People's Republic of Korea. Level after level of seating radiated concentrically around its perfectly circular center. As in each of the many buildings in the Trench, in place of windows were digitally placed scenes of beauty so the base's inhabitants didn't have the constant view of artificial materials and didn't disturb the structural integrity of the buildings in the immensely pressurized depths of the Pacific.

Civilians from the base descended to the auditorium at a constant rate of flow. Spouses and families of soldiers, and others gathered for the memorial. Military units waited to enter until they were prompted since they would be marching in a parade-style fashion. The ceremonial entrance allowed for all units garrisoned at the base to receive their well-deserved admiration by all civilians present who rely on them for protection. Units that will be deploying in the early hours of the operation the next day will be marching in last, so the other half of the total military force in attendance can salute them off. Once all cohorts of troops have entered the voluminous arena, then the memorial detail with the fallen enter with the eyes of the living descending homage upon them.

"All right, folks, let's move."

It was time for Colonel Maddox to take his brigade into the auditorium, with the four other complimentary brigades from his division following in sequential order.

Captain Tannis and Lieutenant Hoover were placed in the same company, which was intentionally ordered by Colonel Maddox. Sergeant Deems, Private Yalu, Private Bex and the other remaining members of the Auckland outpost were also assigned to the same company due to their already well-established reputation and unit cohesion. They were all members of Dogcart Company, First Battalion, First Brigade, of the Second Infantry Division, with Captain Tannis leading them. It was nice for them to be part of a larger force again. In Auckland, they had no backup, no reinforcements. When things went south, they were out of luck, except for the one Accendia intervention that saved a half dozen of them.

Colonel Maddox led his brigade into the Grand Auditorium and was met with a cascade of rolling applause that never seemed to end. The grateful men, women, and children stood in fervent support of their protectors, and gazed down at the thousands of men and women in their FAF Combat Uniforms, which included their ceremonial tricorn hats.

"Look around, soldiers. This may be the last friendly crowd that we see for a while. Take it all in. Sure feels great, doesn't it?" Maddox yelled out while marching forward, so few of his words could actually be heard by his troops because of the overwhelming volume of noise. Only the nearest battalion officer and the first few rows of troops behind him could discern his words.

Tannis, standing next to Hoover with his head and eyes still facing forward, called to him, "Isn't it awesome, brother?"

"I feel so good. I haven't felt this good in a long, long time. Great way to send us off," Hoover responded in the same way.

Yalu and Bex kept their heads still, but their eyes were jagging in all directions. With each step they took, they felt intensifying pressure waves upon their bodies from all the clapping, hollering, and celebrating. Wave after wave struck them in a way that muted their own heartbeats.

"This is nuts, dude!" Yalu exclaimed to Bex.

"Oh, yeah!" Bex couldn't seem to find any other words to describe the environment and his reaction to it, nor could he manage to hear much of what Yalu said.

The troops poured in line by line through several of the entrances on the lower level, so they could all be witnessed by the over one hundred thousand people already in the stands. Unit after unit continued in the same methodical and systematic way that Colonel Maddox's brigade did. Each group of men and women continued their marching around the periphery of the stadium to their designated spots, clearing the way for the final group to enter.

General Marion, his staff, Chief Champion Barclay, and the Accendia civilian leader, Representative Barclay, led the memorial detail into the stadium. The cheering and clapping stopped, not because of the presence of the highest ranking military members being present, but because of the caskets being escorted directly behind them. Those standing in the crowd, civilian and military alike, stood in silence. Those in uniform stood at attention with their right hands drawn up in a rigid salute, while civilians put their right hands over their hearts. Besides the stepping of the memorial detail, there was absolute silence within the auditorium.

Two different flags draped over the coffins, depending on which cause the individual was a part of. The caskets of the four Accendia servicemen and Peter had the Accendia flag, and the thirty-nine people from the massacre at Auckland, including Lieutenant Hoover's wife and daughter, donned the FAF flag. The twenty-six soldiers killed at Auckland also had the FAF flag draped over their caskets.

The Accendia flag had the powerful winged lion with two feather-laden chevrons beneath it, and was surrounded by a bold red diamond. The FAF flag had at its center, a thirteen-pointed blue star surrounded by thin white and red outlines, and was contained within a circle. Both of the flags and their combined symbolic meaning were the antithesis of the currently presiding flag flown over the globe, which represented the sinister forces of the United People's Commonwealth.

The procession continued with the pallbearers ceremonially placing the caskets in their designated places while the leaders proceeded to the rostrum nearby. General Marion walked to the middle and began to speak into the voice amplifier.

"Ladies and gentlemen, military and civilian alike, we gather today to remember the seventy lives who were taken from us in recent days. They could have been any one of us. Some were soldiers, some were civilians. Regardless of title, rank, name, or place of origin, they all supported the same cause. All that the thirty-nine civilian men, women, and children resting in these caskets before me did on that beautiful, sunny day in Auckland, was attend a church service. They risked their earthly lives with the understanding that going to that service would help them inherit their eternal reward, and give thanks for their blessings in this life. As they knelt in reverence toward the altar, they were gratuitously murdered. Each one of them had their own story, many whose stories intertwined with our own. We will remember their courage for continuing their way of life in the midst of the climate of hatred which rules our world. We will all remember their example and carry it forward to help stop the evil which now controls so many aspects of our lives."

General Marion named each one in alphabetical order with a deliberate and monotonous voice. Not a sound could be heard, except for an intermittent sob. Lieutenant Hoover was one of them. Captain Tannis helped to provide some consolation the best he could.

"The twenty-six soldiers here served at their Auckland post with distinction and valor. They were stationed in Auckland, but were from many locations around the world—like many of you here today. After the murder of the civilians, these men rushed to confront the forces that carried out the atrocity. Little did they know they faced a heavily armed company of specialized warfighters. Undermanned and outgunned—instead of running—they chose to fight. They fought valiantly even as their casualties mounted. Their acts of bravery saved six of their fellow soldiers with the assistance of our allies, who provided vital support and rescue. Those surviving six are present today and have combined with the remaining elements of the Auckland outpost in addition to receiving troop strength supplementation. Colonel Maddox, please have your brigade stand so we can all honor your troopers and you."

After a long applause and standing ovation, General Marion proceeded to read the names of the fallen.

"As the commander of all Federated Anti-Colonial Front forces, I take our proposition very seriously and personally know the great risks involved. Many have lost their lives in a similar way to these people who lay in front of me here." Marion waved his hand across each of the caskets in front of him. "We that decide to stand up against tyranny all have a price to pay. Some pay more greviously than others, but we stand unified. Fighting with us are men and women of the Accendia, who risk just as much as we do. Standing next to me are the civilian and military leaders of the Accendia. To my right is Representative Lucille Barclay, and to my left is her husband, Chief Champion Peregrine Barclay, head of all Accendia military forces. I have come to know these two wonderful people over the past several years, absent my time in captivity. I assure you all, we have no greater allies than they. Let us all give the Barclays, and all Accendia military and civilian advisors present today, a round of applause."

The clapping lasted about ten seconds and then Representative Barclay stepped forward to speak.

"Thank you, General Marion, for the kind introduction and warm words about our group. Chief Champion Barclay and myself are here to address you about two things. The first, is that as the elected civilian leader of the Accendia movement, I am greatly appreciative of all that you and your families have gone through to be here. My husband, Chief Champion Barclay, has been honored to work with the brave men and women of the Federated Anti-Colonial Front from all over the world. We are both here today to extend our prayers for protection and safety to those of you who are about to go into harm's way." The FAF civilians and military were intrigued by what Lucille Barclay had to say and dedicated their complete attention to her.

"We have also recently experienced a more personal loss. Our son, Peter, was recently put to death in Chicago. We are still grieving the loss of our only son the best we can, and do realize that many of you have lost your children as well. May we all have the strength to endure and persevere.

"Peter was arrested and quickly executed because of his beliefs. The premier himself had a hand in our son's murder because Peter's mind couldn't be contained, and because the flag which he had in his suitcase was too dangerous to be allowed in public—that flag was the American flag. Some of you here remember what it stood for, while others may not have the personal experience with or knowledge of the extinct nation and the flag which represented its values. My husband and I know, and Peter most certainly knew that looking back to the American founding is our greatest hope for restoring the world with freedom. The beginning of the reinstitution of liberty starts tomorrow morning with Operation Cloudburst. We start with the liberation of America."

The folks up and down every row in the auditorium erupted with thunderous applause and chanting. Chief Champion Barclay and Representative Barclay showed respect for the old United States of America with a salute and hand over the heart, respectively. General Marion and his staff also displayed their arms out of reverence.

Representative Barclay closed her remarks and then allowed for the priest near the rostrum to bless the recently departed and pray that the souls are granted their heavenly reward.

Chief Champion Barclay provided his presence for a show of support. He was still having such a difficult time with Peter's recent death that he did not want to speak. His military position was such that he didn't want to risk crying in front of the entire auditorium since he wanted to remain as composed as possible.

Chapter 21

SPECTER WAVE

Billings, the more realistic and reticent of the duo, tried to get lost in his own mind to help pass the time. Brody's temperament was on the other side of the spectrum, he tended to let his mouth get the best of him. Physically, the two men appeared quite similar—typical military-style haircuts, meticulously groomed, and twenty-one years old. Their facial expressions, though trained to be limited in frequency, were nearly identical.

"So, how many more days you figure till we get some action around here?" Brody rhetorically spouted.

"Could be any day, man," Billings uttered, transfixed by one of the many monitors surrounding him.

"You really think so? I didn't expect much action here, but I figured if I did a good job, then I might get to deploy to a hot spot like Auckland or somewhere like that."

"Oh, yeah?" Billings didn't think Brody knew what he was asking for.

Brody continued, "You hear 'bout that Robocorps company that got wasted by some new weapon? Some crazy stuff goin' on down there. I wish I could help with the fight."

"I'm not sure what I think about that." Billings decided to turn his head to the now eerily excited Brody. "All I'm sayin' is you never know. Those guys you mentioned in Auckland—they're the baddest of the bad. Cutting edge. Hardcore. They probably thought they'd never have a problem engaging a band of uncivilized noncons, and look what happened to 'em. They let their guard down, got complacent. They let their technology get in the way of using their heads. We can't do that here. We can't be off in fantasyland thinking about what ifs somewhere else, when we have our own jobs to do right here and right now. It only takes one mistake like that and game over."

"Okay, okay. I see whatcha mean. So you really don't know for a fact that somethin's going down or not, right? I mean, you don't have intel or anything, right?" Brody asked worriedly.

"Of course not. Did you hear anything I just said?"

The two Maritime Defense soldiers inharmonious ended the conversation, and focused on the commercial freighters moving in and out of the Coastal Defense Zone that encompassed the large Los Angeles port. Nearly twenty-five percent of all shipboard freight bound for North America passed by this seven island military archipelago. The Commonwealth's investment in defending the port with all the latest military capabilities further illustrated its strategic importance.

* * *

"General, our amphibious troops are in place along their Great Lakes and Mississippi River tributary targets," reported a senior signals officer with the FAF.

"Excellent. Tell Admiral Perry we're ready for his forces to surface," General Marion replied while looking at the earth from a distance back aboard his flagship, the *Lexington*.

General Marion's plan to liberate the territory once called America will begin with a swift and devastating amphibious assault along the strategic and symbolic Los Angeles shoreline. The first prong of the attack will be naval bombardment, then a massive landing of seaborne and airborne troops. Over fifty thousand troops will land in the area stretching from Santa Monica, Long Beach, Huntington Beach, and south to Laguna Beach. The landings at the beaches along the Los Angeles coast will demonstrate the FAF's ability to mount a large scale operation against one of the Commonwealth's most heavily defended ports. Commonwealth leadership should be completely stunned, and more importantly, Premier Kerioth should be terrified.

"This is Admiral Perry. All systems are ready. Officers, lead the fleet to rally points for ascent and operational striking distance. Remember folks, stealth and complete surprise are of the utmost importance—we can't afford any mistakes." The admiral, aboard the *Lexington* in the Naval Operations Center, directed scores of men and women to prepare the beginning phases of Operation Specter Wave.

The semi-autonomous ships and subs had no crews, and only followed the commands of their designated sailors from the control center aboard the *Lexington*. Each strike group leader for the various vessels called out.

"Stargazers ready."

"Eagle Rays ready."

"Mullaways ready."

"Viper swarms ready."

Admiral Perry viewed the uplink of each tactical asset with his staff to ensure all systems were in place and at the appropriate depth.

* * *

"Hey, Billings, are you seeing this?" Brody anxiously pointed out on a sonar readout.

"Seeing what?"

"Come here, quick."

"All right, all right. Hold on," Billings haphazardly meandered over, thinking that Brody was overreacting to a school of fish again or maybe a little on edge from their last conversation. "What've you got this time, Brody?"

"You tell me, man."

Billings knew it definitely wasn't a school of fish. It couldn't be—it was way too big.

"Oh, man. Well, it looks like it's five hundred meters out and about fifty meters long. Get a visual on it," Billings instructed.

"Okay, okay. Let's see what we have here." Brody looked into a high powered rangefinder with magnification. "I see its shadow. Could be a FAF mini-sub or USV (unmanned submersible vehicle)? They have been known to recon harbors. Should I call it in to Colonel?"

"Just wait and see. We don't wanna cry wolf again. He was really pissed the last time we called in something that turned out to be bogus. Remember the group of divers?"

"Well, what if this is an actual threat?" Brody didn't want to miss out on an engagement with a potential enemy, especially with some of the powerful anti-ship and anti-submarine systems at his disposal.

"I thought you were the tough one here? Just watch it, see what it does. Don't freak out yet. We need to know what we're dealing with."

Brody's eyes were still transfixed on the anomaly. "It's moving up. The shadow's getting bigger."

"Okay. Let me know if you see it breach the water."

Within a split second of Billings waiting for confirmation, Brody yelped out, "Breach! Breach!"

"What is it? Brody?"

Hesitating for a moment, Brody painfully uttered, "Whale."

"Seriously? A whale? Not again. You're drivin' me nuts. I'm glad Colonel didn't find out about this one, can you imagine how peeved he'd be?"

"This is coming from the same guy who told me about just waiting to get whacked like those poor suckers in Auckland. What'd you expect?" Brody jabbed.

"Well, I didn't mean to be paranoid. I just meant to try not to be complacent," Billings responded.

The two stepped away from their duties, even though their orders mandated that one soldier was to be attentive to their detection apparatuses at all times. Billings and Brody had another mandate in mind—spring rolls—Minh's Restaurant's specialty spring rolls.

"I suppose we should head back. I feel weird even being away from these screens for a minute, but dang these rolls hit the spot," Billings confessed.

"There's a gap in traffic. Don't worry about it. After what I put you through, I think you deserve it." Brody was effective at mitigating Billings's compunction. His guilt melted away, at least for the time being.

* * *

Back at the *Lexington*, final communications were being made to ensure progress with all aspects of the upcoming operation.

"General, my forces are ready and in position. When will our space forces take out Commonwealth global comms and ISR (intelligence, surveillance, reconnaissance)?" Admiral Perry asked General Marion.

"Admiral, at the outset, your strike group will disrupt Los Angeles-area comms, ISR, and detection assets, but continental and global assets will remain intact. Since your assault remains a diversionary action, we don't want to completely disrupt their logistical support right away. We want Commonwealth forces from North America to flood the Los Angeles region to allow our primary invasion forces to take the Great Lakes and Mississippi River regions."

Admiral Perry needed some last minute clarification about the overall mission that lay beyond his naval operations. As supreme allied commander of the FAF, General Marion reminded his chief naval commander.

"Are we still anticipating they'll reinforce other ports, like New York and New Orleans?"

"I'm sure they will, but it won't matter. Our troops are already well beyond the ports and positioned inland along major population centers. They'll disembark from your subs and civilian vessels after your Los Angeles beach landings are well underway. At that time, our space command will eliminate the Commonwealth's satellites and other space-based systems."

"Very good, sir." Admiral Perry rarely had the opportunity to address General Marion in person, especially since being back from his captivity.

"Oh, and Admiral?"

"Yes, General."

"Your strike group is expendable. It would be nice to salvage most of the bigger vessels for future operations, but with no human lives at stake on our side, your ships and machines can be lost. Just be sure to take out as many Commonwealth forces as you can. Surprise them and send a message that shakes Kerioth's foundation."

"Will do, General. They won't know what hit 'em."

The two saluted one another and then carried on to their combat operations command centers.

Admiral Perry's staff and fellow combatant commanders used a large proportion of the Naval Operations Center on the *Lexington*. The majority of FAF naval vessels were being utilized for the upcoming submissions of Operation Cloudburst, with Operation Specter Wave using a large percentage of the semi-autonomous vessels available. The Accendia only had so many available materials and personnel to appropriate for FAF naval strength.

"All right, folks—it's time. To each one of you who has waited for this moment to come. To each one of you who has longed for the day to take back our rights—that moment of that day is now!" The Admiral's crescendo roused the men and women who briefly broke their concentration to acknowledge their leader.

"Let's do this. You all know what to do. We've trained for this day for countless months." The several hundred or so people let out a brief and affirming yell, then proceeded to launch the specter wave—the first phase of Operation Cloudburst.

* * *

"Hey, Billings, I just lost my surveillance consolidator screen. It's weird. Sonar, radar, gravitational wave mass—they're all down," Brody reported in a less hysterical pitch than the last encounter.

"Strange. Let me know when it comes back. I'll try San Clemente and Santa Catalina posts and see if they're down too." Billings was a bit suspicious of this phenomenon.

"Will do. Let me know what they say. Could be another software glitch."

Billings tried syncing his comms pack with the two nearby island outposts to no avail. He tried reaching out to the four other island installations. Nothing.

"Brody, we've got a problem—all seven keys to the harbor are down. I'll use the shortwave to tell Colonel about the malfunction. Just use your rangefinder for visual read if your systems are still down."

Neither of them had a good feeling about this. Billings was eager to talk to his Colonel for troubleshooting and reassurance. Brody was petrified to be relying on his own eyes instead of the state-of-the-art Commonwealth technology.

"Here we go," Brody thought to himself as he took a big gulp, putting his eyes to the lenses.

"Colonel, it's Billings. All our detection sensors and comms are down. What's happening?" Before the colonel could respond, Brody let out a shout.

"Billings! Get down!" Brody dove to the floor, pulled his weapon off the back of his chair and covered his head. Billings spun around and saw a flurry of incoming missiles skim the surface of the water's plentiful waves. Based on their incredible speed, they had to be hypersonic missiles.

"Colonel! Colonel!"

"What now, Billings? I'm working on the glitch."

The hundreds of missiles increased their speed as they approached the defensive islands. Some changed their trajectory to veer upward at an angle, while most continued on their straight approach toward the shoreline. Billings saw several dozen of them whiz past the buildings to his right and left.

"Attack! We're under attack!"

"Billings, repeat. Now calm down. Did you say we're under a…." The transmission went static. Billings knew that one missile had the Coastal Defense Zone headquarters as its target. The colonel was gone.

Brody remained on the ground, which was now violently rumbling from all the sonic booms and explosions that were rocking the harbor.

"Brody—look." Billings pointed out the panoramic, curvilinear ballistic glass. Brody knelt up, slowly lifted his head from a crouched position, until his eyes could see above the bottom of the window's base. The distant explosions from the coast were deafening. Several blasts shook the island, nearly knocking Brody back down to the ground.

"We just lost our defenses. Anti-ship and anti-air systems, they're all gone."

Billings was just waiting for some ordnance with his name on it to find him.

"We're screwed, man. We can't do a thing, maybe just wait to die is all." Brody set aside his eager belligerence for submission.

"I know. I know. Just shut it. The least we can do is gather intel on what's happening. We need to focus and get with it," Billings reasoned.

Momentarily convinced, Brody stood back up and managed to stow his paralyzing fear, and gave Billings a confident look which indicated his return to duty.

Wave after wave of projectiles continued to pummel the region. The ocean seemed to bubble up the speedy missiles from numerous locations. Some destroyed coastal defense installations, while others honed in on incapacitating air and sea-based Commonwealth assets in the area. Many ships docked at the naval base in the harbor were sunk or severely damaged. Aircraft sitting on runways and in fortified hangers met the same fate. Despite the FAF's ability to jam Commonwealth defenses, some countermeasures succeeded in destroying a handful of the incoming missiles. This degree of success, however, only worked for one volley, as the next wave targeted and destroyed the countermeasures with a high level of accuracy.

"It's been what, a few minutes since this started?" Billings estimated.

"I think so," Brody affirmed.

The two trapped troopers attempted to orient themselves to the ongoing situation in their less conspicuous location amid the rubble. Brody began to speculate, "Is this attack some noncon way of terrorizing the port or testing our defenses?"

"Or the start of an invasion?" Billings conceded.

"Invasion? With what—a few hundred men and a couple sailboats? The FAF is a land force only, everyone knows that," Brody chided Billings.

"Maybe they've kept their real strengths a secret until now."

"I doubt it, but I guess we'll have to wait and see."

The two looked out, trying to identify the approaching missiles and their intended targets. They tried to assess the situation the best they could so they could report it up the chain of command if comms came back online.

* * *

Back at the Naval Operations Center aboard the extraorbital *Lexington*, the men and women who operated the submerged armada worked diligently.

"Admiral Perry, preliminary Stargazer sub squadron cruise missile barrage has concluded with maximum effectiveness. Shall we proceed with surface operations?" a mid-ranking officer asked.

"Proceed. Commence with the next phase."

"Yes, sir."

The other officers in the room paid close attention. The men and who were responsible for the next stage of the operation carried on with their preparations.

"Admiral, Viper swarms one, two, and three are in position."

"Excellent, Captain. Move 'em out."

"Lieutenants, surface Viper swarms now. Search and destroy military assets—plain and simple. You may also encounter elements of Commonwealth first wave reinforcements." The Captain oversaw the sailors who controlled the sixty small and highly maneuverable Viper attack boats.

Admiral Perry ordered the crews of all other semi-autonomous ship classes on standby since Operation Specter Wave was approaching its zenith. All crews were ready for the imminent invasion.

* * *

"You think the civies are all okay?" Brody earnestly inquired as he thought about his wife of one year.

"Oh, I'm sure they're fine. You hear those sirens blaring? I'm sure the city's mostly locked down by now. At the very least, brought to shelters where they're safe," Billings tried to reassure his brother-in-arms.

"I just can't lose her—Clair's my everything. We're still waiting for our childbearing application to come back, so you know what that might mean."

"That's great, man. I'm still waiting to find the right girl, but I would love to be at that point too."

Even if for half a minute, Brody and Billings relished the chance to shift from ultra-vigilant, hair-standing tension, to the more personal aspects of life. As they were finally able to take a full, recuperative breath, they noticed something happening in the sea.

"Billings, what's that out there?"

"Looks like another school of rockfish or something. Maybe another whale forcing 'em up?"

The thousands of fish began to violently thrash closer and closer to the water's surface, with many jumping into the sea-drifting air atop the waves. The school of fish appeared to grow and grow, spanning several hundred meters. As the group of panicking pycine reached critical mass, it finally erupted.

"Whoa, whoa, whoa! Here we go again!" Brody bellowed out as Billings keenly watched with his eyes tripling in size.

The Vipers landed on the water's surface after leaping from the blue oceanic depths. They wasted no time in fulfilling their propensity for destruction. Cruising at whiplash speed, they began to engage what little Commonwealth naval assets remained from the missile attack along the defensive island perimeter, as well as the ships docked in the naval yard and ashore. Speeding along in pairs or trios, they unleashed a variety of munitions. Some launched torpedoes and heavy mortars, while others used electromagnetic chain guns or medium-caliber cannons. Each weapon served its own purpose and was directed to targets identified by hundreds of small aerial drones that hovered in a vast, web-like pattern over the entire battlefield.

Billings kept trying the radio, "Is there anyone out there? Anyone alive?" Just static. No apparent signs of life. "This is Staff Sergeant Jarot Billings, Commonwealth Coastal Defense Force, does anybody copy?" Billings had to speak at a low whisper to avoid detection by the swarms of Vipers, which continued to wreak havoc all around his position.

"Knock it off, dude. Yer gonna get us killed," Brody ever so tactfully asserted.

"I'm trying to get us help," Brody interrupted Billings's retort.

"You think there's anyone left to help us? We're done. Look out there, man—we're finished."

"I have to try," Billings insisted.

Billings kept trying to call for help several more times. Each time yielded the same ominous silence. The silence, however, was broken by several unfamiliar sounds. A few Vipers were destroyed by some low flying hellidrones and armored vehicles making their way to shore. Commonwealth reinforcements from nearby bases were starting to arrive to stop the naval assault.

"You see that Billings—we took some out! Eat that! Yeah!"

Billings conceded, "We're in the fight, but I still have a bad feeling about this."

* * *

Admiral Perry waited for the right moment to deliver the next blow to the Commonwealth forces in the Los Angeles Coastal Defense Zone. "Send 'em all. Now."

A rear admiral heard the message and quickly ordered, "Surface Eagle Rays and Mullaways." The rest of the sailors who eagerly awaited their orders went into high gear to guide their semi-autonomous naval vessels upward.

Unlike the Vipers, the much larger Eagle Rays, and larger yet, Mullaways, surfaced through the water more gradually. As they rose up, the water rolled farther and farther down as the ships revealed themselves to the open air. Their curved and angular hulls, which were perfect for navigating while submerged, began to change. Large turrets moved upward from their protected compartments, and hypersonic munition pods became available for use after their armored shields slid to the side. The twelve Eagle Rays, heavy destroyers by class, positioned themselves between the thirty rapid assault Mullaway ships and what remained of the protective islands outside the Los Angeles harbor.

"Sir, most of our Vipers are down. Enemy aircraft and self-propelled howitzers are knockin' 'em out," an intelligence senior chief petty officer reported to Admiral Perry.

"Thanks for the update, Senior Chief."

Perry relayed to his other subordinates, "Ladies and gentlemen, it seems the Commonwealth is taking our little incursion seriously. They've got attack and bomber aircraft inbound, and at least four divisions of armor and infantry, including two Robotics Corps regiments en route from nearby regions."

"Admiral, Eagle Rays are operational," another captain reported.

"And the Mullaways?"

"They're ready too."

Admiral Perry's smile was instantaneously fixed after hearing those words. He giddily ordered, "Launch 'em!"

* * *

Billings's guttural uneasiness came to fruition as he watched the largest cannons and lasers of the drone fleet open fire on their targets. Remaining defensive systems were bombarded as well as reinforcements traveling by land and air. Eagle Ray lasers also provided defensive capabilities to the fleet by destroying incoming missile and artillery fire from the shoreline, while their hypersonic missile systems provided long-range strike capabilities and another anti-air deterrent against drone swarms. The dozen dreadnought-size destroyers protected their sister ships, which had since retracted their domed outer hulls along their entire lengths. The Mullaways were ready for their vital role in the mission.

"Billings, we've got troop carriers inbound!" Brody screamed.

"What are you talking about?" he responded.

"Look, man!" Brody pointed to the large Mullaways that surrounded their destroyed outpost. They watched squadrons of smaller aircraft depart each of their home vessels and head toward the shoreline. Billings was quick to point out strange streaks running through the water. They hadn't been there before and they didn't seem to be natural occurrences.

"Are those some sort of jet streams?" Brody guessed.

"I don't think so," Billings slowly answered as he continued to analyze the many parallel, streaking lines darting toward the shoreline. The linear anomalies became more prominent as they approached the sandy beaches. As it became apparent, Billings uttered, "Invasion."

The two men, barely able to blink, watched what appeared to be hundreds of amphibious assault craft fanning out of the shallowing waters as they made it to four beaches along the Los Angeles area coastline.

"This is Sergeant Jarot Billings of the Commonwealth Coastal Defense Force, Los Angeles Zone. All systems are down. There are amphibious and airborne troops moving ashore. I say again, enemy troops a...." The speaker went static. Billings and Brody were gone. Only a plume of billowing smoke and flames remained.

* * *

With the Los Angeles region in chaos, the only sets of ears that paid attention to Billings's final words of warning were many miles away.

"Your Eminence, we have a situation along the Los Angeles coastline," a trepidated staffer reported to Premier Kerioth.

"What kind of a situation, Beesley? And tell me it's not another quasi-tsunami, is it?" The premier had utter contempt for any notion of instability under his rule.

"I'm afraid not, sir. There are nonconformist troops storming the beaches from Santa Monica to Laguna Beach outside of Los Angeles."

It took a moment for Kerioth to find the words for an educated response. He closed his eyes and ran his hand through his graying, neatly trimmed beard, restraining his inner tendency toward wrath.

"What did you say?" Beesley was still waiting to be screamed at or physically assaulted by the premier. He didn't want to announce the devastating news a second time.

"I'm sad to report that Los Angeles is being invaded."

This time the premier was ready to respond. "Who is invading Los Angeles?"

"They appear to be tens of thousands of Federated Anti-Colonial Front marines who are coming from air and sea-based vehicles. They completely surprised and overwhelmed all coastal defenses and military units in the area."

"Why haven't our strategic space assets taken them out?"

"It seems we're having unexplainable malfunctions to most of our strategic assets in the region and in orbit."

"I see." Premier Kerioth moved closer to Beesley—so close that each follicle of his moustache's aftershadow was plainly visible. "You get every available division and air wing that we have in North America down there to quell this invasion as quickly as you can." The time for concealing his anger had passed. Knowing that one of his prized North American cities was being taken over by enemies of the state drove him to his breaking point. "Do you hear me, Beesley?"

Beesley's frozen stare was interrupted, "Yes, Mr. Premier. Right away." Beesley ran. He fled to avoid any outbursts by the premier, and to alert the proper command levels of the premier's directives.

Premier Kerioth shouted one final recommendation to Beesley, who was already a stone's throw down the hallway. "I don't care if we have to destroy the whole city. I would rather make Los Angeles uninhabitable than lose it to the rebels. The entire area is expendable,

Beesley. Stop the noncons at any cost!" Beesley knew full well the premier had no regard for the lives of the innocent if it'd cost him even an ounce of his pride.

* * *

"What's our progress with the Mullaways?" the anxious Admiral Perry asked his closest staffers.

"Admiral, all Mullaways have deployed their full contingent of amphibious and airborne troops," a first lieutenant reported.

The admiral paced for a bit as he thought about the various military assets involved in the operation. He continued pacing as he carefully watched the interactive command module, which allowed high ranking officers to view in real time, the activities and maneuvers of a given operation as well as provided a platform for issuing immediate orders. The admiral slowly sipped his double-shot espresso with peppermint flavoring. It was his favorite beverage—one that accompanied him during stressful situations ever since his service in World War V. He sipped, paced, and stopped repeatedly as he observed the large battle unfolding before him.

The mighty Mullaways—thirty in all—managed to complete their entire cycle of surfacing, launching all troop compliments, and resubmerging. Each Mullaway carried onboard a large fighting force that made its way to targets by air and by sea. The ship-based aircraft from each Mullaway comprised of twenty Air Assault Delivery Vehicles (ARDELVs), also called Skimmers, which each held twenty-four combat troops and flew them into battle. Waterborne craft from each Mullaway consisted of two types. Forty Rapid Assault Submersible Craft (RAPS), also named Grunions, carried their payloads of thirty-one marines to shore and inland to fight. Next, there were ten Groupers, a larger variant of the Grunions that delivered combat vehicles alongside the troops in the Grunions. In all, the Amphibious Task Force participating in Operation Specter Wave involved one thousand two hundred Grunions, three hundred Groupers, six hundred Skimmers, nearly fifty-two thousand FAF troops, and one thousand eight hundred semi-autonomous combat vehicles. It was a massive force, indeed—one the Commonwealth had not expected, nor was prepared to fight.

A lieutenant described the current situation to Admiral Perry, "As you can see, sir, our final waves of Grunions and Groupers are making their way onto shore, while the first wave is advancing to reinforce Skimmer positions. All Skimmer platoons are currently engaging in heavy contact with preliminary counterassault reinforcements."

Admiral Perry kept his eyes on the interactive command module, only acknowledging the young, baby-faced lieutenant with a slow and deliberate, "Very good." The other officers looked at each other somewhat surprised. "What's the Commonwealth chatter lately? Are they still taking the bait?"

"Admiral, it looks like they're sending all available combat forces to the region. We're even seeing hypersonic air, sea, and ground-based cruise missiles en route toward our forces. Space-ground attack munitions have been jammed, so we don't have to worry about those hitting us."

"Are our air defenses still holding?" Perry had to know if his anti-air weapon systems remained viable to defeat Commonwealth missile counterstrikes.

"Yes, sir. They're taking out all immediate threats; however, as more enemy missiles make their way, our air defenses will likely be overwhelmed and run low on munitions," the air defense commander reported.

The admiral replied, "This is what's supposed to happen—remember that, folks. We've gotten their attention. They're responding with overwhelming numbers to annihilate our invasion force. They don't know that this *invasion* is the snare that will ultimately lead them to their own destruction."

Perry's words resonated with his staff and all present, especially those that had forgotten the larger objectives at work during the operation. Many of them felt they were standing on top of the world. More specifically, standing on top of Shinar Palance with their weight crushing the heart of the Commonwealth beneath them.

Battle attrition was taking its toll on the FAF ground and naval forces. Over half of the Eagle Ray heavy destroyers sank to the depths of the Pacific. Several Mullaway assault ships were severely damaged as they were resubmerging with the others to escape the fiery onslaught. The Stargazer submarines were long gone, having fired their payloads and already heading back to the Trench and other strategic locations. With little naval support left, the one thousand eight hundred semi-autonomous vehicles and specter troops fighting inland were left more vulnerable from the air, despite having their own short-range air-defense capabilities. It wouldn't be long before more reinforcements would arrive to engage and destroy the FAF expeditionary units that had recently landed.

"Do we know if they've figured out our little secret yet?" Admiral Perry asked a senior intelligence officer.

"Quite possibly, sir. I've got a live feed from a Robotics Corps Head Assault Leader engaging our 6th Specter Marine Brigade in Santa Monica."

The Admiral exclaimed, "Let's hear it!"

* * *

The beleaguered Robotics Corps company commander informed his ranking officer of the serious problems facing his mechanically-integrated combat company. "Senior Assault Unit Leader, this is Whiskey, Alpha, four, nine, Head Assault Leader James Higgins. I'm facing a regiment to brigade size enemy with dozens of armored vehicles, indirect and direct fire capabilities, and highly trained infantry. I've lost thirty percent of my men so far, and have been able to take out at least fifteen infantry fighting vehicles with our guided, high-explosive mortars and shoulder-fired rockets. Enemy infantry losses have been negligible."

"Head Assault Leader, why aren't their infantry goin' down?" the senior assault unit leader skeptically replied.

"I don't know, sir. We're hitting them with everything we've got. I know we're making direct hits, but they're still not dropping." The perplexed and angered head assault leader was equally worried about what his senior assault unit leader would say as he was reporting his unusual circumstances.

"Have every man and machine in your unit make sure their cameras are on. I've got to see this for myself." Head Assault Leader Higgins paused his exchange with the senior assault unit leader as he gave the order.

"All right, sir. They're all on."

"Roger that, Higgins. I've got all feeds live. I'll get back to ya in three mikes. Over and out."

The incredulous senior assault unit leader sat in the recently erected Forward Operations Command Center (FOC) about five miles east of Los Angeles. He shared the impromptu, yet sophisticated building with other battalion-size commanders up to several senior group leaders. The FOC provided the command structure for the divisions of the Commonwealth Land Forces hastily making their way to the southern California coast to repel the FAF invasion. As the counterinvasion forces's proximity to Los Angeles closed, so swelled the ranks of the senior officers at the FOC.

"Let's see what we have here," the curious senior assault unit leader soliloquized while sitting among several enlisted staffers. He honed in his attention on one of the fireteams in Head Assault Leader Higgins's E company. The Robotics Corps junior assault leader, along with his five WAMs, were firing from behind a large vehicular roadblock. The sextet were heavily outnumbered as they faced a thirty-one man platoon which had exited their Grunion and began to engage. Two other semi-autonomous infantry and cavalry fighting vehicles provided them additional cover and heavy weapons support.

"Poor suckers," the Corps senior assault unit leader let out as he watched the fireteam hanging on by a thread. He focused on the machine railgunner WAM, Tommy, and even looked down its sights to view the targets that it fired upon. To his disbelief, what Head Assault Leader Higgins reported was absolutely true. Dozens of rounds appeared to pass right through the three noncons who were aligned perfectly within its sights. Its aim was dead on, but the men on the receiving end didn't even flinch.

"What the hell?" He even saw the rounds hit an armored vehicle parked behind their immaterial bodies. "How can that be? Something else is going on here."

A FAF Grunion amphibious assault craft spraying machine gun rounds and cannon fire was hit by a missile from a close air support Commonwealth jet. A climbing column of flame shot upward. The senior assault unit leader almost had to look away from his screen because of the blinding flash of pyrotechnical precision, but he didn't. Instead, he kept focused. He noticed another anomaly the moment the vehicle was destroyed. A bunch of the FAF marines who were in view disappeared at the same time. He figured it out—ghost soldiers. The vehicles somehow projected the holographic soldiers to give the illusion of a large invasion force. "But why," he thought to himself. "Diversion. It's a diversion!" He couldn't believe it. How could it come to this?

"Head Assault Leader Higgins, tell your men to only target the vehicles! The infantry can't hurt you—they're not real!"

"Uh, sir?" Higgins didn't understand at all what was going on.

"Just do it!" the senior assault unit leader barked.

"Roger that, sir. We'll only target enemy vehicles," he affirmed, although somewhat sarcastically because of his disbelief in the accuracy of the orders. How could he possibly order his troops, being cut down by the minute, to ignore the dozens of Tricorn marines who were firing on them?

The senior assault unit leader quickly ended his exchange with Higgins to go up the chain of command to inform them of the urgent news. "Get me Group Leader Briggs, immediately!" The visibly upset senior assault unit leader was beside himself, knowing full well that his men, as well as the entire Land Force counterinvasion army, were falling for a diversionary trick.

"This is Group Leader Briggs."

"Group Leader, sir. This is Senior Assault Unit Leader Kwarters. This invasion is a decoy. The marines swarming our beaches aren't real."

Group leader Briggs had to willfully suspend his disbelief so he could understand what he heard. "Senior Assault Unit Leader, can you tell me how these marines, who you say aren't real, are managing to inflict a fifty percent casualty rate on our earliest counterassault companies? Surely these ghosts can't possibly be firing live ammunition into our men?"

It was clear he was losing the group leader's confidence regarding the matter. "Sir, I know what this sounds like—but please, I have direct evidence to support my claim."

The conversation went on much slower than Senior Assault Unit Leader Kwarters had hoped. His convictions needed a much more thorough analysis by Group Leader Briggs for any of the information to change the strategy of the Commonwealth Land Forces.

* * *

This was exactly what the FAF officers were waiting to intercept. Admiral Perry was listening, word for word, to the initial transmission relayed to Senior Assault Unit Leader Kwarters from Head Assault Leader Higgins, and then Kwarters's conversation with Group Leader Briggs. They wanted suspicion and doubt to run rampant, but they would not allow for the knowledge of specter troops to disseminate beyond laughable conspiracy theory. Operation Specter Wave needed to continue its vital role in creating confusion and attracting the maximum number of Commonwealth defense forces available in North America. The greater goal of liberating the former American mainland—Operation Cloudburst—had to be maintained and protected. Of course, the larger mission afterward is to bring down the Commonwealth at its hive in Trier.

One phase needed to happen prior to the next. A deliberate, concerted effort, which required focus and discipline, was needed every step of the way. Only then could a world free of the totalitarianism of the Commonwealth be possible. The chains which enveloped the world needed to be removed, link by link.

"Inform General Marion that it's time. Ask him what more he needs from me?" Admiral Perry ordered his second-in-command. The message relayed to the *Lexington's* communications officers and was then transmitted to General Marion's staff.

Shortly thereafter, the general gave his responding order. "Knock 'em out, now." The simple and direct message cascaded down the myriad channels to initiate a crushing blow to the Commonwealth military apparatus.

Unbeknownst to Premier Kerioth and the rest of his underling enforcers of the Commonwealth, General Marion's flagship—the *Lexington*—was already making its way to earth. Completely hidden from detection, the *Lexington* launched dozens of hunter-stunner drones that identified and disabled Commonwealth navigation, ISR, communication, and weapons-based satellites. Their technological backbone which heavily relied on satellite-based logistics, and command and control, instantly turned to space junk.

The massive interchronological cruiser charged beyond the lunar distance threshold toward North America. By this point, the units fighting the specter troops near Los Angeles lost their long range communication capacity, and all troops quickly deploying to the area were left all but blind. Chaos ensued and talk of ghost troops coming ashore was soon replaced by silence. The psychological warfare that the notion of phantasmic fighters had on Commonwealth soldiers was firmly implanted. It seemed the premier was losing his unshakable grip on his empire by the minute. His already low level of patience continued to fall with the news of each setback.

* * *

The unfortunate aid tasked with delivering the most current update about the fighting near Los Angeles slid past the partially open door to face the already exasperated premier.

"What is it this time?" the snarky voice preemptively asked.

"Your Highness, it's regarding an important radio transmission that was interrupted before its message could be completed."

"What was it and why was it lost?"

"Your Eminence, it was from a Robotics Corps head assault leader fighting in Santa Monica. He reported to his superior officer, who then reported to a higher ranking officer that the nonconformist incursion is completely unmanned." The slender, thirty-four-year-old aid didn't have a chance to finish.

"How can it be that I am witnessing a full-scale invasion outside of one of my epitomizing cities and you have the audacity to tell me the tens of thousands of enemy soldiers killing my troops are an illusion?"

"Premier Kerioth, based on our latest intelligence analysis, the partial transmission we obtained indicated that the various semi-autonomous combat vehicles on our shores are the sources of the holographically projected infantry."

"How can you be sure of it?" the incredulous Kerioth inquired.

"It appears that once a vehicle is destroyed, the troops in its vicinity vanish. As more and more vehicles are being taken out, the infantry forces are proportionately reducing. Furthermore, there are no signs of any bodies of the infantrymen being left behind. Some of these ghost troops gave the appearance of being wounded and killed, but that appears to be illusory as well."

The premier believed the staffer. He had little choice but to accept this compelling evidence as truth. What most concerned him now was the reason for the ghost troops landing near Los Angeles. That was far more disturbing to him than the news of the ghost forces being used.

"What more do we know about this rebel operation?"

"Your Eminence, we have a total operational blackout. Our satellites are either being jammed or destroyed, possibly both. Same with our troops in North America—we cannot communicate with them. They're cut off from the rest of our military and intelligence apparatus."

Premier Kerioth had little reaction besides being dumbstruck. He couldn't think of a good question to respond with this time. He was always used to gaining control, not losing it. He had greatly enjoyed the usurpation of more and more power for himself and his allies. This latest news reflected an impossibility in his mind. As the burden began to weigh the premier down, there was an inverse relief to many civilians living under his tyranny.

"Assemble my council immediately, and tell military command to reinforce our most valuable ports and highly-valued installations.

Any sign of resistance, crush them right away. I cannot allow this monster to grow."

"Very well, Your Excellence. I will do so right away."

"Move! Now!"

The premier pondered to himself as his obsequious staffer scurried off. Complete satellite disruption to invade one string of beaches in southern California? Not likely. If the noncons could amass an invasion force this quickly and with no prior detection off the coast of Los Angeles, they could do the same just about anywhere. "What was to come?" he uttered under his breath while scanning a robust world map on the wall. "Where will you come next?" Puzzled and angered, the premier impatiently waited for his high council to be convened and his orders disseminated. He had no idea what was in store for the rest of the former United States of America.

* * *

General Marion continued his descent toward earth's atmosphere aboard the *Lexington*, the ship that would undoubtedly be instrumental in the liberation of the land of the liberators. Meanwhile, the primary invasion divisions awaited their orders to launch their surprise attack from the clandestine ships and subs. Every piece was in place, and every spring waited to be sprung.

The entire idea of renewing America's independence began with General Marion. He knew for some time what might be needed to pull it off, and with the support from the Accendia, the dream showed the potential to become a reality. Accendia technology and tactics changed the dimensions of the mission. Accendia engineers and scientists led faux companies and filled various Commonwealth government positions to ensure the requisite logistical work could be in place by the critical times needed to carry out their missions. They assisted in expanding the Mississippi and Ohio River basins and deepening the canals to and through the Great Lakes. All were necessary projects used to ostensibly improve commercial shipping for vital Commonwealth economic activity in North America. The FAF and Accendia needed the waterway augmentations to support the vessels and equipment needed for the invasion—not to mention the tunnelling underneath the Panama Canal, and the construction of the base at the Horizon Deep, which also served as enormously important strategic assets.

General Marion and the other FAF military planners thought of Operation Specter Wave and the more expansive Operation Cloudburst as missions of liberation, as opposed to an invasion. The general knew full well of America's history and the liberation which its national policies sought. He knew FAF recruitment and training would be easiest in America, where there still was a dormant vein of liberty. It was in America where a foothold could be achieved to rise up against the ubiquitous Commonwealth and its stranglehold on the world's people.

"General, my fleet is out of there. Managed to salvage most of 'em, so that was a plus. The gators and other fighting vehicles are still givin' 'em hell on the beaches. They're down to about thirty percent, but they'll keep fighting until every last bullet, rocket, and missile are spent."

"Very good, Admiral Perry," the grimacing General Marion responded after the subtle, jocular-natured transmission. "I know my troops are chompin' at the bit for some action too. Your men get to play their video games in their quantum control rooms as their vehicles engage the enemy—my men shed blood when they fight."

Admiral Perry wasn't too happy with the figurative shot taken at his sailors.

"General, I know that the thousands of crewmembers operating the subs and ships that your troops are currently riding have some skin in the game—some risk to be had. Sir, by air, sea, land, and space, we all play a role in this mission."

"Admiral, you're right. I'm sorry. You and I both know it's been a tough year for our forces. Hundreds killed, hundreds more imprisoned, likely never to be seen again."

Perry interjected, "General, I understand. Army's always borne the brunt of casualties. I know it's tough—we've both lost men and women. Far too many. You know I'd do anything to bring em' back."

Marion acquiesced, "I know you haven't had it easy either. We've all suffered under this regime. Until we have complete and absolute victory, I'm afraid the suffering won't stop. I just pray we can win swiftly and with the absolute minimal loss of life, both for our folks and civilians."

The two men, strongly opinionated, circled back to their fraternal roots. It didn't take long at all. It happened quite frequently as their passions got in the way, and their pride waned and waxed. Their senior rankings, at times, seemed to foster a rivalrous relationship instead of one bonded by collaboration. It'd been that way for years—even before the formation of the Commonwealth. Both military minds from their respective branches, will be absolutely critical to the success or failure of the FAF in the coming days.

General Marion represented the FAF Army Command and served as the Supreme FAF Commander, Admiral Perry represented Naval Command, General Banning represented Air Command, and General Napal—Space Command. The four cardinal commanders of the FAF and their Accendia counterparts sat down for their daily briefing in the Joint Operations Command Center (JOCC) aboard the *Lexington*, with the meeting primarily focused on Operation Specter Wave and the current transition to Operation Cloudburst. The chiefs and their staff prepared for their parts of the briefing at their workstations, which were adorned with northern pine. How rare it was to not use a plastic polymer, especially after the Commonwealth claimed dominion over all wildlife, including every tree on every parcel of what used to be privately owned property. Unless one was properly aligned with Commonwealth authorities, privately owned was an abandoned idea.

Their meeting lasted about an hour, with highly classified operational details being explained about the upcoming mission to overtake the Commonwealth occupation of North America. Each branch—Army, Navy, Air force, and Space force contributed their pertinent information for mission planning purposes. Subdivision commanders from Cyber Command, Logistics Command, Marine Command, and Strategic Weapons Command were also present for their input. Altogether, the plan was ready, and the forces were deployed. The time to launch the attack was approaching. They were ready, and they all hoped the Commonwealth was not.

* * *

The premier's level of vexation was chronically high in recent days. Beginning with General Marion's escape from Central Stadium, then Peter's arrest and execution, followed by the Accendia and FAF incursion at Chicago, and finally in the landings near Los Angeles—much had transpired. Even the premier's high council couldn't do a thing to mollify him. The prospect was no more likely in light of the new findings, which were just relayed from Los Angeles.

"Your Excellency, I am pleased to report that all ground enemies have been eliminated, and what remains of the rebel fleet has resubmerged and retreated. There are a few—how should I say—anomalies, though," the Provincial General of Land forces reported.

"What kind of anomalies, General?" the premier monotonously asked.

"Sir, there are three noncombatant ships that remain. They each have a large sail, which displays the apparent name of each ship. You may find them significant, but none of us are aware of any meaning at the moment."

"What are the names?"

"The Dartmouth, the Eleanor, and the Beaver. Interestingly, each of them is emanating a substance that has colored the entire shoreline. At first, we thought it was a biological attack, but our analysts have determined that the ships are excreting several types of teas from them: Bohea, Congou, Souchong, Singlo, and Hyson."

"You have to be kidding! You're lying! You have to be!" the premier shouted as he began to chuckle.

"Your Excellency, I don't understand—"

"General, do you have any idea what you're telling me? Please entertain me."

"Sir, I'm not sure what to say. Of course, I'm telling the truth. I wish I knew about what you're referring."

Premier Kerioth abruptly stopped his communication line and looked around to the members of his high council. "Do any of you have any idea of what is going on?" No councilmember was ready to address him during the current verbal assault on them.

"This is a new American Revolution in a sense—a new revival. The ships and the tea are exactly what were used at the Boston Tea Party of 1773. This symbolizes their ideology, their resolve. More importantly, this tea party off the coast of Los Angeles represents what we have feared would happen. This is not just some nonconformist, tricorn-wearing group propped up by their allies. We are fighting a movement that is focused on removing our power. Their fight for liberty means that we will lose everything. Don't you get it you morons?"

The premier's words struck an eerie chord for those that vaguely knew what he was talking about. Those within the confines of Shinar Palace who did not know—the so called enlightened and aristocratic rulers of the world who had no recollection of history's lessons or significance—were unaware of the magnitude of what was fomenting.

"This is not some simple rebellion that can be quickly extinguished. This is an all-out revolution to unseat us and crush the Commonwealth. We cannot and will not allow this to happen. Do you understand me? This is not a joke. In fact, this is the greatest threat we've faced since taking power."

The room was completely silent. The racing minds of the council flurried about as the premier slowly walked over to his world map. He stared at it, looking over that which he controlled in anticipation of losing it all—piece by piece.

About the Author

Patrick D. Carlson was born and raised in suburban Minneapolis, Minnesota. He received his bachelor of arts degree from Hamline University in 2009 and his doctor of physical therapy degree from Sacred Heart University in 2013. He currently lives in the Twin Cities metropolitan area. When not working as a physical therapist, he can be found reading, cooking, or spending time with his wife and children.

CPSIA information can be obtained
at www.ICGtesting.com
Printed in the USA
LVHW111351290420
654731LV00001BB/211

9 781645 842835